A tall, dark-haired man appeared across the room...

Meg's mouth went dry, her prepared speech forgotten. *What was she supposed to say next?*

She swallowed. The pause lengthened. People were staring curiously now, and to Meg, their eyes appeared hostile.

"I...know that this new hotel will be the jewel of my—husband's—hotels...." Meg stammered. "I am delighted to welcome you all...."

The man in the back stared at her with eyes as dark and compelling as obsidian. Completely unnerved, Meg grabbed the scissors and cut the ribbon, officially opening the hotel.

Flashbulbs exploded, and she found herself engulfed with people offering congratulations.

All at once the crowd fell back and the dark-haired man stepped forward. He walked up and took her in his arms, swept her backward and kissed her full on the mouth. A long, intimate kiss that stole her breath away....

When he released her, the guests were smiling, clapping.

"Surprise, surprise!" the hotel manager exclaimed. "I swore my staff to secrecy. Mrs. Chastain had no idea you would be coming, Mr. Chastain!"

Mr. Chastain. Jake Chastain.

Her "husband," who was supposed to be in London.

Dear Reader,

I was intrigued by a real-life trial that occurred in California in 1997 involving two women. The premise of the actual case was far too unbelievable to use in a novel (!) but when I thought about what one woman was accused of in that trial, I began to ask myself *"what-if"* questions.

What if I used the barest detail of her plan, but changed her motive? *What if* I created two fictional women, a dynamic man and a completely different outcome?

I was surprised by what happened when I put these characters in motion, and hope you will be, too.

With my very best regards,

Paige Phillips

A Stranger's Wife
Paige Phillips

HARLEQUIN®

TORONTO • NEW YORK • LONDON
AMSTERDAM • PARIS • SYDNEY • HAMBURG
STOCKHOLM • ATHENS • TOKYO • MILAN • MADRID
PRAGUE • WARSAW • BUDAPEST • AUCKLAND

For the newest member of our family, Amanda Dial

ISBN 0-373-22508-3

A STRANGER'S WIFE

Copyright © 1999 by Joan Dial

Printed in U.S.A.

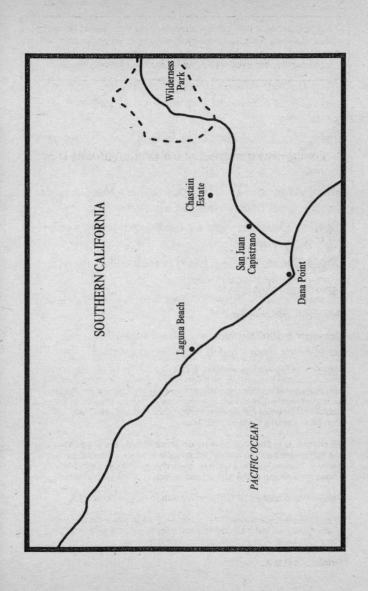

CAST OF CHARACTERS

Meg Lindley—She agreed to a simple masquerade—would she wind up in jail for murder?

Jake Chastain—He was a killer's target—but was the villain a stranger, or someone much closer to home?

Mike Aragon—The P.I. approached Meg in good faith—would he die for his efforts?

Jessica Chastain—Jake's mother refused to stay out of the way.

Rhea Chastain—She hired a look-alike, then conveniently disappeared.

Sloan Pensby—Rhea's foster brother was sick and dying—or was he?

Mason—Did the butler suspect more than he knew—or know more than he suspected?

Rick—A man of many faces.

Huxley—The Doberman's sudden love of Jake's wife seemed very strange indeed.

Chapter One

He had been following her since she left the market. Sure now, Meg Lindley quickened her pace. Only two blocks to go, but the dark street was deserted and a muffled footfall told her he was gaining on her.

Dead leaves, a legacy of an unseasonal Santa Ana wind, crunched under her feet as she broke into a run. Overhead, drifting clouds formed a vaporous army, overpowering the moon.

Gripping the grocery bag tightly, she heard the can of beans clunk against the jar of peanut butter. She twisted the handles of the swinging plastic bag twice around her fist.

She knew she couldn't maintain her speed; her right foot was already dragging. Splints and casts in early childhood had stretched her Achilles tendon to the point that no one would have guessed she'd been born with a clubfoot, and she rarely limped unless she was extremely tired. But she'd been on her feet for twelve hours, and adrenaline couldn't overcome the aching fatigue.

Even if she made it to the house, there was no way she'd be able to unlock the door before he caught up with her.

My only chance is to surprise him, she thought. *I've got to do the unexpected.*

Stopping dead in her tracks, she wheeled around to face him.

She had a quick glimpse of a man whose shoulders strained the leather jacket he wore, and whose expression registered surprise as she swung the grocery bag as hard as she could.

He was too tall for her to reach his face, but she heard him grunt as the bag struck his chest, winding him. Groceries crashed to the pavement, the jar shattering, as Meg and turned sped away.

Headlights turned the corner ahead, the twin beams momentarily blinding her. Desperately she ran out into the street, waving her arms. The car swerved, accelerated around her and roared off into the darkness.

Meg raced down the center of the street, breath grinding in her throat, right past her house. He wasn't going to trap her on the shadowed porch, she decided.

Nobody walked after dark in this neighborhood of modest houses, most with security bars on the windows. She doubted anyone would come to her aid if she screamed.

A barking pit bull leapt at a chain-link fence as she sprinted past. She briefly considered flinging herself over the fence and taking her chances with the dog, but fending off ravaging teeth seemed more daunting than fighting off a rapist.

She was certain that was what her pursuer had in mind, since he must have known from observing her in the market that she wasn't a candidate for robbery—she'd spent her last ten dollars on groceries and had to rummage through her pockets for enough change to pay the bill.

Meg forced herself to run faster. If she could circle back to the boulevard, with its traffic and lights, surely he'd give up the chase—

"Wait!" a surprisingly civilized voice called after her. "I'm not going to hurt you."

Right.

She didn't see the gray cat streak across the street until it was too late. The cat darted under her feet, tripping her. She sprawled on the ground, wincing as she scraped her hands on the blacktop.

In the seconds before her pursuer caught up with her, she grabbed her keys from her pocket. Damn him, he wasn't going to get his way without a fight.

His shadow loomed over her and she rolled aside and scrambled up on her knees, her keys raised ready to rip his face.

The moon sailed out of the clouds, its pallid glow illuminating his face. Her heart pounding, Meg was surprised to see there was nothing sinister about his features, which under other circumstances she might have described as pleasantly rugged.

He took a step backward, reached into his pocket, withdrew something. "I'm sorry, Mrs. Lindley. I didn't mean to scare you. I've not been able to catch you at home and I didn't want to approach you at work. I'm a private investigator."

She saw now that he was dangling some sort of badge from his outstretched hand. He extended the other hand toward her. "Please, let me help you up. My name's Mike Aragon."

Meg hesitated, then stood up on her own, keeping her distance. "What do you want? And what's the big idea of stalking me?"

"Could we at least get out of the street? This isn't the choicest of neighborhoods."

She backed away, keeping her eyes fixed on him. He followed her to the sidewalk.

"Just what are you investigating, Mr. Aragon?" Meg asked. "If you're a skip tracer looking for my husband, you're out of luck. I've no idea where he is."

"I'm not looking for your husband. I was sent to offer you a proposition that would be mutually advantageous to you and my client."

"And who is your client?" Meg asked, curious.

"Look, we can't talk out here on the street. I noticed an all-night coffee shop back there near the market. How about I buy you a cup of coffee and explain? I'll be glad to replace those groceries you tossed at me, too."

Torn between curiosity and bone-weary fatigue, she rubbed her grazed hands on her jeans. Curiosity, and a sense that her situation couldn't get any worse, won out. "Okay, let's go."

They walked back down the street. Several lean cats were licking at the spilled peanut butter; the dented can of beans had joined the flotsam in the gutter. She made a mental note to come and clean up the mess in the morning.

The coffee shop was empty except for a bored-looking waitress and a couple of short-order cooks arguing in Spanish behind the kitchen partition. Meg led the way to a table in the window, but Aragon said, "How about that booth in the corner?" and made for it without waiting for a response.

Once seated, he asked, "You want something to eat? Go ahead and order anything you want. I'm on an expense account."

Meg ignored the offered menu. "Hot tea."

He ordered a pot of tea, black coffee for himself, and when the waitress left, he placed a manila envelope on the table in front of her. "Prepare yourself for a surprise."

Meg opened the envelope and slid out a photograph.

She stared, blinked, then leaned closer. "This is—I don't

understand. I never wore my hair like that, I don't own those clothes...yet...''

He remained silent as she studied a portrait of a woman with ultra-short blond hair, wide-set blue eyes that regarded the camera as if it were an inquisitor, and full lips that pouted rather than smiled. She wore an expensive-looking jacket unbuttoned over spectacular cleavage, and her long fingers, posed under her chin, were decorated with several rings, one of which was a wedding band.

Aragon still hadn't spoken. Meg whispered, ''This is eerie. It's me—yet it isn't me.''

''Exactly,'' Aragon confirmed, picking up the picture and slipping it back into the envelope as the waitress brought their drinks. When she left, he said, ''She's my client, and your double, Mrs. Lindley. Oh, your hair is longer and more of a honey color. But your eyes are the same shape and color. If we could replace your worried look with that damn-you sneer of hers, your features would be nearly identical.''

''Who *is* she?'' Meg asked, still staring at the envelope.

''She's the former Rhea Pensby, who married Jake Chastain about eighteen months ago. And if the name *Chastain* doesn't mean anything to you, he's an entrepreneur who builds hotels, resorts and shopping malls here and in Europe.''

''What does she want of me, and how did you find me?''

''Let me answer the second question first. A friend of hers saw you when you and your husband catered a wedding up in Santa Barbara about a year ago. The friend had pictures of the wedding and you were in one of them. My client was traveling and busy with other things, and several months went by before she asked me to find you. By then your catering business had gone under—I guess when your husband took off. I found out you were working for another caterer and moonlighting at the movie theater.''

Trying to pay off the debts Hal had left in his wake, Meg thought. Just thinking his name scalded her soul.

''You lost just about everything, didn't you?'' Aragon's tone was sympathetic. ''Your business, your house, your car.''

''Never mind that. What does my look-alike want? If it's to baffle her guests with a caterer who's her double, I'm up for it.''

''It's a little more complicated than that.''

''How complicated?''

''She's willing to pay well—''

''If it's something illegal, immoral or fattening, forget it.''

''No—it's just a minor deception. She wants you to take her place for a couple of days. Pretend to be her. No one will be hurt by the masquerade—you'll simply go to the opening of a new hotel in the Caribbean, cut a ribbon and attend a party afterward. None of the people there have met her personally.''

Meg frowned. ''So why can't she go herself?''

He leaned forward, his voice low. ''Before I go into any more detail, I'd like to know if you're interested and also if we can count on your complete discretion. As you can imagine, if it got out that she sent a ringer, people would be upset—especially her husband.''

''So he doesn't know? This is beginning to sound fishy.''

''If I can give you valid reasons for secrecy and for her wanting you to impersonate her, would you be interested?''

''Maybe,'' Meg said hesitantly. ''I don't know.''

''What if she'd pay you ten times what you can earn in a month working two jobs? Not to mention a nice trip to the Caribbean? All for a couple of days' work.''

"It sounds too good to be true, and in my book that usually means it is."

"What if, as an added inducement, I were to find your missing husband for you?"

Meg blinked. "Did your client authorize you to do that?"

"As a matter of fact, yes, she did. You have to understand, she's a woman who has almost unlimited funds at her disposal. Paying you—and me—is small change to her. She can hide our checks in her monthly clothing account."

"But how did she know Hal had left me?"

"I gave her a full report on you before she asked me to contact you with the proposition."

Meg sipped her tea. She was beginning to feel a surrealistic fog closing in, probably due to fatigue, she decided. Maybe she was dreaming this whole encounter. She'd certainly fantasized even more exotic ways of paying off their creditors and finding Hal—if only to ask him why, *why?*

"If you agree, we'll have to move fast. You'll have to be in St. Maarten the day after tomorrow. We'll need to get you to a hairstylist and pick up the clothes you'll need, which, of course, will be yours to keep."

"Look, I am interested—who wouldn't be, in my situation? But I need to hear a good reason why Rhea Chastain wants to deceive her husband over this. And what if he shows up?"

"He won't. He's in Paris and then going on to London, on business there. He isn't due back here for a couple of weeks."

"Why isn't she with him?"

"Because he wants her to open the Caribbean hotel for him. She may fly to London to join him after the opening ceremonies."

"So why doesn't she want to go to the Caribbean?"

"Her brother is dying. She wants to go to him in San Francisco. But her husband...well, let's just say he doesn't approve of her brother's life-style, or of the disease that's killing him. Her brother isn't expected to live more than a matter of days, and Rhea doesn't see the need to upset her husband by canceling the Caribbean trip to go to San Francisco—not when she has a look-alike who's desperate for extra cash."

"What sort of a husband would be upset that his wife went to see her dying brother?" Meg couldn't imagine such cruelty. But then, she hadn't foreseen that the man she loved would walk out without a word, leaving her with massive debts, a failed business and a house in foreclosure.

"Well, there was more to his dislike of her brother than his disease. He was involved with drugs and mixed up in a lot of other illegal activities, and he'd served time."

"I see. But still...if the man is dying—"

"Rhea told me she had been able to slip away to see him a couple of times without her husband's knowledge when he was away on business, but now they've run out of time and it's a matter of saying goodbye."

"Why can't she tell the people in St. Maarten that she's sick and can't go? She could tell her husband the same thing."

"You know what I personally think? I think if this little impersonation works out this weekend, she might ask you to stand in for her again in the future when she doesn't want to be bothered with some chore. Her husband is a self-made man, of the old school, who thinks a wife should also be a helpmate. He expects her to pull her weight, but she thinks hosting fashionable parties in Orange County is her only obligation, and that she shouldn't have to be bothered with the little people—i.e., the staff of a Caribbean hotel and a few local dignitaries."

Meg thought of the hours she'd slaved in a kitchen today, preparing salads and vegetables and making soup for fifty people, followed by an evening of selling movie tickets and popcorn....

"Mrs. Lindley—what do you say, will you do it?"

"This woman—Rhea Chastain—her life is so different from mine. I'm not sure I could play the part of rich society wife."

Aragon's eyes flickered over her face. "Believe me, she wasn't born with a silver spoon in her mouth. Before she married Chastain and moved out here, the differences between you might have been more noticeable. She's more tanned and toned now, and she's lost most of her Southern drawl—in fact, she's worked hard at losing it. Besides, you aren't going to be playing the part of a society wife. You're just going to cut a ribbon and attend a party. You'll probably do both with more class than Mrs. Jake Chastain."

"You don't sound as though you particularly like her."

He shrugged. "I hardly know her. I just don't admire the parasites of the world, especially the beautiful ones who use people."

"But she's doing this in order to see her dying brother. Doesn't that count for anything?"

"Yeah, I suppose her motives, this time at least, aren't completely selfish."

"If you checked my situation, I suppose you know I'm hanging on by my fingernails. I'm trying to pay off debts. I wouldn't want my creditors to think I've skipped out, too. I'd need time to contact them, and the people I work for, to ask for time off."

"You're only going to be gone a couple of days. There's no need to contact creditors. You'll be back before they miss you. You can call in sick, or plead a family emergency to the caterer and the movie theater."

Meg played with her teaspoon. Doubts nagged, but refused to coalesce into rational objections. "All right," she said at length. "I'm probably crazy, but I'll do it."

"Before you leave I'll need your husband's social security number, driver's license number if you know it, credit card numbers, a picture, general description and anything else you can think of that would help a search—names of any family and friends, for instance."

He glanced at his watch. "It's after midnight. Maybe I'd better walk you home." A faint grin plucked at his mouth. "We wouldn't want any stalkers following you, would we?"

WATCHING AS THE PI and the woman left the coffee shop, the man in the shadows nodded to himself, satisfied that all was going according to plan. Yes, he thought, she'll do nicely. And since she's alone in the world, she won't be missed after she's served her purpose.

Chapter Two

Meg caught a glimpse of her reflection in a window as she walked into LAX with Mike Aragon.

The stranger she had become wore a casually elegant cream linen pantsuit and soft kidskin shoes, which, although brand-new, were luxuriously comfortable, even on her right foot. The nape of her neck felt strange minus her mop of hair, and the unaccustomed jewelry felt awkward, heavy. Having her hair shorn to within a couple of inches of her scalp had been less traumatic than the bleaching process. She'd closed her eyes and assured herself it would all grow out.

Mike Aragon wheeled a cart bearing monogrammed leather suitcases. She hadn't seen the contents; there'd been no time. In her shoulder bag was what appeared to be the real Rhea Chastain's passport, credit cards Meg didn't expect to use, and a bundle of cash. There was also a gold cigarette case and matching lighter.

"But I don't smoke," she'd protested to Aragon.

"Rhea's been trying to quit—Chastain hates the habit," he'd replied laconically.

"I don't know enough about her," Meg fretted, as the enormity of what she was doing hit home.

"You've got the prepared speech I gave you. Memorize it on the plane. Other than that, smile a lot."

He led her to the first-class check-in and she was asked for photo ID. Handing over Rhea's passport, she held her breath until the clerk returned passport and ticket and wished her a pleasant flight. The monogrammed suitcases disappeared down the conveyor belt, en route to San Juan. From there she'd fly in a private jet to St. Maarten.

"I'll walk you to the gate," Aragon said. "You don't have much time before your flight leaves."

She walked beside him in silence, fighting an urge to turn and run. A couple of passing flight attendants—female—gave him appreciative glances. *Must be those shoulders,* Meg thought.

When they reached her gate, he turned to her. "Well, good luck. The weekend should be a piece of cake. The money in your purse is your advance—you'll get the rest when I meet your return flight on Monday."

"How can I be sure you'll be here?" she asked nervously.

"I'll be here. I don't get my final payment until then, either. But if you're worried, this may reassure you." He handed her an envelope.

Inside was a receipt for a five-hundred-dollar retainer to be applied to a search for one Harold Lindley, formerly of Lindley Catering of Los Angeles, signed and dated by A. Michael Aragon, Licensed Private Investigator, with a Santa Ana address, and phone and fax numbers.

"Good luck, Mrs. Chastain. See you Monday."

In the instant before she started down the concourse, Meg noticed a muscular man standing at one of the pay telephones, looking over his shoulder at her. Their eyes met for only a second, but there was something chilling and malevolent about the way the man's flat gray stare flickered over her. Meg felt another qualm as it occurred to her that the woman she was impersonating had a circle of friends, relatives, acquaintances…and possibly, enemies.

MEG HAD EXPECTED smiling, dusky-skinned islanders to meet her in St. Maarten, and was ashamed of her own ignorance when her driver—a freckled, red-haired young man—greeted her by saying, ''Welcome to two countries, Madame Chastain…Holland and France. We will drive through Phillipsburg, the Dutch capital, and then proceed to Le Marigot, which is the French capital.''

''I've had a long flight,'' Meg said. ''I'd like to leave any sight-seeing until tomorrow, after tonight's grand opening. Perhaps we should go straight to the hotel?''

''*Oui,* madame—but the route I mention is on the way. I merely thought you would like to know where you are going, and naturally, if you have any questions I would be pleased to answer them. I was born here, you see.''

Feeling both wilted and chastened, Meg followed him to a waiting car—a French model she couldn't identify.

They left the quaint town and followed the coast, the car window framing lovely secluded coves, sparkling water and emerald foliage splashed with vivid blossoms.

Glancing at her in his rearview mirror—somewhat disdainfully, Meg felt—her driver remarked, ''When we reach Orient Bay, you will see the French Riviera of the Caribbean. There are no finer white-sand beaches anywhere in the world.''

Jet lag, added to tension and fatigue, was beginning to catch up with Meg. She hadn't slept the previous night, and was five hours out of sync with California time. She would have to be careful not to limp when she emerged from the car. She tended to favor her right foot when she was tired.

Her driver hadn't exaggerated the beauty of the beaches,

which were fringed by coconut palms and sea grapes. She blinked as several bare-breasted women strolled nonchalantly by. Then the car drew to a halt on a wide brick driveway beside a trellis trailing purple bougainvillea.

Waiting to greet her was a short, compact man, dressed in a white shirt, bow tie, a dark jacket and gray-striped trousers. His attire looked uncomfortably hot and formal, a sharp contrast to the bare-breasted tourists on the beach.

The red-haired driver opened the car door, and Meg stepped out into warm, humid air.

"Welcome, welcome, Madame Chastain. May I address you as Madame Rhea, since our lovely 'otel is named for you?" The short man bustled forward, took her hand and raised it to his lips. "André Ducane, at your service. This way, *s'il vous plaît*."

Ducane. The hotel manager, she reminded herself. He led her into a marble-floored lobby filled with white rattan furniture, bright chintz pillows and a veritable jungle of plants.

"Your suite is ready, madame," Ducane said. "I am sure you will wish to rest until the opening ceremony, which will begin at sunset. I have taken the liberty of ordering a light meal for you."

"Please, no food," Meg said quickly.

Ducane looked hurt. "But the chef 'as prepared your favorite."

Meg gave him a weak smile. *Rhea's favorite what?* The prospect of tonight's dinner loomed ever more menacingly. Why hadn't she thought to ask about Rhea's preferences? Was she knowledgeable about wines? What if she slipped up and exhibited a caterer's know-how of food and wine— would that give the game away?

The Hotel Rhea consisted of individual bungalows set into the verdant hillside. Each bungalow had its own terrace and small pool, complete with jacuzzi. All would have a spectacular view of the indigo ocean. Lobby, lounges, banquet and exercise rooms were housed in a long, low brick building softened by lush plantings.

Ducane and a pair of bellhops carrying her luggage hovered nervously as she was shown into her bungalow, and she realized they were expecting her to inspect every inch of the luxuriously appointed suite of rooms.

Her feet all but disappeared in the thick carpeting of the living room, which was fragrant with masses of fresh flowers. Baskets of fruit and boxes of French chocolates were also liberally scattered throughout. A bottle of champagne was chilling in an ice bucket next to a three-tiered dish of *petit fours.*

She walked into the bedroom, which was dominated by an enormous circular bed covered with a satin spread. A quick glance into the adjacent bathroom revealed gold fixtures, a sunken marble tub, a separate shower and more flowers.

French doors opened to a terrace. Frosty drinks were set out on an umbrella-covered table, and delicate white flower petals floated on the surface of the pool.

"Very nice," Meg told Ducane inadequately. "Now if you'll excuse me…"

The manager looked disappointed, and Meg wondered if she should have offered tips, despite Mike's instructing her that the owner's wife would not do so. Perhaps Ducane had been expecting more lavish words of praise for his efforts?

He quickly ushered the bellhops out of the room.

Meg exhaled slowly.

CITING SHORTAGE of time and Meg's need for a lengthy session in a beauty salon, Mike Aragon had asked for her dress and shoe sizes, and Rhea had provided clothes for the trip—so unpacking proved to be interesting.

Rhea's taste in clothes apparently ran mainly to tailored trousers and shorts. One suitcase yielded silk-and-lace underwear, two sheer nightgowns with matching peignoirs and three thong bikinis. It seemed overkill for a two-day trip.

After she showered and washed her hair, she dressed in fitted white satin leggings and a matching tunic decorated with tiny seed pearls. In Meg's mind, any further jewelry was unnecessary, but Mike Aragon had instructed her to wear outsize gold-and-pearl earrings, a matching necklace and trio of bracelets.

Meg thought that psychologists might have an interesting take on the man-tailored suits worn over feminine underwear, not to mention the excess of jewelry.

She winced as she unpacked spike-heeled rhinestone-studded evening sandals, and hoped she'd be able to make it through the party without limping. The evening clothes were such a far cry from the day wear; she wondered if husband Jake had selected the satin outfit for his grand opening.

When she was dressed, except for the sandals, she noted that, as usual, she was ready way too early. She went out onto the terrace to study Rhea's speech, but her mind soon wandered. She realized then that this was the first time since Hal had left her that she'd had a moment to sit and think.

She was stunned by the wave of pain that washed over her. Hadn't she put behind her, months ago, all the denial and the rage and the grieving? But no, it came rushing back—from the day she returned from taking a wedding order to find Hal and all his clothes gone, to the frantic phone calls, the rationalizations, the fruitless searches, the midnight tears, the humiliation of seeing her house and car repossessed.

If only Hal at least had talked to her first, or left a note or phoned.

"No!" she said aloud, sharply. *No more agonizing. It doesn't help.* Determinedly she picked up the prepared speech again, but the words blurred.

As the setting sun splashed the sky with vermilion and gold, the manager tapped on her door and announced it was time for her to accompany him to the lobby for the opening ceremonies.

Meg was glad of his short strides as she hobbled on the high heels. Aragon had not briefed her on whether the guests had been checked in prior to the ribbon-cutting, but she presumed they had, since it would have placed a damper on the party if they had to stop the festivities to register.

When she reached the lobby, she saw that the terrace beyond was crowded with dinner-jacketed men, women in designer evening dresses, and waiters dispensing champagne and hors d'oeuvres.

A wide red ribbon had been draped across the entrance, and a flower-bedecked dais was positioned behind the ribbon. Surveying the scene, Meg felt panic rise in her throat. She couldn't remember her speech, indeed had never spoken in public before. Hadn't she read somewhere that public speaking was the number-one fear of the entire population of the world?

Ducane led her to the dais and she saw an outsize pair of silver scissors nestled amid the flowers. He rang a bell and the guests fell silent.

"Ladies and gentlemen, it is my honor and privilege to present Madame Rhea Chastain, whose name graces our magnificent hotel. Please, let us welcome her to the St. Maarten Hotel Rhea...."

Polite applause greeted her as she wobbled up to the dais. She cleared her throat. "Good evening, ladies and gentleman. I am so happy to be here with you..." Her mouth was dry, the prepared speech completely forgotten.

The sea of faces blurred, receded, returned. "This is the finest of all the Chastain hotels and my husband and I want to thank you all for coming..." *What am I supposed to say next?*

She swallowed. The pause lengthened.

People were staring curiously now, and at least one pair of eyes seemed hostile. Their owner, a waiter with a sun-streaked ponytail, moved away quickly when he realized that she was looking in his direction.

"I...I know that the Hotel Rhea will be the jewel of my husband's hotels..." Meg stammered. "I am delighted to welcome you all..."

At the far side of the terrace, a tall, dark-haired man in a black dinner jacket emerged from behind a cluster of potted palms. The latecomer stood still, staring at her with eyes as dark as obsidian, a faintly mocking smile hovering about his sensually full lips.

The dark-haired man's stare was the last straw. Completely unnerved now, Meg grabbed the scissors and approached the ribbon. Flashbulbs exploded as she snipped the ribbon, then handed the scissors to Ducane. Suddenly she found herself holding a glass of champagne, engulfed by people offering congratulations and good wishes.

She hadn't eaten since breakfast on the plane, and the first sips of champagne caused her head to swim. Minutes passed as she responded to the compliments of the guests.

Then all at once the crowd fell back, and the dark-haired man stepped forward. She saw now that his features were lean, chiseled, and his dark eyes were hooded, the kind of eyes she imagined should belong to a hypnotist—or maybe a Mafia hit man.

He didn't smile at her. He simply walked up to her and took her in his arms, bent her backward over an arm that felt like a steel coil, and kissed her full on the mouth—a long, intimate kiss that forced her lips apart, his tongue insinuating itself between her teeth.

When he finally released her, she was too breathless to speak, or even react. She realized then that the surrounding guests were laughing and applauding wildly, and that Ducane was jumping up and down, unable to conceal his glee.

''Surprise, surprise!'' Ducane exclaimed. ''I swear my staff to secrecy. Madame 'ad no idea that you would be coming, M'sieur Chastain. Ah, it is so romantic that now you spend your second 'oneymoon in our beautiful 'otel!''

M'sieur Chastain. Jake Chastain.

Rhea's husband, who was supposed to be in London.

CARRYING A TRAY of hors d'oeuvres and moving inconspicuously among the guests, the ponytailed waiter was as startled as Meg by the appearance of Jake Chastain. Something had obviously gone wrong. Discarding his tray, the man headed for the nearest phone to report to his boss.

Chapter Three

Jake Chastain snapped his fingers, and a trio of musicians magically appeared. They began to play a throbbing rhumba.

Taking Meg's hand, Jake said, "Shall we dance?"

Meg felt color flood her face. She had no idea how to dance, especially not a Latin number. She thought rapidly and then said, "I—twisted my ankle."

He glanced down at her slender ankles above the spike-heeled sandals, and raised a quizzical eyebrow.

She said quickly, "It isn't bad…I mean, I can walk okay, but I was hoping to sit down soon."

For an interminable moment he stared at her, and she held her breath. Ducane and the other guests were still close enough to overhear their conversation; otherwise, she might have been tempted to blurt out there and then that she was not his wife.

Jake slipped his hand under her elbow. "Then let's find a place for you to sit, angel." Was there a touch of mockery in his tone? Meg wished she knew.

He led her to one of the chintz-cushioned rattan sofas. When she was seated, he bent down to unfasten her sandals, then slip them off. "Which ankle? Neither seems swollen."

Her cheeks flaming now, Meg answered automatically,

"The right," then immediately wondered if he would be able to detect that it was not his wife's foot that he was holding and gently massaging.

She said, "Please…it's nothing. I wouldn't have mentioned it, except I didn't think I could dance."

Jake straightened. His movements were smooth, effortless, and she sensed he would be a wonderful dancer. Absurdly, she felt a twinge of regret that she'd never learned to dance. Self-consciously, she began to slip her feet back into the sandals.

"Leave them off," Jake ordered. "You'll twist your ankle again if you try to walk in those ridiculous things."

So much for the theory that Jake selected the outfit, Meg thought.

"Stay here," he said. "I'll go and find some flats for you to wear."

Scooping up the evening sandals in one sinuous movement, he was gone before she could speak.

Meg stared after him, her thoughts racing. He must have known she was not Rhea. The way he touched her ankle, that kiss… Her cheeks grew hot again. How could he *not* know? But he hadn't said anything. No doubt, like her, he didn't want to make a scene in front of the hotel guests and staff.

In the back of her mind an intriguing question posed itself. *What if he actually believes I'm Rhea?* After all, the likeness was amazing, especially since the makeover. What if she could maintain the masquerade until she could call Mike Aragon and have him contact Rhea in San Francisco so she could fly out here and switch places with her?

Even the slightest chance that she could pull off the impersonation until Rhea arrived tempted Meg to try it. The whole point of the deception was to keep Jake from finding out she'd gone to visit her brother, and Meg was being handsomely rewarded to make sure that didn't happen.

She decided to adopt a wait-and-see policy. If, as soon as they were alone, he asked her who she was and what she had done with his wife, then she'd simply have to tell him the truth. But if he didn't…

A prickly, someone-is-watching feeling made her turn her head. The same ponytailed waiter she had seen earlier moved hastily away, but she was certain the man had been hovering nearby. Had he been eavesdropping?

She looked up to see Jake returning with her kidskin flats dangling from one hand. He was a man who came into a room like a matador entering a bullring: all lithe grace and lethal purpose.

His dark eyes locked with hers, and she tried in vain to interpret the glance. Puzzled? Suspicious? Knowing? Or was she looking for something that wasn't there?

He dropped to one knee and slipped the flats onto her feet, stroking her ankle as he did so in a way that sent a ripple up her spine.

"We should get some ice on your ankle. I'll take you back to our bungalow and order a dinner tray for you. I'll dine with our guests, and explain. I'm sure they'll be as impressed as I am that you didn't let a twisted ankle keep you from the grand opening. Do you think you can walk?"

He looked up and gave her a sly smile as his fingers continued to move rhythmically. "Or shall I carry you?"

"I can walk," Meg said, wanting nothing more than to be alone so she could call California—but wondering how the real Rhea would behave. She decided a mild protest might be in order. "But I think I could hold out until after dinner."

To her disappointment, he said shortly, "Good, I was hoping you would." He rose and signaled Ducane, who silenced the musicians and announced that dinner would be served.

The guests were ushered into a charming walled courtyard with a tiled fountain at one end and a softly lit bar at the other. Mosaic tables were set out under the stars, but tonight the adjacent banquet room would be used for the large number of guests. Round tables for eight beneath crystal chandeliers, turned romantically low, were set with antique silverware and delicate china.

Meg vaguely recalled Ducane introducing her earlier to the three couples now sharing their table, all of whom were apparently island residents. To her dismay, Jake addressed them in what seemed to be flawless French.

She sat stiffly in her chair. *Can Rhea also speak French?* Recalling Mike Aragon's advice, she smiled at everyone and picked up her water goblet. How little she knew about Rhea Chastain. She could never maintain this charade, it was impossible.

To her great relief Jake said, "But let's continue our conversation in English, shall we, so my beautiful wife can join in?"

Wine was served—a premier Chablis—and one of the men proposed a toast to the Hotel Rhea. Ducane accompanied the waiter who served an appetizer of grilled vegetable terrine, and the manager returned again after lamb chops were served and sampled.

Ducane hovered nervously, and Jake murmured, "You'd better comment on the food, Rhea. Put M'sieur Ducane out of his misery. Your reputation as a *bon vivant* preceded you."

Everyone smiled and watched her expectantly. Unsure exactly what *bon vivant* meant, Meg decided it must mean that Rhea was a gourmet.

In familiar territory now, Meg smiled at the manager and

said, "The vegetable terrine was excellent—I liked the colorful layering with eggplant and sweet red peppers, served with a dab of *tapenade,* and the vegetables had set long enough for the flavors to meld beautifully."

Ducane relaxed visibly. "And madame's opinion of the lamb?"

"Wonderful," Meg assured him. "The mustard-and-rosemary sauce was perfection, and the potato and celery-root gratin delicious. Please give our compliments to the chef."

Ducane bustled away wearing a satisfied smile, and Meg picked up her fork again, acutely aware that Jake was staring at her. Had she said too much? Too little? She wished she knew.

Under other circumstances Meg would have thoroughly enjoyed the meal, but her throat seemed to have fused shut. Jake, on the other hand, ate heartily and obviously relished the food.

Walking back to the bungalow shortly after midnight under a star-studded sky, with Jake's hand firmly under her elbow, Meg felt such a complete sense of unreality that it was difficult to think. Ducane's arch comment about a second honeymoon reverberated around her mind like jungle drums. Dare she plead that old standby: a headache? Menstrual cramps?

A sudden quarrel followed by the silent treatment had been Hal's solution when he wanted to sleep in the guest room, but Meg loathed that particular ploy. Still, she would have to do something to ward off any amorous advances. She couldn't sleep with another woman's husband, even though she was uncomfortably aware that Jake Chastain exuded an animal magnetism that appealed to some hitherto untapped primitive urges within her.

"Beautiful night," Jake commented.

"Yes. The hotel is magnificent, by the way. You must be very pleased and proud."

He turned his head to look at her. "You're showing a side of yourself tonight I've never seen before."

Alert to possibly dangerous ground, Meg didn't comment.

He added, "I've never known you not to find fault with either a meal or its presentation. I didn't think you were capable of unabashed praise. And I'm curious about your unexpected analysis of the food. How did you manage that?"

Damn, she *had* said too much. "Oh, I checked on the meal ahead of time so knew what the chef was doing," she said, aghast at how quickly she was acquiring the unwanted ability to lie.

"I was especially surprised at your compliments after the way you picked at your dinner."

"Oh, the food was wonderful. I just wasn't very hungry. The long flight…"

"And twisting your ankle, of course. You're limping a little even in the flats."

Meg was glad the concealing darkness hid her guilty flush.

They turned onto the brick pathway leading to their bungalow, which was set off, away from the others. Screened from the rest of the hotel buildings, the only sound here was the gentle soughing of the ocean, and Meg turned her head as another sound intruded. A soft footfall on the bricks behind them.

"What is it?" Jake asked.

"I thought I heard somebody coming this way."

He looked back. "I don't see anybody, and I doubt any of the staff would dare disturb us. This is our honeymoon hotel, remember?" Again, the mocking tone.

But Meg was more concerned with whoever was surreptitiously following them, convinced now that she, or more likely, Rhea, was under surveillance.

They reached the bungalow, and Jake unlocked the door.

Her heart beating rapidly, Meg went inside.

In the living room she turned to face him. "I'm really tired, Jake. I hope you understand—I am very happy to see you—but..."

Jake yanked off his bow tie, shrugged out of his dinner jacket and tossed it to a chair. "Just what the hell are you playing at?"

Meg's stomach lurched. So he *did* know, after all.

Jake said, "Let's cut the pretense, shall we?"

"I'm sorry," she said inadequately.

He looked at her sharply, and she had the distinct impression he had not been expecting an apology. She was about to plead with him to try to understand Rhea's motives, when he suddenly caught her wrist and pulled her close to him.

His face was so near hers that she felt his breath fan her cheek. He said softly, "If I thought you really meant that..."

Feeling the intensity of his emotions and empathizing with his shock at the deception, Meg couldn't speak, but she looked down at his hand enclosing her wrist. A fine shading of dark hairs almost disappeared into his tanned skin, and if it had not been for his perfectly manicured nails, she would have guessed that those strong fingers with callused tips were accustomed to heavy manual labor.

At her glance, he released her and a mocking smile replaced the raw emotion she had just witnessed. He said, with elaborate casualness, "Perhaps we could maintain the charade for a couple of days, so as not to destroy the ambience of the hotel we're touting worldwide as the idyllic honeymoon hideaway.''

He paused, and she saw something flickering in his eyes that suggested he was not as controlled as he wanted her to believe. ''What do you say, Rhea? Shall we pretend our marriage isn't on the rocks?''

Chapter Four

Jake said lightly, "Don't look so stricken. I don't expect any conjugal rights. We'll simply put on a show for the guests and the staff. I'll sleep out here on the sofa."

Meg found her voice at last. "Yes, that would be best."

"I'll just take a shower first, then you can have the bedroom and bath to yourself."

"I noticed extra bed linen in the closet," Meg said, her voice slightly breathless. "I'll make up the sofa."

He gave her a bemused glance before disappearing into the bedroom.

Meg listened until she heard the shower running, then closed the bedroom door and grabbed the phone.

It took precious minutes to access an outside line, then learn the dialing codes for California. With a five-hour time difference, making it only a little after seven o'clock in California, she hoped she'd catch Mike Aragon at home.

His phone rang six times and then to her dismay his recorded voice announced, "A. Michael Aragon, private investigations. I'll get back to you." She then listened to a tinny ragtime tune until the message machine beeped that it was ready for her to speak.

She whispered into the phone, "Call Rhea. She has to fly out here immediately. Her husband arrived tonight."

The water had shut off in the shower. She dropped the phone and ran to the closet, pulling out sheets, a blanket and pillow. She was spreading the sheet on the sofa when Jake reappeared, a towel wrapped around his middle, his dark hair damp.

Her heartbeat thundering, Meg averted her eyes from a sculpted chest and well-developed biceps. She plumped the pillow and placed the blanket at the foot of the sofa. ''There's another blanket if you need it.''

''What happened to your voice, Rhea? It seems to have dropped about an octave.''

''I think I may be catching a cold.'' She resisted an impulse to cross her fingers behind her back.

''That's too bad. I hoped that voice coach was finally earning his fees.'' He paused. ''You haven't commented on my unexpected arrival.''

''I was surprised, of course,'' Meg answered, wondering if she should ask why he had changed his plans. But that might bring a response that was for Rhea's ears alone. Perhaps it would be better to say as little as possible. ''I thought you were going to be in London at least a week.''

''I managed to wrap things up early.''

''Jake, I'm really wiped out. Good night.''

She had to brush past him as she entered the bedroom. It was a little like passing too close to a panther who had not yet been fed. He murmured softly, ''Sleep well. We'll talk in the morning.''

MEG AWAKENED with a start in the unfamiliar bed. She could hear the ocean breaking on the shore, but the sound that had brought her from shallow sleep was Jake's voice, speaking softly in the adjacent room. He was on the telephone, and his tone was urgent, concerned.

"...have they caught him? Anyone see or hear anything? Damn, I thought the hotel had better security."

The luminescent dial of her bedside clock showed 2:10 a.m. Slipping out of bed, she pressed her ear to the connecting door.

Jake said, "No, I didn't authorize Roland to use my suite. He's a new man in London, and I believed our people there had checked him out. Yes, I suppose it's possible he let an assailant into the suite himself."

There was another pause, then Jake asked, "Was he dead when they found him? What? Uh-oh, execution style. You'd better see what we missed in his background check. No, I don't think there's any connection to Chastain Enterprises—let's not get paranoid. Be sure to find out if Roland had a wife or dependents and take care of them, okay? I'll talk to you tomorrow."

Meg leapt across the room and back into bed.

A phone call in the middle of the night about a murdered employee would surely be sufficient reason for a husband to come and talk over the tragedy with his wife, despite their personal problems. But there was silence in the next room and minutes ticked by without Jake knocking on her door.

Too troubled to relax completely, Meg dozed intermittently. Then just before dawn she awoke to find sunlight gilding the window shutters.

"YOU'RE DIFFERENT," Jake said suddenly.

Startled, Meg looked up from a crystal dish of sliced mango and papaya. They were having breakfast on the patio under a brilliantly blue sky.

Is Rhea a bacon and eggs woman? Meg said, "I just felt like fruit this morning..."

"I'm glad to see you eat *anything* at this hour, but that wasn't what I meant—and you know it."

She waited tensely, wondering if this was the moment he'd end the masquerade. Was he playing cat and mouse with her? Had he known from the start? *Why didn't he tell me about that late night call from London?*

He said, "I'm glad you've quit smoking."

Feeling some comment was necessary, Meg said, "So am I."

He was watching her so intently that she looked away, her gaze sweeping the beautiful bay. Perhaps he was keeping the grim news from London to himself so as not to worry his wife, or spoil the interlude on this perfect island.

After a moment, to break a silence that was heavy with unspoken feeling, she said, "The view is spectacular. This is a wonderful place for a hotel."

"You can stop acting now," he snapped. "We're alone."

She said quietly, "I meant what I said. This is a beautiful island."

He leaned forward, his expression hard. "Let's cut to the chase, shall we? Last night I gave you time to get over the shock of my unexpected appearance. Now I want to know if you're ready to discuss the situation calmly."

"I...don't know," Meg answered. Her hand was unsteady as she picked up her coffee cup.

He gave an exasperated sigh. "I meant what I said the night before I left for Paris. We can't go on eating each other alive. You wouldn't listen when I said our marriage was a mistake and we should file for divorce. But I was deadly serious."

Meg listened in stunned silence.

"I agreed to wait until this hotel had been officially

opened because I figured a couple of weeks apart would give us both time to make our decisions about the future.''

Jake pushed aside his plate and stood up, pacing slowly around the small patio. A breeze caught his black hair and tousled it, and his tanned features momentarily lost the expression of cool detachment and looked strained.

''I couldn't stand the waiting, Rhea, the uncertainty. We agreed there'd be no phone contact, and I didn't want to discuss our problems long distance anyway. But I have to know if you're ready to end this marriage amicably, with as little publicity as possible, to avoid a media circus. That's why I cut my trip short and flew here.''

Meg felt like a non-swimmer, out of her depth in a raging torrent. Incredibly, he really believed she was his wife. But how could she possibly respond to the revelation that they were on the brink of divorce?

She cleared her throat. ''I...didn't expect you to come to St. Maarten. I thought we'd talk about it at home. I suppose I've fallen under the spell of the island, but...do we have to discuss it here?''

He stared at her for a long minute, then said slowly, ''No, I guess not. Breaking up a marriage is a serious step. Maybe a honeymoon hotel isn't the right place to arrange a divorce.''

Questions hammered Meg's brain. If they were on the verge of divorce, why was Rhea so concerned about keeping her visit to her dying brother secret? It didn't make sense.

During her sleepless hours the night before, she had also wondered if, when Jake learned she was not his wife, she could be charged with some crime. She would have to stall somehow until she could contact Mike Aragon.

Drawing a deep breath, she said slowly, ''Jake...could we just pretend to be friends until we get home, so that we can both think over what we really want? You know, not talk about our problems, or our marriage, or anything... Make believe we've only just met.''

He gave her a mocking smile. ''Not let passion get in the way, you mean? Our problems are way beyond fixing with a roll in the hay, Rhea. I know you don't want a divorce. But I do.''

No, Meg thought, *this can't be happening. I can't be a party to their breaking up.* Her mouth was dry. She said hesitantly, ''Surely we could postpone talking about it for twenty-four hours? Couldn't we just act like friends until we're home?''

His detached expression slipped back into place and he shrugged indifferently. He walked to the edge of the patio and stood looking across the pool toward the sweep of white sand beach glimpsed through the palms.

''You know, Rhea, while I was in Paris I'd begun to consider the possibility that passion was all we'd ever had. I even wondered if all the fights were some sort of twisted prelude to sex and if our marriage could survive without either.''

Turning to face her, he said, ''We never were just friends. You realize that, don't you?''

''Perhaps it's time, then,'' she suggested softly.

He gave a short derisive laugh. ''Since we're leaving tomorrow I guess we can be friends for a day. Maybe I need to prove to myself I'm not a complete slave to the dark gods of the loins.''

He walked back to the table and stood looking down at her. ''You are different, you know, in some way I can't quite define.''

She didn't dare hold his gaze.

''You seem so much...calmer,'' he went on. ''Yes, that's

the word I want. Less restless. What happened while I was gone to cause this metamorphosis, Rhea?''

''I don't know what you mean,'' Meg said warily.

''For one thing, you've stopped constantly fidgeting with yourself, running your hands through your hair, twisting your ring, smoothing your clothes, touching your body. Even your voice is more modulated—by the way, *are* you catching a cold?''

''No, I think it was just the long plane ride. Made me a little dehydrated, you know.''

JAKE STARED at his wife, marveling at her ability to project an appealing softness, not only in her voice, but in her entire attitude, that he had never seen before. What a damn fine actress she was! His asking for a divorce, of course, had jolted her. It might be interesting to allow her to play out her little charade, to see how long she could keep it up before she reverted back to the demanding, self-absorbed virago he had avoided as much as possible these past months.

He allowed his gaze to linger on her face for a moment. Her beauty still had the power to heat his blood, even now that he knew that beauty was indeed only skin deep.

In unguarded moments, Meg thought, he looked at her as if he still cared for Rhea—and he was solicitous of her well-being. Perhaps it was just a fight they had had that got out of hand. She had to steer him away from the subject of divorce before he divulged any intimate details of his relationship with Rhea that were none of her business. Drawing a deep breath, she said, ''Jake, if I seem different, perhaps it's because I missed you.''

She realized her mistake when he frowned. ''Don't play that game with me. It no longer works.''

''I'm sorry. Truce, okay?'' Meg said quickly. ''But since

we are here to promote your honeymoon hotel and have to spend the day together for appearance's sake, perhaps this would be a good time to find out what it would be like to just be friends.''

He shrugged. ''So be it. What would you like to do today?'' An ironic grin appeared. ''As friends, of course.''

Meg glancēd at the azure sweep of the sea. ''I'd love to have a picnic on the beach and swim in the ocean.''

His look of astonishment was instantly replaced by a ferocious scowl. ''You're suggesting that because you know that's what I like. Damn it, don't cater to me, Rhea. I don't want to feel like a charity case. You've always hated the sand.''

''What's wrong with trying something your partner enjoys? That isn't catering.'' Meg almost choked on the word, but he couldn't know catering was her profession. ''It's called give and take. Who knows, perhaps I'll find sand isn't so bad after all.''

Jake considered for a moment, then nodded. ''All right. I have a few business calls to make, then I'll call the kitchen and order a picnic hamper.'' His expression remained skeptical.

Needing a private moment to call Mike Aragon, Meg decided to take another chance. ''No, don't do that. I'd like to see the kitchens. I'll go and order lunch. What would you like?''

Jake's dark eyes lit up with amusement. ''Surprise me. You seem determined to do that at the moment. Since when are you interested in kitchens?''

THE GLEAMING HOTEL kitchen was bustling with early morning activity, but Meg was glad to find the head chef was not yet in his private office, which was separated from the cooking area by a wall of glass. A telephone sat temptingly on the chef's desk.

This time there was an immediate response to her call to California. "Aragon."

Unfortunately at that moment the office door opened and the head chef appeared. Meg waved nervously at him and said into the phone, "Hello, St. Maarten calling. Did you get my message?"

"Meg? Damn, I've been calling you for hours but the manager wouldn't put me through. He said you were sleeping. What's going on? Can you talk?"

"Not exactly."

"Okay, answer questions. Is Jake there with you?"

"No." She partially covered the receiver with her hand and said to the chef, "I'll be just a moment." He reluctantly retreated, leaving the office door open.

Mike said, "I get the picture. Jake isn't there, but you aren't alone. Does he know?"

"Not yet." Unsure if she could be heard out in the kitchen over the clatter of pots and pans, she asked, "Is the other party en route?"

"No, she isn't. I haven't been able to locate her. I've been up all night trying to track her down."

Lowering her voice to a whisper, Meg said, "Can you hear me? I'm worried the kitchen staff might be listening."

"The kitchen staff?"

"Just listen—Jake doesn't suspect me. At least, he's acting as if he believes I'm his wife."

"Holy sh—" Mike began.

"Not literally his wife. Mike, what we didn't know was that they talked about divorce before he went to Europe. He wants to discuss the breakup, but I said it would be better to do that at home in California. Meantime, for the sake of appearances, I've suggested we just act like platonic friends on vacation for a couple of days.''

"Smart thinking. Did he go for it?"

"Yes. But you've got to get her over here as fast as you can."

"When are you due to leave?"

"Tomorrow afternoon."

"Back to California?"

"Yes."

"It might be easier if you could hold out until you got back here. Two Mrs. Jake Chastains on a small island would be hard to hide. That would also give me more time to find her."

The chef walked back into the office, looking impatient. Meg's voice took on a slight edginess. "I suppose that would be all right."

"Somebody came back into the kitchen?"

"Yes."

"What the hell are you doing in the kitchen anyway? Are you on some sort of busman's holiday?"

"I'll call you when I get home."

"Be careful, Meg. And if you have to, tell him the truth. We can always say we thought the whole thing was an innocent prank that his wife wanted to play on him."

"Yes, of course. Goodbye."

Meg smiled apologetically at the chef, wishing she'd had time to tell Mike of Jake's horrifying phone call from London. Jake had sounded concerned, compassionate, but hadn't seemed to see any connection to himself or his company, despite the fact that the man had been killed in his suite. But Meg was beginning to wonder if Jake Chastain was facing a greater peril than a faltering marriage and a deceptive wife.

MEG HAD NEVER worn a thong bikini in her life. Why hadn't she remembered what Rhea had packed before rashly suggesting a picnic on the beach? There was nothing suitable to use as a cover-up, so evidently Rhea intended the bikinis for sunbathing and swimming in the suite's private pool.

Slipping a robe over the bikini, Meg opened the bedroom door. Jake, wearing swim trunks and a matching shirt, sat on the sofa, waiting. He wore reflective aviator-style sunglasses, so she couldn't see his eyes.

"I forgot to pack a cover-up. Could I borrow one of your shirts?"

"Sure. I'll get you one. I noticed your tan is fading a little, so it's a good idea not to soak up too many rays."

Meg considered how many differences he'd tallied between her and Rhea, and wondered again if he was playing cat and mouse. But perhaps the differences between his wife and herself were more subtle than she imagined.

He handed her a white long-sleeved shirt. She went back into the bedroom to put it on, rolling up the sleeves, glad of the tails that covered her bare derriere.

Meg had assumed they would walk the short distance to the beach, but a valet was waiting with a car. Jake said, "I know a little cove where we won't have to share the sand with tourists and cruise ship passengers. It's just a short drive."

He was right. The cove was deserted, the sand pristine, and a cluster of palms filtered the sunlight, providing shade. Jake unloaded beach chairs and towels from the trunk of the car, along with the hamper of food.

He discarded his shirt. "Ready for a swim?"

Meg had longed to plunge into the sea, and was glad that she and Rhea at least both liked to swim.

Taking off his shirt she felt his eyes flicker over her.

"Well, some things haven't changed, I see. You still like to show off your body. I suppose you know that's why I wanted to come here instead of using the beach in front of the hotel?"

She dropped the shirt onto the beach chair and raced for the water. Splashing through the shallows, she was glad when she was submerged up to her neck.

Jake caught up with her and they began to swim parallel to the shore. For Meg the gentle swells were tame compared to California's surf, and while she enjoyed the swim, she missed the challenge of riding the breakers.

When they returned to shore she quickly dried off and put on the shirt.

Jake raised his eyebrows slightly. "Do you need that now? We're in the shade. You're not afraid I'm going to seduce you, are you? Didn't I agree to be friends only?"

"I know. For some reason, I'm suddenly shy."

He raised a mocking eyebrow. "If you say so. I'll refrain from pointing out that you packed a thong bikini when you thought I wouldn't be here to see you wear it."

Spreading his towel on the sand, he lay on his back with his hands folded under his head, staring up at the palm fronds fluttering in the breeze.

For a split second Meg felt the skin of the absent Rhea slip over hers, and she said with some spirit, "If you hadn't been here I'd have swum in our suite's private pool and no one would have seen me."

"Touché. I'm sorry."

He rolled over onto his stomach, propped himself on his elbows and looked up at her. "So what do we talk about? Since we're accustomed to either flirting or fighting, it might be difficult for us to have an ordinary conversation."

"Let's try, shall we? Would you like to tell me about

business?'' *Perhaps even mention a murder in your London suite?*

''No, I'd rather talk about you. You could tell me about your childhood. You've never spoken of it since the first time I woke you from the nightmare and you told me about the abuse.''

Meg stiffened. *Abuse.* Her vision of Rhea shifted slightly.

Jake said, ''I've never pushed you for more details, but I can't help thinking those early experiences must have a bearing on the troubles we've had in our marriage. It must have been difficult—probably still is—for you to trust people. I wish I could get you to see that your relationship with Sloan—shared childhood trauma or not—is unhealthy.''

Sloan. Rhea's adopted brother, dying in San Francisco. How could Jake be sympathetic about a murdered employee in London, and yet so callous about his wife's brother?

Meg was tempted to remind Jake that Sloan was terminally ill, but decided it would be impossible for her to express Rhea's feelings about her brother. ''I'd rather not talk about Sloan, or my childhood now, Jake. It's just too beautiful here to dredge up unpleasant memories.''

He sat upright, his face set in tight, angry lines. ''You saw Sloan again, didn't you? Despite your promise not to.''

''No. I didn't,'' Meg said quickly. ''Even though he's so ill.''

To her astonishment, Jake burst out laughing. ''Ill? After pumping up with weights in prison for two years? He looked healthy as a horse when he was paroled two weeks ago. I suppose his sudden illness requires a specific drug to treat it? Cocaine, perhaps? For pity's sake, Rhea, wake up and see him for what he is.''

Bewildered by this outburst, since it had the ring of truth,

Meg said quickly, "Let's not quarrel about him now. I'm hungry, how about you?"

"Sure." He reached over and lifted the lid of the hamper, surveying the contents, then glanced up at her. "Did you have the chef pack this, or did you have a hand in it?"

She was unsure how to respond, since she had selected every item: chilled apricot soup and a salad of tiny shrimp tossed in fresh greens, all packed in ice; cold roast chicken; crusty French bread and Gruyère; hazelnut torte; and fresh fruit. Meg mumbled, "Well, it was a cooperative effort."

Jake looked at her for a moment. "You forgot the wine."

She managed to stop herself from responding, *Wine in the middle of the day gives me a headache.*

At the same instant she caught a flicker of movement between the palms on the cliff above the cove: a silhouetted man who swiftly drew back out of sight. Meg's heart skipped. Someone had been watching them. For how long? And why?

She stared up at the cliff. The sand under her was still warm, the sun high in the sky, but she suddenly felt cold.

Sure now that it was not her imagination, that she—in her guise as Rhea—had been under surveillance since leaving LAX airport, Meg's skin crawled. And Jake had just blown a hole in Rhea's "sick brother" story, so what was Rhea *really* doing this weekend?

Chapter Five

"Do you remember that weekend in Capri?" Jake asked.

Meg said cautiously, "Of course."

"Well?"

The afternoon was hot, the sunlight shimmered on the sand and cast sparkling diamonds on the sea. "Well, what?"

He gave a sardonic smile. "Nothing, I guess. Aren't you hot in that shirt?"

"I was thinking of going back in the water."

"Isn't it too soon after lunch?"

"Did your mother warn you about that?"

He laughed shortly. "Hardly. I'm surprised you ask, knowing how unmotherly she is."

Meg blinked behind her sunglasses. She hadn't pictured a mother in Jake's life. She wondered how Rhea got along with her.

Another quick check of the cliff revealed no further sign of the watcher. Still, Meg had the uneasy feeling that he was still up there, keeping out of sight but observing them.

"Lunch was incredible," Jake mused. "If that's a sample of the chef's expertise maybe I should transfer him to California. Since he made it to your specifications, we've obviously been wasting your talents. How would you like

to plan some menus?'' He added quickly, ''A business arrangement only, of course—unaffected by our marital
status, or lack thereof.''

''I'd love to—'' Meg realized almost at once that she
was responding as herself. Would Rhea have loved to?
Probably not, from what Mike Aragon had said about her.
She objected to doing any kind of chores, preferring to
spend her time with personal trainers and voice coaches,
attending fashion shows or hosting parties.

But it was too late. Jake was nodding his approval.

''If you think I'm capable,'' she added.

''After today's lunch? Rhea, that lunch blew me away.
I knew you liked good food, but I thought your only talent
was the ability to reduce a chef to tears—sorry, that slipped
out. You're trying to be nice and I keep delving into the
past.''

''No delving,'' Meg said. ''Per our agreement.''

Glancing up at the cliff again, she saw no sign of anyone
spying on them, so peeled off the shirt and ran to the water,
the sand burning her feet. She'd worry later about the rash
promise to work for Chastain Enterprises. There were more
pressing problems to handle.

JAKE WATCHED HER splash into the water, his blood churning. This new Rhea continued to puzzle him. It was going
to take every ounce of control he possessed to keep his
hands off her. She must know the effect her near nakedness
was having on him, which was only enhanced by the brief
glimpses of her body that he had caught when she discarded
his shirt before swimming. Was this a test she was putting
him to, to see if he could still feel desire for her? Or was
it his punishment for asking for a divorce? Either way, Jake
vowed not to play her game. Rhea obviously believed she

still had the power to captivate him. She was wrong, but it would be amusing to watch her try.

MEG AND JAKE DINED that evening in the walled courtyard of the hotel beside a softly lit fountain, separated from a pair of honeymooners by several large urns trailing flowers. The moon had not yet risen and the sky was studded with stars.

The impossibly romantic setting was having an unexpected effect on Meg. She was dining with a handsome, dynamic stranger who was charming, witty, and attentive to her every need. She told herself that Jake was obviously trying to keep to their agreement and that no man could consistently be this well-behaved.

But it was impossible for her not to compare Jake Chastain to Hal, and to see, perhaps clearly for the first time, that her marriage had been doomed from the start.

Hal had been one of the stars of culinary school who expected to become a world-famous chef, but wasn't willing to climb the ladder step by step. He refused to accept the dismal statistics of new-restaurant failure, persisted in borrowing money long after it was no longer propping up the business, wouldn't cut back on his extravagant lifestyle, alienated everyone who tried to help him, and closed his eyes to the ruins around him.

Meg was sure that they could have made a go of the catering business, but Hal was devastated by what he perceived as loss of status. He missed strolling through the restaurant, greeting people, being complimented, flirting with the women. In the catering business he was expected to inconspicuously provide the food and then fade into the background. There simply wasn't enough glory for him.

Still, Meg had not seen his defection coming.

She sipped champagne and wondered how many setbacks Jake had overcome to get where he was today. She was also becoming intensely curious about Rhea. What sort of woman was she that she could resist this man's incredible appeal?

She looked across the table, and Jake's eyes met hers.

He smiled enigmatically. "We should have come here months ago. Something about this island has transformed you." His jaw moved slightly and he added, "I know I'm not blameless in the mess we made of our marriage. Workaholic that I am, I thought I didn't have to court you after I married you. We didn't spend enough time alone together. Except for that weekend in Capri."

He glanced away, but not before Meg caught a glimpse of regret in his eyes—and she wondered what had happened in Capri.

Feeling some comment was called for, Meg said, "You mustn't blame yourself, Jake. Your business is time-consuming."

Surprise flickered in his dark eyes. He said slowly, "I demanded a lot of you—business dinners with people you didn't know or have anything in common with. Wanting you to learn more about my various enterprises. I felt you were wasting your time with frivolous pursuits when you could have been doing something useful. That's why I was so delighted today when you agreed to do some menu planning for the hotels."

Meg made a noncommittal sound. That rash promise would be difficult to explain to the real Rhea.

Jake went on. "I couldn't understand your obsession with making yourself over. It seemed you were never satisfied with the way you looked, dressed, spoke, walked. You'll never know how it irritated me to come home and find a personal trainer or a voice coach or a hairstylist following you around. And by the way, I wish you'd let your hair go back to its natural color. "

He gave an exasperated sigh. "There I go again. Trying to tell you what to do, how to live. It's too late for that now. It's just that for the first time you seem to be open to discussion about what's wrong between us."

"Perhaps it would be a good idea to talk about what was *right* between us," Meg suggested. "Apparently we do know how to relax together, when we have time."

Jake raised his glass of Dom Pérignon. "To a perfect day, Rhea. I don't remember when I felt this relaxed." He quoted lightly, "It's almost like being in love."

She tried to look away, but found she couldn't. She thought she might have said his name, but wasn't sure. There were warning signals buzzing in her ears, and perhaps she'd had too much champagne, because she was imagining what it might be like if Jake *were* falling in love with her—with Meg—and there was no Rhea waiting to snatch him back.

Jake smiled, his teeth very white against his swarthy skin. "I don't ever remember seeing that look on your face before. There's a softness there that's wreaking havoc with my resolve. You've never looked at me like that before. What's happening here, Rhea?"

Meg hastily lowered her eyes. "It has been a lovely day, hasn't it?"

"Yes, it has…and we still have tonight."

There was no mistaking the smoldering promise in his dark eyes.

Chapter Six

As they walked back to their bungalow, Jake took Meg's hand, and the gesture seemed natural, right. She felt a quiver travel up her arm, even when he said offhandedly, "We have to keep up appearances. Our guests could be watching."

They strolled through the scented night in silence, but Meg's thoughts and emotions were caught in a whirlwind. She couldn't be falling in love with this man. He was another woman's husband.

In the bungalow, the bedroom door was open and soft lights illuminated the round bed. The satin coverlet had been turned back and a single red rose adorned the pillow.

Jake saw her glance in the direction of the bed. "This is a honeymoon hotel, remember?" he said. "We wanted romantic ambience, and the usual mints on the pillow didn't do it."

Meg nodded, afraid that any comment she made might be misconstrued. What was happening to sensible, feet-on-the-ground, play-by-the-rules Meg?

"Thank you again, for a perfect day, Rhea." His voice was husky with an unspoken question that Meg recognized only too well. The physical attraction between them was a

palpable force that they were both having trouble concealing.

Jake's carefully orchestrated attitude of indifference was
more evident in his words than in his body language, and
the look in his eyes made her heart begin a slow dance
against her ribs. She longed to melt into his arms, and only
when he called her by his wife's name did her conscience
kick in again.

As calmly as she could, she said, "Good night, Jake."
Her heartbeat was surely loud enough for him to hear.

A raw flame flickered in his eyes. The small space between them resonated with yearning.

Slowly he reached out with one arm, encircled her waist
and pulled her close to him.

Knowing he was about to kiss her, she couldn't move or
speak. Her eyelids felt heavy although she was wide-awake,
and a tingling she had never experienced this intensely was
working its way insistently to nerve endings too long ignored.

She swayed toward him and his mouth found hers. Her
arms went around him and she pressed closer, returning his
kiss, even as distant warning voices clamored to be heard.

His kiss was like nothing she had ever known. It came
close to being an act of love in itself. All rational thought
vanished as their mouths blended, and Jake held her so
closely that she couldn't tell which was his heartbeat and
which was hers. She felt as if they were soaring through
the cosmos, alone together in the universe, and she never
wanted the kiss to end, never wanted to lose the magic of
his nearness.

The phone rang, the sound shrill, shocking.

"Damn," Jake muttered. "I'll unplug it."

Reality rushed back for Meg. "No, wait, it could be important." *It could be your wife, calling to tell you I'm an imposter.*

"More important than this?" Jake asked, holding her closer.

Meg slipped out of his arms and picked up the phone. Ducane's voice, agitated and apologetic, came over the line. "Madame Rhea, forgive the intrusion—I am so sorry—a police officer is calling. It's regarding M'sieur's mother."

She handed Jake the phone. "You'd better take this."

He took the phone and listened for a moment. Then he said quietly, "I'll charter a plane immediately."

To Meg he said, "My mother's had an accident. She's in the hospital." He was already punching numbers into the phone.

MEG GLANCED NERVOUSLY up and down the hospital corridor as she waited for Mike to answer his phone. She cut his greeting short. "It's me. I'm at the Mission Trauma Center. Jake's mother was hurt in a freeway pileup. You've got to—"

She broke off and hurriedly hung up the phone as she saw Jake emerge from his mother's room. He hadn't argued when she suggested that he see his mother alone first.

Jake glanced at the telephone, his eyes narrowing. Then he said curtly, "Keep her company for a few minutes while I speak to her doctors. Don't let her rile you—or vice versa."

THE WOMAN LYING in the hospital bed in a private room filled to overflowing with flowers swiveled her exotic dark eyes in Meg's direction. "Sorry to disappoint you, Rhea. They say I'm going to live."

One side of her face was bruised and there was a cast on her left arm. She had Jake's chiseled cheekbones and sensual mouth, but Meg's attention focused on her remark, which spoke volumes about her relationship with her daughter-in-law.

Meg said, "I'm so glad you're going to be all right."

"Of course you are, dear." Jessica Chastain's voice was drugged, but still managed to drip with sarcasm.

"Is there anything you need?" Meg asked, feeling inadequate and wishing Jake would return.

"You will take care of Huxley, won't you?" There was a sly gleam in the dark eyes that looked so unnervingly like Jake's.

"Yes, of course." *Who is Huxley?*

"I mean, personally. You, Rhea. Not a maid."

Huxley must be a pet. A dog? A cat? *Please,* Meg thought, *not a boa constrictor.* She said, "I promise."

Jessica tried to laugh, but it turned into a choking cough that caused I.V. tubes to shake alarmingly.

Meg grabbed the nurse's button and pressed.

"I'm…all…right," Jessica wheezed.

But the door burst open and two doctors, a nurse and Jake appeared.

"It only hurts…when I laugh," Jessica said.

Meg grinned, in spite of her concern. She had a feeling that, given the opportunity, she would like Jake's mother.

"A BROKEN ELBOW, scrapes and bruises," Jake said as they rode the elevator down to the parking garage. "It could have been a lot worse."

"Yes, it could. Those chain-reaction freeway pileups can be deadly. How long did the doctors say she'd have to stay in the hospital?"

"Just a couple of days, all being well. They want to run a few tests."

"Your mother asked me to take care of Huxley," Meg

said, wondering how Rhea addressed her mother-in-law. During their visit, Meg had carefully avoided calling her anything.

Jake gave her a sidelong glance. "She was baiting you, as usual."

"Even so, perhaps I'd better…"

"We'll stop by her house. I'm sure Carmelita will stay with him until Jessica goes home." Jake opened the car door for her. He was looking at her strangely, and Meg was unable to interpret what the look meant.

His mother's house was a two-story redwood with wraparound balconies, clinging to a hillside that overlooked the architecturally quaint and charming town of Laguna Beach. There would be a white-water view of the spectacular bay from the balconies, probably all the way to Catalina, Meg thought enviously.

Carmelita proved to be a petite woman of about fifty, her salt-and-pepper hair swept into a smooth coil on top of her head. She was already speaking even before she opened the front doors.

"…and she knows better than to be anywhere near the El Toro Y in rush hour. How is she? They wouldn't tell me nothing on the phone, just that she's satisfactory. Satisfactory! What does satisfactory mean? Oh, wait, you've got Mrs. Rhea with you. I'd better put Huxley outside before you come in—oh, no!"

The last exclamation was made as an enormous black-and-tan Doberman came skittering across the slate entry at full gallop.

Jake stepped in front of Meg, but Carmelita, surprisingly strong for her diminutive size, had pushed Meg aside, and in the resulting confusion the dog skidded to a halt in front of her.

Meg promptly dropped to her knees and offered her

hand, palm up, avoiding the dog's eye. "Hi, boy, hi, Huxley." She spoke softly, calmly. "Down, boy. Good dog. Good boy."

For a moment the dog seemed puzzled. He sniffed her hand, then whined softly. Meg slowly moved her hand closer, first stroking his chest with one finger, then sliding her hand upward to rub behind his ear and fondle his head.

For what seemed an endless moment, nobody spoke. Meg had already concluded that Rhea either didn't like dogs in general or Huxley in particular, and that the feeling was mutual. The chances were that she had just given herself away, but she had acted instinctively and it was too late to worry about the consequences. She looked up at Jake expectantly.

"That's the first time he hasn't growled at you." There was pleased wonderment in his voice. "Wait till Jessica hears about this. She'll never believe it."

Huxley was now nuzzling Meg and licking her hand. "I just thought…it was time to make friends."

Jake stared at her. "You seem obsessed with making friends lately. First me, now Huxley. Next thing I know you'll have Jessica eating out of your hand."

Carmelita shrieked with laughter, then clapped her hand to her mouth and gasped, "Oh, excuse me!"

JAKE PERSUADED Carmelita, who normally only worked days, to stay at the house with Huxley for a few days, then suggested they go to an ocean-side café for brunch.

As Rhea examined the menu, he studied her, trying to make sense of the transformation in her. Outwardly, she looked the same—albeit perhaps more serene than before. But it seemed every other aspect of her personality had undergone a radical change. Most noticeably, her former terror of Jess's Doberman had been replaced by a fearless gesture of friendship that had turned Huxley into putty in her hands.

Jake reflected grimly that the same was probably true of himself and he couldn't help but wonder, in view of her past history, just what Rhea was up to. Suspicion of his wife's actions had become a way of life. She'd tricked him too many times in the past for him to trust that she was sincere now in anything she did or said.

So why, knowing this, did he want her more than ever before? This past weekend he had felt desire for her that was so intense it dominated all of his thoughts and actions. He had even come close to forgetting that he had flown to the island to discuss the terms of their divorce.

The memory of their kiss last night haunted him. Recalling the taste of her mouth and the scent of her skin threatened to inflame his senses again, and he quickly looked away, forcing himself to question her motive for melting so sweetly into his arms. Especially since she hadn't been able to wait to call somebody from the hospital. For once, she hadn't been able to hide her guilty expression when she saw him approaching, and had practically flung the phone down.

Jake wasn't sure whether he would prefer that she'd been calling Sloan, or a lover. Either way, that surreptitious call served to confirm his suspicions that her new attitude was all an act, put on to forestall a divorce.

They were both too tense to be particularly hungry, and after picking at his food Jake said, ''I'd like to get Jess a box of Godiva chocolates and a dozen roses, and check on her again.''

He expected Rhea to complain that she wanted to go straight home, but she surprised him. ''Yes, of course.''

MEG HAD BEEN in Jake's company practically every second and hadn't had a chance to call Mike, so she didn't know when to expect Rhea. It would be embarrassing in the extreme if they arrived at the Chastain residence to find her there.

"You're very quiet," Jake remarked as he blended into traffic on Pacific Coast Highway.

"I was just thinking about your mother," Meg said, giving in to an impulse. "Most people would have been feeling sorry for themselves, under the circumstances, rather than kidding around as she was."

The long night without sleep must have affected her judgment, Meg thought when she heard herself add, "I'd really like to get to know her better."

What am I doing? Remaking Rhea's life for her? A reckless sense of entitlement seemed to have overcome reason.

Jake gripped the steering wheel in mock alarm. "Don't shock me like that while we're in traffic, please!"

"She doesn't like me very much, does she." It wasn't really a question, since it had been obvious.

Jake responded, "You're both strong-willed women. You were bound to clash. But if she gets an opportunity to observe your brand-new persona, Jess is going to be as enchanted as I am—trying not to be."

"What new persona, Jake?" Meg asked cautiously.

He glanced at her out of the corner of his eye. "Either the past year or so was some kind of act, or the past two days were, Rhea. This weekend, you've managed to become the woman I've dreamed of all my life. If I didn't know you better, I'd be inclined to hope you've really changed. But that would be a vain hope, wouldn't it? I don't know how long you can keep this up, Rhea, but don't overestimate your allure."

Meg tried to think of some way to steer the conversation away from the intimate subject of the Chastains' marriage.

Back in California and in the light of day, she felt like the imposter that she was.

"Jake, let's not hold any postmortems right now. We're both tired, and you're upset about your mother."

"We weren't tired or upset last night, Rhea. There was much more than simple lust involved in that kiss. For one mad moment I even dared think about reconciliation." He paused. "Or perhaps a whole new beginning. But that's out of the question, isn't it?"

Meg tried to read the deeper meaning behind his words. There was both regret and a certain wistful longing in his tone. Rhea had obviously hurt him, but was he really ready to divorce her? On the long flight home Meg had given a great deal of thought to what she would say about that passionate kiss, when she had come close to yielding to desire.

Now she wondered if her rehearsed response sounded wooden. "Why don't we wait a few days, until your mother is out of the hospital, before we make any decisions? A few days to settle back into our regular routine will put everything in perspective."

Watching his profile, she saw his expression harden. He drummed on the steering wheel with his fingers. "Sure. But don't harbor any false hopes that I'm going to change my mind about the divorce. And don't stall too long. As you well know, I'm not a patient man."

He drove in moody silence for the rest of the journey.

Their destination proved to be an oceanfront house shielded from the coast highway by a dense barrier of trees and shrubs.

As he slowed for the turn, Jake said, "This is closer to the hospital and Jessica's house. I'm going to stay here until she's back on her feet. Of course, if you'd prefer to go home…"

"Home" was evidently somewhere else. She had no choice but to answer, "No, I'll stay here."

He flashed her a questioning glance. "I know you've never cared much for this place. Are you sure you wouldn't rather take one of the cars and drive home?"

"No, I'd prefer to stay." Apart from the fact that she didn't know where "home" was, Meg didn't want to have to deal with the occupants of the main house.

Unlocking the front door, Jake said, "Fortunately Mason's been sending a cleaning woman over, so we shouldn't have to face any cobwebs."

They entered a house that to Meg screamed "bachelor pad." An older, wood-frame structure that surely was underbuilt for the pricey location, the house had taken on an abandoned atmosphere.

"I'll call the hospital and check on Jessica," Jake said. "Then I should make a fast trip down to Dana Point and check on the project there. Perhaps you could order in some food for us."

She nodded her agreement, and he asked, "Do you want to call Mason and have him send over one of the maids, or shall we just camp out for a couple of days until Jess can leave the hospital?"

"We'll manage," Meg answered, not knowing who Mason was or how to reach him and certainly not prepared to deal with a maid.

"Good. I'll see how Jess is doing and then take off."

When he finished his call to the hospital, Meg walked with him to the door. He paused, his dark gaze locked with hers, demanding the truth. "You'll be here when I get back?"

"Yes, of course. I said I would stay."

"Why do I get the feeling you're going to slip away at any second? Or at least, that this new you will disappear."

Meg felt her face flood with color. Not knowing what else to say or do, she said, "If you could give me an idea of how long you'll be, I'll plan dinner."

He stared at her with that questioning look that she wished she could interpret, then finally said, "I'll probably be gone all afternoon. I'll take the rental car. If you do need to go out, at least one of the cars in the garage should be gassed up and in running order. If it isn't, Mason is in trouble. The keys are in the top drawer of the desk."

THE MINUTE JAKE left, Meg called Mike Aragon. She got his answering machine, listened to Groucho Marx sing "Hello, I must be going," then left word that she was at Jake's beach house just south of Laguna Beach, that she had no idea of the address, but that he had to get Rhea down here within the next couple of hours.

Waiting, she explored the rest of the house. Three bedrooms, three baths, a study, a room filled with exercise equipment. The kitchen looked unused, as did the rest of the house. Outside, a flagged patio led to a flight of steps cut into the cliff face. The descent to the beach was steep, but there was a wooden handrail.

The phone rang inside the house. Hoping it was Mike, she raced to pick it up. "Hello?"

"Mrs. Chastain?" It was a female voice—no discernable accent, a little sharp.

"Yes," Meg answered, startled that it wasn't Mike calling back. After all, who else knew anyone was here?

A soft chuckle on the line, smothered almost at once. "Are you alone?"

"Who is this?"

"Rhea." She made her name sound like a warning.

Meg said, "Thank heaven. Can you come right away?"

"Aragon said you want to leave. I'm calling to find out what it would take to get you to stay—just for a few days."

"Mrs. Chastain, your mother-in-law had an accident, she's in the hospital. Your husband needs you."

"I don't suppose the old witch broke her neck, did she?"

Meg tried to keep revulsion from creeping into her reply. "She broke her elbow."

"So, she'll recover. Look, I'm in San Francisco. I can't come right away. I have to stay here with a very dear friend who is dying. Just hang in for a couple of days, that's all I ask."

"Friend? I thought it was your brother who was dying."

"Just between us, Meg—" the voice was low now, conspiratorial, wheedling "—I told Aragon it was my brother, but it's really the man I was with for years before I met Jake. He's got nobody, only me, and the doctors say he could go any day now."

"That wasn't all you misled us about, was it?" Meg asked grimly. *There's the little detail of a possible divorce.*

"Okay, so Jake and I had a little tiff. We always make up, but we won't if he knows I deceived him. Will you stay one more day? My friend needs me."

"Mrs. Chastain, I really feel your first duty is to your husband. You've got to come home. He's already suspicious of me."

"Honey, if you'd blown your cover Jake would have said something by now. Whatever you're doing, just keep doing it. Where is he now, by the way?"

"He said he was going to Dana Point to check on a project."

"And there'll be other projects tomorrow and the next day. He'll run from one to the other. You'll hardly see him, and when you do he'll drag you to the hospital to see the old bat."

"Your mother-in-law seemed anything but an old bat. But I'm sure she's suspicious of me, too. I didn't even know what to call her."

"Jessica. Everybody calls her *Jessica*. Jake calls her *Jess*."

"I don't know enough about your life. Who is Mason?" Meg knew she shouldn't be asking such questions, which implied she would agree to stay, but she couldn't seem to stop herself.

"He's the butler. He takes care of the main house. What's the deal with going to the beach house? Jake wants to be near Jessica, I suppose?"

"Yes. At least until she's out of the hospital. He asked a lady named Carmelita to stay at her house with Huxley."

"Miserable mutt. I hate that dog. Carmelita is day help— she's been with Jessica for years. She won't have a live-in. Jessica is an artist, in case the subject comes up. She and I don't get along, so she won't expect you to visit her. In fact, why don't you leave Jake at the beach house and go to the main house?"

"No...no, this is all wrong. We can't go on deceiving your husband like this. When I agreed to the arrangement, he was supposed to be in London."

"He was. How could I have known he would fly to St. Maarten? Look, just stay another day. Twenty-four hours, okay?"

Meg thought of the way Jake looked at her and the way she felt when he was near. "No. I can't. Mrs. Chastain, you've got to come back here immediately or I intend to confess my part in the deception to your husband."

There was a gasp on the line. "My God, no! You can't tell him—there's no telling what he might do, to you as well as me. You don't know him like I do. He's a violent man—he's beaten me in the past...oh, please don't tell him!''

Meg grappled with the image of Jake beating a woman. Was it possible that he was a Jekyll-and-Hyde? She said, ''I'm not sure I believe that.''

''Then believe this—if you tell him we deceived him you'll wreck our marriage. Do you want that on your conscience?''

Meg bit her lip. ''I'll stay until you get here, as long as we can change places today.''

There was a pause, then an exasperated sigh. ''All right, I'll see if I can get a flight out today. But like I said, I'm in San Francisco. It's going to take awhile. Maybe I can get there some time this evening.''

''I'll stay until then. We need to plan how we're going to switch places,'' Meg said.

''I'll call you as soon as I know when I can get there. Then we can arrange to meet somewhere.''

''All right,'' Meg said reluctantly. ''But please, hurry.''

Replacing the receiver, Meg went into the kitchen. The refrigerator was running, but empty except for a six-pack of cola and a bottle of mineral water.

The doorbell rang.

Meg froze.

Chapter Seven

Meg didn't move. The doorbell rang again. A moment later, a male voice crackled over an intercom inside the house.

"Come on, open up. Rhea sent me."

Meg hesitated. She had just finished speaking to Rhea on the phone when the doorbell rang. How could she have sent somebody that fast?

Uneasy, Meg went to the door. No security viewer or chain.

But whoever was out there knew how to access the intercom.

"Your name," the intercom voice said, "is Margaret Lindley—usually called Meg. You were hired by Mike Aragon. Now open up."

Easing the door open, she faced a giant with a shaved head and thin black mustache. He wore an Armani suit, and there was a sleek black Porsche parked on the driveway.

If she was surprised by his appearance, the feeling was evidently mutual as his pale eyes flickered over her and he shook his head disbelievingly. "No doubt about it. You're a dead ringer for Rhea."

Meg cleared her throat nervously. "And you are?"

He grinned. "I'm your 'brother,' Sloan."

Meg remembered then. She had seen this man before—

at the airport the day she left for St. Maarten. She also saw
now why Jake had laughed at the notion that Sloan was
terminally ill. He was the picture of health, with the phy-
sique of a prizefighter. He ran deep-set eyes over her in-
sinuatingly, and cold fear immobilized her. She didn't want
him in the house with her, but couldn't slam the door on
him when his foot was over the threshold.

Sloan said, "I need to check out the house while Chastain's gone. Rhea's on her way, but she's only been inside
this place once, over a year ago. She'll call me from the
plane, and I'll fill her in on what to expect."

"I don't understand—" Meg began.

"You're here, you're familiar with the house. When
Rhea arrives, her husband will expect her to be. What's to
understand?"

"There's nothing unusual about the house. Except for
the location I'd think it fairly modest by Chastain stan-
dards—" Meg began, but he pushed past her.

Heart thumping, she went to the phone.

Sloan snapped, "Who're you calling?"

"I'm going to see if I can get some groceries delivered.
Jake asked me to before he left."

There was some comfort in having the phone in her hand,
but having this muscular giant prowling through the house
terrified her. He grunted in response, then moved toward
the study, where she heard him moving about.

When he came back into the living room, Meg said,
"I'm going to have to ask you to leave now, because I
can't get groceries delivered. I'll have to go and pick them
up."

Eyes like gray marbles flickered over her. "You're not
bailing, are you? Rhea needs you to stay until she gets
back."

Meg put down the phone. Her hand was trembling. "I

told you I was going grocery shopping. I'll be back. But I need you to leave so I can lock up.''

For a long heart-stopping minute he stood staring at her. Then he moved closer, licked his lips and reached out with one finger to trace the contour of her cheek. Her skin crawled.

She forced herself to look him in the eye without flinching, although every nerve in her body was screaming. She said sharply, ''If Rhea wants me to continue this masquerade, you'd better go. Now.''

At length he gave her an evil grin. ''Okay. I'm done here.''

She didn't let out her breath until she heard the sports car's engine start up outside. Then she called Mike.

MEG HAD FILLED a grocery cart and was testing the ripeness of a couple of avocados. She looked up with a relieved smile as Mike approached.

His glance took in her white sleeveless blouse and pleated walking shorts, supplied by Rhea. He murmured, ''The first time I saw you it was in a supermarket. The difference this time is the display cases feature higher-priced items and the shoppers—including you—are better dressed. You look cool and elegant, by the way.''

''I feel tense and tired,'' she said. ''We had a long overnight flight.''

''Well, your weekend in the Caribbean has given your skin a peach glow, and that high-voltage smile of yours is enough to send a ripple up the spine of every man within range. I'm finding it hard to believe you were able to keep Chastain at arm's length.''

''Nevertheless,'' Meg said, ''I was.''

Mike eyed the loaded grocery cart. ''This is a cosy domestic scene. What are you going to do with all that food?''

"Take it back to the beach house and fix dinner."

"Why? You said on the phone that Rhea was on her way. There's no need for you to go back there. I'll follow you back to the house, you can leave his car in the garage and then I'll take you home."

Meg put down one of the avocados. "Is that why you insisted on meeting me when I called you?"

"Absolutely. You've got to call it off now, Meg—okay if I call you that?—too many complications. It's over."

"I have to wait for Rhea to get here," Meg said firmly. "If I walk out now, the whole weekend will have been for nothing. I can't count on her being able to get a plane from San Francisco and arriving here before Jake returns from Dana Point. She promised to call me the minute she arrives, and then I'll slip out and meet her. We'll change places and then it's all over."

"Every minute you spend with Chastain, you risk him realizing you are not his wife. How long do you think you can be with him on his home turf—with no hotel guests and staff as buffers—before he decides he wants a real wife again, not a friend?"

"You don't understand. They're talking about divorce."

"Yeah, you already told me that. But he's a man, and you're a beautiful woman."

Meg felt herself flush and she looked away quickly.

Mike caught his breath. "Damn, you're not attracted to Jake Chastain, are you? I guess I should have warned you about his reputation. He was a bachelor a long time, and I hear his powers of seduction are legendary. Not to mention his almost unlimited wealth and power being the ultimate aphrodisiac."

Angered that he dared question her morality, Meg snapped, "To me, nothing matters beyond the fact that he's someone else's husband."

Obviously deciding to take a different tack, Mike said, "Speaking of which, I may have a lead on *your* husband."

A not-so-subtle reminder that she was also married, Meg thought. She didn't answer immediately, because a mother with a young child in her cart stopped to check the avocados. After they moved down the aisle, Meg turned to him. "You know where Hal is?"

"Not exactly. The usual checks—DMV, credit cards— didn't pan out. Since there was no paper trail, I explored the possibility he'd bought a fake ID. I'll be showing Hal's picture to somebody later who may be able to help. Look, Meg, we can go back to the house, leave Jake a note—"

"In Rhea's handwriting, I suppose? No, I've thought this through very carefully. I just have to hang in until Rhea arrives sometime this evening. I'll make dinner, then I'm sure Jake will want to go back to the hospital to visit his mother. I'll suggest she'd rather see him alone, and I'll stay home. It's pretty obvious that his mother and Rhea didn't get along, so he won't be surprised."

Mike considered for a minute, then said, "I'll find your husband for you, even if Rhea cuts us loose."

"Thank you, but that isn't the reason I want to stay. I won't do anything to jeopardize the Chastain marriage."

"I thought you said it was over anyway."

"Jake mentioned a possible reconciliation."

"With you—not with Rhea."

Meg knew from Mike's expression that conflicting emotions were registering on her face, not the least of which was a startled recognition of the truth of his statement.

Mike muttered, "What have I put in motion here?"

They stared at each other. He was clearly waiting for her to reassure him that, to her, Jake Chastain was merely part of a business arrangement she'd made with his wife. But all Meg could truthfully say was, "When Rhea returns, she can deal with their problems. I won't add to them."

"I don't like it, Meg. I feel responsible for getting you into this. I think she lied to us."

"Look, Mike, whatever Rhea's reasons were for asking me to take her place, I still have an obligation to play the part until she comes back. Jake would never forgive her if he found out we'd deceived him."

"What about your jobs? Aren't you expected back at work tomorrow?"

"Carrie Hooper, who owns the catering service I work for, calls me when she needs extra help—I'm not on a regular schedule. I'll be able to make the matinee at the theater tomorrow. Rhea will be here by then."

"She asked you to stay on, didn't she," Mike said heavily. "And you're considering it."

"If I were, I wouldn't have demanded that she come back today, would I? Come on, Mike, be reasonable. I'll probably spend no more than an hour with Jake over dinner, then he'll go to the hospital and I'll bow out of the picture."

As SHE PREPARED an asparagus salad, Meg thought of her meeting with Mike and wondered why she had avoided telling him of Sloan's visit. Probably because the shaven-headed muscle man's arrival would have added an even more compelling reason for Mike to insist that she call off the masquerade immediately.

She rinsed a bunch of cilantro and was about to start chopping it when the doorbell rang again. At a seldom-used beach house, the arrival of a second visitor seemed ominous.

A dog barked outside, and Meg was pretty sure that she recognized the bark. When she opened the door, the first thing she saw was Huxley, his tongue lolling and his tail wagging. Carmelita, holding a large bag of dog food and looking flustered and upset, was halfway through a recital.

"...so I called and called, but you didn't answer the phone and I thought maybe you'd turned off the ringer and I didn't know what else to do..."

Standing aside to allow them to enter, Meg asked, "What happened? Is it Mrs. Chastain—did you hear something from the hospital?"

Carmelita's face crumpled. "No, no! Is my sister. Oh, why do troubles come in bunches, like grapes? I have to go right away and I couldn't leave Huxley alone. You know he'd tear up the house. I thought Mr. Jake would be here and tell me what to do."

"Mr. Jake had to go to a business meeting," Meg said.

"Lucky for me, you make friends with Huxley, right?"

The Doberman was busy licking Meg's hand and snuffling happily. Meg led them into the living room. "Sit down. Would you like a cup of tea?"

Carmelita shook her head. "No time. I must leave."

"Your sister is ill?"

"Very sick. Maybe die. Troubles in bunches. First Jessica, now Consuela. Gotta go to Guadalajara right away. You take care of Huxley, okay?"

Knowing she could hardly refuse, Meg didn't dare imagine what would happen when Rhea arrived and learned she had to board the Doberman. She said, "Yes, of course. How did you get here? I didn't see a car."

"Don't drive. Caught a cab. Boy, he didn't want no dogs in his damn cab but I told him I'd report him if he didn't take us. The nerve of him. Anyway, it was an emergency and you wouldn't answer your phone and I didn't have no time to fool around. I gotta go, right away. You drive me to Orange County airport now?"

"Have you called the hospital to tell Mrs. Chastain you're leaving?" Meg asked.

"Sure. She said bring Huxley to you."

I bet she did, Meg thought. "Okay, let's go," Meg said. She would have liked to call Jake, or at least leave him a note, but she had no idea how to reach him, and couldn't leave a note in her own handwriting. Maybe she could make the trip to Orange County airport and be back before he was.

HUXLEY SLURPED her neck all the way to and from the airport. By the time she arrived back at the beach house it was just about dark, but she was glad to see Jake had not yet returned. The question was, had Rhea arrived back in southern California and called while she was out?

The telephone had a built-in message machine, and she pressed the retrieval button in case Jake had called. He hadn't. But there were a couple of beeps that indicated somebody had called and hung up. Rhea?

She washed the dog drool from the back of her neck, then found a large bowl and filled it with water, piled some dog food onto a china plate, and watched Huxley make both disappear. He then settled down for a nap.

Meg turned her attention to finding table linen and setting the table. There were a couple of bottles of wine in one of the kitchen cabinets, and she considered whether or not to get it out, since Jake had expected wine with lunch the previous day. She decided to pretend she hadn't found the wine, in order to keep a clear head.

At the supermarket she had bought salmon steaks, which she would broil and serve with a cilantro-mushroom sauce. For a fast dessert she could caramelize bananas.

Handling the food, as always, relaxed her. She had made an asparagus salad earlier, but as the evening chill settled along the coast with the return of the marine layer, she thought an asparagus soup might have been better, especially served with a dollop of *crème fraîche.*

Crème fraîche…why had she thought of that now?

She and Hal had come together because of *crème fraîche.*

Hal Lindley had been the handsomest student at the Culinary Institute, with his fiery bronze hair, jade green eyes and cleft chin. He had the added distinction of having lived in France for a couple of years with a French mother who had left his military father, taking Hal with her.

Their class was still studying basics when Hal asked Meg out on a date. His opening gambit had been, "I'd like to see what your hair looks like. Will you go to the movies with me?" They were required to wear chef's hats, with all of their hair covered.

Meg had grinned and agreed. She'd carefully washed, conditioned and brushed her hair that day.

The film had been a lighthearted romp, and afterward they'd gone to a little Mexican place that made great fish tacos. Hal had been charming, funny, with a certain sophistication that most of Meg's contemporaries lacked. She had been instantly captivated.

"I'm making *crème fraîche* next weekend," he'd told her. "Would you like to join me?"

She'd never heard of the dish, but hadn't wanted to admit her ignorance and definitely wanted to pursue their acquaintance.

"I live a block from the beach," Hal added. "We'll get the *crème fraîche* started, then hit the surf."

A man who shared her love of cooking *and* her love of the beach had seemed almost too good to be true. She had bought a new bathing suit.

He was renting a room in a house owned by an elderly widow in Santa Monica, who gave him free access to her kitchen. The widow was away, visiting a friend in Pismo Beach, and so they had the house to themselves.

In a tiny immaculate kitchen Hal had warmed five cups of heavy whipping cream. "The first time I had *crème fraîche* was at an aunt's house in Normandy," he told her. "She gave me a slice of chocolate cake with this stuff on top that looked sort of like sour cream but tasted like nothing I'd ever had before."

He removed the cream from the heat. "We want it just about lukewarm, 100 degrees. When it's finished it will have a velvety texture and subtle flavor and it won't curdle in soups and sauces."

Meg watched as he transferred the warm cream to a plastic container and then stirred in five tablespoons of buttermilk. He covered the container loosely and set it aside. "Okay, let's hit the beach."

"You're not going to refrigerate it?" Meg asked.

Hal gave her a slightly superior grin. "No, it stays at room temperature. The lactic-acid-making bacteria in the buttermilk will produce a mellow complexity and luxurious texture."

If he'd quoted a love poem, Meg could not have been more dazzled.

He added, "We'll stir and taste in about eight hours."

"Eight hours," Meg had repeated, blissful at the prospect of being with him all day.

Hal nodded. "It will take twelve to thirty-six hours to thicken. Then it will keep in the refrigerator for up to ten days. But we'll sample it tomorrow."

As Meg prepared dinner in Jake's beach house, and the setting sun painted the flagged patio and west-facing windows with a wash of gold, it came to her with startling clarity that she and Hal had married too young, too soon, and that she had never truly loved him. She'd been dazzled by his expertise in the kitchen and in the surf, and by the time she came to her senses and realized how self-centered and critical he was, it was too late.

And she knew why she was thinking about how she and Hal had gotten together. It was because it would be so easy to believe what had turned out so wrong then with Hal, could be so right now with Jake Chastain.

If only he didn't belong to someone else.

Please, Rhea, call. Call now, before Jake returns. Call before I do something I'll regret.

Huxley stirred and whined softly, then gave a sharp bark. He lumbered to the front door as a key turned in the lock.

THE SETUP WAS PERFECT. *No security system and easy access up steps cut into the cliff. This time there'd be no mistake. He should never have trusted a woman to do the job. She'd been too squeamish to do it herself and had hired some goon instead.*

He'd have gone to London himself if he'd been able to leave the country, but he couldn't while he was on parole.

He waited impatiently, down on the darkening beach, hiding behind the rocks, watching the house. Waiting for the lights to go out.

Chapter Eight

Jake looked at Huxley, groveling at his feet. "How did he get here?"

Huxley wagged his tail and fawned.

Listening to his wife's explanation, Jake battled an urge to sweep her into his arms and carry her into the bedroom. He forced himself to remember the hell of the past months, but the sweetness of the past weekend intruded. Then he reminded himself of their agreement to be "just friends," and when that didn't help he focused on her hastily terminated phone call at the hospital.

This was all part of an elaborate scheme to lull him into a false sense of security. She didn't want a divorce, she wanted to maintain the status quo. And why not? She'd never let her marriage vows get in the way of doing whatever she pleased.

Despite this knowledge, Jake couldn't help but regard his wife with a quizzical half smile. "The old Rhea would have called the nearest animal shelter and boarded him," he said, patting the Doberman's head, "then given Carmelita cab fare. Instead you haul her to the airport and take care of Huxley. You know, I'm beginning to have this secret fear that you're going to rip the mask off your face and underneath you'll be a reincarnated Mother Teresa, or definitely somebody I shouldn't be lusting after.''

There seemed little point in denying that he lusted after her, since he'd made it pretty obvious. Besides, Rhea knew that any deeper feelings he'd had for her were long gone, if indeed they had ever existed beyond the realm of fantasy.

She seemed to bite back a grin. ''Oh, come on, it isn't that big of a deal. Your mother will be out of the hospital in a day or two and I didn't think it was worth upsetting her, or Huxley, by refusing to take care of him. But I am wondering who will take care of Jessica while Carmelita is in Mexico.''

''Maybe she'll let me hire a live-in nurse, although I doubt she will. You'd better call Mason in the morning and have him send one of the maids over to her house.''

Something flickered in Rhea's eyes—a hesitancy, or slight confusion. He'd seen that look a couple of times during the past weekend and it puzzled him, because it was so out of character for her to be uncertain about anything. Was it possible that she was genuinely trying to make amends for the hell she'd put him through these past months?

No. More likely she was trying to assess his reaction to her new facade. Well, let her keep guessing.

She said, ''Dinner can be ready in ten minutes, if you're hungry. I imagine you'll want to visit your mother this evening.''

''I stopped at the hospital on my way home, so we don't need to go back this evening. Jessica had a room full of her Laguna artsy-craftsy types, all of whom regard me as some sort of changeling the gypsies left on her doorstep.''

He sniffed the air. ''Something smells good. Do I have time for a fast shower before we eat? It's been a long haul since we left St. Maarten.''

"Sure, go ahead."

Jake managed to resist asking her to join him.

MEG WONDERED how she was going to be able to take the call from Rhea. Perhaps she'd call while Jake was in the shower, although it was probably too early for her to have flown in from the north.

The telephone was silent while Jake was in the bathroom. When he returned, Meg was carrying the asparagus salad to the table. He went straight to the cabinet where she'd seen the wine, took out a bottle and followed.

"Chardonnay okay?"

"Perfect."

The dining room was furnished in Spanish Colonial style, and he pulled out one of the tall-backed mahogany chairs for her. A wrought-iron and amber glass chandelier over the table cast a golden glow.

Jake paused to look around the room, then shook his head in baffled wonder. "I once thought all this stuff was cool. Did I ever tell you that this was the first house I ever bought?"

"You might have mentioned it," Meg said carefully.

"The furniture belongs in a Mediterranean-style house, but I got it cheap in Tijuana. Jess calls it my Joaquin Murrieta period. She felt I had a lot in common with the wily bandit."

Meg smiled. He poured the wine, handed her a glass and raised his. "To amicable solutions."

The telephone rang. Before she could move, Jake, who was still on his feet, had reached it.

"Chastain." He paused, then said, "Hello?"

He hung up the phone. "Nobody there."

Rhea, Meg thought.

He looked at her levelly. "You expecting a call, Rhea?

Are we dealing with that old cliché—if a man answers, hang up?"

"No, I'm not expecting any calls," Meg said, feeling the lie flood her face with color.

He sighed audibly. "Why do I bother to ask?"

Returning to the table, Jake sat down. "We'll have to answer the phone, since Jessica might decide to call. After we've eaten, I'll call the hospital and tell her about Huxley."

"She didn't mention that she'd sent Carmelita here with him when you were at the hospital?"

"No. I imagine she expected you to turn them both away. I'm looking forward to telling her he's here."

At the mention of his name, Huxley eased himself down beside Meg's chair and laid his head protectively over her right foot.

Jake raised an eyebrow. "If I didn't see it, I wouldn't have believed it."

As he began to enjoy the food and wine, it seemed to Meg that he relaxed, became less hostile. Several times Meg looked up to find him watching her and thought she saw regret in his eyes. *He doesn't really want to divorce his wife,* she thought. *He's hoping they can reconcile. It wasn't me he wanted last night, it was Rhea.*

The telephone rang again just as they were finishing eating. Meg leapt to her feet. "I'll get it. Have some more dessert."

Grabbing the phone, she wondered how to let Rhea know that Jake was with her. But it was Jessica's voice that came over the line. "Have you killed my dog yet?"

"Hello, Jessica," Meg said. "Huxley's fine. How are you feeling?"

"Like I was hit by a truck. Oh, silly me. I was! Let me speak to my son."

"It's your mother," Meg said, handing him the phone.

As she began to clear the table, she heard Jake say, "Yes, I know, me too. Now, Jess, be nice. They're getting along famously. Did you eat anything? Yes, I know all about hospital food. Shall I send something over? Rhea ordered in the best meal I've had lately. I could call and have them—what? All right. Tomorrow perhaps."

Meg slipped the plates and cutlery into the dishwasher. She had washed all of the cooking utensils earlier. *He thought I'd ordered the food in.* Rhea evidently didn't cook. Why hadn't she surmised that? Was it because she secretly wanted to impress him? Meg felt a wave of guilt wash over her. What was she *doing?*

She was still standing in front of the dishwasher when Jake came up behind her and slipped his arms around her waist. He kissed the nape of her neck, the warm pressure of his lips sending a shiver through her entire body.

He murmured, "Just a little thank-you kiss, Rhea, for the perfect dinner. How about I light a fire and turn on some music? Let's just relax this evening. No postmortems on dead marriages, no recriminations or explanations."

Meg nodded, without turning around. He lingered, his arms around her, for a moment. Then he withdrew, and she heard his footsteps cross the tiled floor.

When she joined him minutes later, the living room was filled with flickering firelight and the soft strains of Debussy. Jake was sitting on one of two couches arranged on either side of the brick fireplace, and she took the opposite one.

In the firelight his expression was watchful, brooding. "It isn't possible for us to be detached from one another, is it? We generate too much electricity for that. More than ever, it seems, since we talked of divorce."

Meg said cautiously, "We're both tired and wound up tonight, Jake. We need to be home and rested before we...before—"

"How easy it would be to fall in love with you, Rhea. Really in love this time. When we first met I believe we both mistook physical attraction for love. But now...I didn't think it was possible to feel this way after all you've done, but how I want to believe this change in you isn't just superficial."

His simple declaration, from across the room, stunned her with its sincerity. *He loves Rhea, not you,* a voice in her head warned. But the demon on her shoulder pointed out that he had been about to divorce Rhea.

She had to respond. As Rhea. Not as Meg. She said, "I believe we can love each other again, Jake. But we need to have some serious discussions about our problems. Not tonight, though. Let's just be friends for one more evening."

The mask descended over his face again. "Sure. Whatever you say. Is the music all right?"

She replied without thinking, "I love Debussy. 'Afternoon of a Faun,' isn't it?"

Jake was silent for a long minute, then he asked quietly, "Who *are* you?"

Meg's stomach lurched. She was about to babble something, anything, when he started to speak again.

"You've been an enigma since the day we met. I never knew what to expect from one day to the next, which new facet of yourself you would be showing. But this past weekend...you've shown me what I always hoped was your true self. And I believe I could love you more deeply than you'll ever know."

He stood up and walked over to a cabinet, opened it to reveal a CD player. A moment later the music changed. A Latin beat, sensual, compelling.

Turning, he extended his hand to her. "Will you at least dance with me? If you won't let me make love to you, at least let me hold you in my arms for a tango."

Chapter Nine

Meg didn't move. The log crackled in the fireplace, the flames sending golden images dancing on the walls in accompaniment to the erotic beat and dramatic pauses of the tango.

Jake still stood, his hand extended toward her, waiting.

In that instant Meg would have given anything to be able to stand up, slip into his arms and dance with him.

"No ulterior motives," Jake said. "We always danced well together, at least."

Meg rose slowly, and he took her hand.

Now he's going to realize I'm not Rhea, and I can't do anything to prevent it, Meg thought.

As if in a dream she felt his arm slip around her waist. He took her right hand in his left, but before she realized what was happening there was a pause in the music and he bent her backward over his arm in a dip almost to the floor, his mouth so close to hers that she held her breath, anticipating a kiss. But he merely smiled and pulled her upright again.

Several months earlier she had helped cater a party at a dance studio and had caught fascinating glimpses of dancers demonstrating the graceful turns and dips of several ballroom dances, including the tango. There was no way she could fake the complicated steps.

Jake's arm tightened around her, and as the music resumed she felt his left thigh press against her as he tried to move forward. But when she didn't slide her right foot backward as he expected, he stopped short, looking at her in surprise.

JAKE STARED at his wife, seeing confusion and a certain wistful longing written on her lovely face, and for an instant he had the odd feeling he had never really known this woman. He had slept with her and they had fought like tigers...but he had never truly learned what drove her, what was important to her, nor had he come close to understanding her mercurial moods. Yet in this one moment, as she went rigid in his arms, ignoring the music, the expression on her exquisite face told him that she might finally be ready to reveal herself to him.

The tango forgotten, Jake held his breath, waiting.

She said, "Jake, this isn't a good idea. I'm really too tired to dance."

Disappointment and anger surged through him then, and before he could contain it his fingers were digging deeply into the soft flesh of her back, holding her in a viselike embrace that expressed more power than passion. Her breasts were crushed against his chest and her eyes widened in shocked surprise.

He said harshly, "What if I were to use you the way you've used me all these months, Rhea? You know damn well I want you—and after all, you are still my wife. Maybe I'm tired of this platonic bunk."

"Jake, please let go of me." He felt a tremor pass through her body, but her gaze was level and her voice calm, with an edge that suggested that she would fight if he stepped out of line. "I'm too exhausted to either dance or argue with you tonight."

He didn't release her. "Did you really expect me to remain indifferent to your sweetly seductive act of the last couple of days, Rhea?"

"I didn't mean to be seductive...I just wanted us to try to get along."

"Sure you did. Now tell me, who did you call from the hospital? And who did you call from St. Maarten? Don't look so surprised, or so innocent. When I interrupted the hospital call, I decided to check to see if you made any calls from the island. You called southern California several times. Since Sloan was up north in San Francisco last I heard, I have to assume there's a new man in your life."

"No!" The word was wrenched from her like a cry of pain.

An ominous possibility flashed into Jake's mind. Rhea genuinely had tried this past couple of days to make amends. She obviously wanted to stall any discussion about the divorce. What if one of her lovers were blackmailing her?

Jake finally relaxed his grip slightly. Maybe he would adopt a wait-and-see attitude while keeping tabs on her bank accounts until they were legally separated.

THE TELEPHONE RANG. Grateful for the distraction, Meg twisted free and almost dived to answer the call. Jake remained motionless, his gaze following her.

"Hello," Meg said. Her voice sounded tense, slightly hoarse.

Rhea's voice whispered over the line. "I know he's there with you. I'm down on the beach. Get down here as soon as you can—I'm getting the damn sand in my shoes."

Meg put the phone down, relief washing over her.

"Another hang-up?" Jake asked grimly.

"Yes."

"That's strange. Other than a maid coming over to clean, this place hasn't been occupied for almost two years."

"Probably wrong numbers."

His face was a mask. "If you want to call somebody, Rhea, go ahead. I'm beyond caring."

"I don't need to call anybody," Meg said miserably, wishing she could shed the cloak of Rhea's misdeeds and tell him that she understood why he had lost his temper, and that he deserved love and loyalty and truth. But then, who was she to talk about truth? She was living a lie, and if she was hurt by it, then it served her right.

Jake said, "I'm sorry the tango degenerated into something akin to an adagio dance. I apologize for manhandling you."

"You've been under strain. I understand."

Huxley ambled into the room and nuzzled Meg's leg.

She said, "He probably should go outside for a while."

"I'll take him," Jake said.

"No, please!" Meg said quickly, visions of Jake descending to the beach and running into Rhea flashing before her eyes. "I mean, you've been working all day and didn't sleep last night. Let me take him."

Huxley wagged his tail, his tongue lolling.

"We can both go," Jake said. "It's dark and you're not familiar with the cliff steps."

"I don't have to go down to the beach to take him for a walk."

Jake gave her the puzzled look that indicated she had said something odd again. "Rhea, the only alternative is the Coast Highway—all kinds of traffic and no sidewalk. Had you forgotten?"

So that's why Rhea wanted to meet on the beach. Meg murmured, "Oh, yes, of course."

"He doesn't need to go for a walk," Jake said. "I'll just take him out into the backyard to do the necessary."

"All right. I think I'll get ready for bed," Meg said, giving an elaborate yawn. "I'll leave the master bedroom for you."

The hard glint returned to his eyes. "Very well, I'll say good-night. Tomorrow, Rhea, we decide how to extricate ourselves from this farce of a marriage. Living like brother and sister may be easy for you, but it's hell for me."

"Tomorrow, Jake, I promise."

He said, "Come on, Huxley."

"Good night, Jake," Meg said, a catch in her voice. *Goodbye, Jake.*

After he and the Doberman went outside, Meg ran to the bedroom farthest from the master bedroom, where she had left the luggage provided by Rhea. She changed into one of Rhea's pantsuits and slipped the kidskin flats under the bed, then pulled back the duvet and lay down.

She heard Jake coming back into the house, then water running. Finally there was only the roar of the incoming tide on the beach below. Remembering Rhea's chilling statement that Jake had beaten her, Meg thought of the savage way Jake had held her, and of his taunting threats. Why hadn't she felt frightened of him? Was it because on some level she was sure that he wouldn't hurt her? Other more complex reasons for her lack of fear wouldn't bear close examination.

After a while fatigue crept from her body to her mind and she longed to close her eyes and drift off to sleep to the sound of the surf. She had to fight to stay awake.

When half an hour without any sound from Jake had

passed, she got up, picked up the shoes and tiptoed from the room.

Huxley was sprawled in front of her bedroom door. He raised his head and thumped his tail.

"Stay," Meg whispered, patting his head. "Good boy, stay."

The Doberman got up, stretched, then followed her to the French doors leading to the patio.

"No! *Stay*," she whispered sternly, pointing to the floor. He wagged his tail and grinned.

She sighed. Rhea was going to love this. Huxley would have to accompany her. He was liable to make a fuss and wake Jake if she tried to leave without him. She grabbed his leash.

Easing open the door, Meg stepped outside into the cool night air and smelled the fresh tang of brine. The Doberman followed, and she snapped his leash onto his collar.

A half-moon sailed in and out of the clouds, briefly illuminating the cliff steps and the beach below. She wished she had a flashlight. Pausing at the top of the steps, she glanced back at the house. No lights. So far, so good.

Waiting for the moonlight to paint her way down the cliff, she wondered what would happen in the morning when Jake and Rhea were reunited. She didn't want to think about her own awakening tomorrow. Back to the little rented house and thrift-shop furniture, back to work, back to the endless bills, back to wondering where Hal was, back to…*being without Jake's dynamic presence. Oh, Rhea, how can you not know how lucky you are?*

The moon reappeared, and she started down the steps. Huxley stayed at her side, like a gentleman. When she stopped, he stopped. She held on to the wooden handrail, and after a minute gained confidence that her feet could find the stairs hewn into the cliff even when the moon hid behind the clouds.

She could see the dark outlines of rocks and the phosphorescent glow of the breakers, but the cove seemed to be deserted. Had Rhea tired of waiting?

Feeling sand under her feet, Meg moved away from the shadow of the cliff and stood in a pool of moonlight. Scanning the beach, she saw that the rocks formed a jagged barrier at the water's edge.

At her side Huxley suddenly growled and flattened his ears. Meg laid her hand reassuringly on the dog's head.

A silhouette detached itself from the dark rocks, moved toward her across the moon-bleached sand. When Rhea was close enough to be heard over the sound of the surf, she said, "It took you long enough. What the hell is that mutt doing with you?"

To Meg's ears, the voice sounded so different from her own that she asked tentatively, "Mrs. Chastain?"

"Who were you expecting? Your fairy godmother?" The silhouette took a few steps toward her.

Huxley growled again. Meg tightened her grip on his leash. "It's all right, Huxley. Good boy, good dog, down. Down."

He sat down obediently but his ears twitched and his distrust rumbled deep in his throat.

"How does it feel to look at a mirror image?" Rhea asked.

Meg realized that she was standing with the moonlight illuminating her face, but Rhea was still a silhouette.

"I can't see you very well. I'm sorry I had to bring Huxley. I was afraid he'd bark and wake your husband if I left him." Meg explained quickly about Carmelita's emergency trip to Mexico, passing along Jake's instructions to call Mason and have him send a maid over to Jessica's house.

Rhea was still staring at her. "They say we all have a double somewhere on earth. The likeness is uncanny. No wonder you fooled everybody. How did you like being me?" Rhea kept a respectable distance between herself and Huxley.

"It was interesting."

"Especially when Jake unexpectedly showed up."

"Yes."

"But he didn't challenge you? He really thought you were me?"

"I think he was puzzled a few times, but no, he didn't challenge me."

"Mike Aragon said you hadn't slept with Jake. I find that hard to believe, knowing Jake," Rhea said.

"Believe it, because it's true. I wouldn't sleep with another woman's husband. I would have told him the truth if it had come to that, but it didn't. As you very well know, you two were on the brink of divorce before he flew to Europe. When he appeared in St. Maarten he suggested we maintain an appearance of marital harmony, for the sake of the hotel guests and staff."

"And what about when you were alone?"

"I told him we should just try being platonic friends until we got home and could talk over our problems. I think he...he may want a reconciliation, Mrs. Chastain."

"Call me Rhea, for pity's sake. Mrs. Chastain makes me sound like his mother. So he wants a reconciliation, does he?"

Meg was doubtful, in view of this evening's ultimatum, but for Jake's sake, she wanted Rhea to return to him in a conciliatory mood. "I hope you two can patch things up."

"Do you, now."

"Yes. I mean that sincerely. Your husband seems to be a very fine man."

"Did Aragon have any luck finding *your* husband?"

Meg shifted her feet in the sand. "No, I'm afraid not."

"Well, I'll probably need your services again soon, so we can keep Aragon on retainer. Will you be available?"

"No, I won't."

"It would just be for some function I'd prefer to skip— no travel to speak of and no Jake to contend with."

"No, I can't do it again. I feel like a criminal."

"Okay. We can talk about it again later on. Maybe you'll change your mind. Look, I've rented a white Pontiac Sunbird for you to drive home. It's parked a couple of blocks from the house."

"Thank you."

Huxley was still growling, deep in his throat, and he pawed the sand, jerking on his collar as he tried to lunge in Rhea's direction—although he seemed more perturbed by the waves pounding the rocks behind her.

"You'll have to take the dog with you," Rhea said. "That mutt will tear me limb from limb if he gets half a chance."

"I can't do that! What will Jake say when he finds him missing?"

"You're not too quick on your feet, are you, Meg? Tomorrow you drive the mutt to the Laguna animal shelter. I'll tell Jake he got out and we should check to see if he's in the shelter. Jake can pick him up and take him to Jessica's house. I'll have a maid over there by then to take care of him."

Meg fondled Huxley's head. "All right, I can do that. But you should know that Huxley and I seemed to hit it off, and Jake knows that. He might bring him back here."

"That's okay. By that time I won't be here, I'll be home.

I've no intention of staying in the beach house. It's way too primitive for my taste.''

So much for their reconciliation, Meg thought, not wanting to imagine Jake's disappointment when his wife abruptly changed her mind about staying with him at the beach until his mother left the hospital.

"If you walk to the far side of the cove you'll find a ramp leading up to the Coast Highway. It's narrow and overgrown with bougainvillea near the top, but you can get through." Rhea tossed a set of keys to her.

Meg grabbed for them but missed, and they fell to the sand. By the time she found the keys, Rhea was already climbing the steps to the house. Meg had never really had a good look at her.

Halfway across the sand Meg glanced back over her shoulder, an uneasy prickle on the back of her neck telling her someone else was watching. But the beach appeared to be deserted and the only movement was of shadows flitting over the silvered sand as clouds scudded across the moon.

When she reached the Coast Highway, Meg realized she hadn't asked which direction to go to find the rental car. She walked three blocks south but didn't find a Sunbird, so turned back and retraced her steps. Huxley was moderately well-behaved.

The Sunbird was parked close to a dense privet hedge, and the Doberman sniffed both the bushes and the car suspiciously as Meg unlocked the back door. The dog seemed particularly interested in the trunk and resisted her tug on his leash when she tried to get him into the car.

"Come on, boy, please," she pleaded, but Huxley whined and sniffed the trunk again.

"All right, I'll see what it is that's bothering you." She had to wrestle privet branches out of the way in order to unlock the trunk.

Inside were four red-and-yellow gasoline cans. Puzzled, she picked up one of the cans and shook it. It was empty. As were the others.

At the same instant she heard the shriek of sirens.

She dropped the can and slammed the trunk shut as a fire engine hurtled past. Turning her head, she saw an orange glow flickering above the trees.

Then she was running, fear grinding in her throat, back to the beach house, knowing long before she reached it that it would be in flames.

Chapter Ten

Firefighters had completely blocked off the area around the house with their equipment. A police officer was attempting to keep traffic moving as motorists slowed down to view the fiery spectacle. Several neighbors, jostling to get closer, were being held back by a fire marshal.

Did Jake get out in time? Where is Rhea? Desperate with heart-stopping fear for their safety, Meg tried to break through the crowd and still keep Huxley under control.

Breathlessly she asked a man standing nearby, "Did they get the people out safely?"

"No one lived there. The place belongs to Jake Chastain but he hasn't used it since he got married. His people keep it in order, but they wouldn't be there this time of night."

"No!" Meg screamed the word. "He was there. Please, let me through." But her plea was lost in the din of sirens as a second fire engine arrived and the crew chief shouted orders.

"Hey, lady!" the fire marshal yelled at her. "Get that dog out of here."

"Did you get the owners out of the house?" she shouted back.

But the marshal had moved away.

Meg looked around frantically. If Jake and Rhea had

escaped in time, surely they would be out here somewhere? There was no sign of them, but she could see Jake's car was still parked on the driveway.

Catching a glimpse of a police officer heading her way, Meg hastily yanked Huxley's leash, pulling him away from the onlookers.

She ran back to the ramp leading to the beach, skidding down the damp concrete in her haste to reach the cove below the house, hoping the wooden handrail on the cliff steps hadn't caught fire.

But the high tide was now crashing onto the foot of the ramp and all the sand was under water. Huxley drew back in alarm, barking at the incoming waves.

"Okay, boy, settle down." She patted his head, then slipped his leash around the handrail and fastened it. "Wait here. Stay. Good boy, *stay.*"

Slipping off her shoes, she plunged into the churning water. It was deep enough to swirl around her waist, and she felt the strong pull of a rip current.

Cautiously she made her way along the cliff face, bracing herself against the rocks as the waves broke.

She was soon breathless from struggling against the current and breaking surf, her hands raw from clutching the wet rocks to stay on her feet as the foaming breakers smashed into her like icy shards of glass. Then between waves she caught a glimpse of the cliff steps, lit by the flickering firelight from above, and the sight gave her strength to keep going.

Another wave slammed into her as she reached the steps and she was almost swept away, but managed to reach out and grab the handrail. Pulling herself free of the pull of the water, she looked up to see a tall silhouette standing near the top of the cliff steps. Jake!

She scrambled up the steps, too breathless to call his name.

He turned just before she reached him. He'd slung a raincoat over his shoulders and it slipped as she flung herself into his arms and clung to him. Above their heads the crackle of flames and sickening crunch of collapsing timbers told their own story.

"Rhea," Jake breathed against her hair. "Thank God! I nearly went crazy when I couldn't find you in the house. Where were you?"

For a split second Meg had forgotten that Rhea should have been in the house. Obviously she had not been. But where was she?

Meg said, "Huxley wanted to go out again. I took him for a walk and—"

The wind shifted suddenly and a shower of sparks from the burning house flew toward them. One of the firefighters dragging a hose across the patio shouted, "Time to leave, Mr. Chastain."

Jake said, "Come on, we'd better get out of here."

He slipped his raincoat over her shoulders and led her around the garage—its roof now burning—to the driveway.

"Huxley's tied up at the bottom of the ramp," Meg told him.

"We'll stop and get him," Jake said, as firefighters cleared the way for the car to leave. As he drove away, he didn't even look back at the blazing house.

It was only when Huxley was in the back seat and Jake was driving south on the Coast Highway that Meg remembered the rental car Rhea had brought for her...and the empty gasoline cans in the trunk.

She also remembered that both she and Huxley had been convinced there had been someone else on the beach. Her last glimpse of Rhea was of her ascending the cliff steps.

Was it possible she had been in the house and Jake had not found her during what of necessity must have been a very brief search? Frightening possibilities and implications flashed into Meg's mind.

Had the fire been arson? If so, was someone trying to kill both Rhea and Jake? *Had they succeeded in killing Rhea?* No, Jake would have found her. Rhea couldn't have been in the house.

Did the gasoline cans mean someone had tried to frame Rhea for setting the fire?

Another chilling scenario presented itself. What if Rhea had not rented the car in her own name, but in Meg's? What if she, Meg, was the one being framed? Show a car rental clerk a picture of Meg and they would surely confirm that she had rented the Sunbird.

Shivering violently, her teeth chattering, Meg pulled Jake's raincoat closer and wished she could awaken from the nightmare.

"We'll be home soon, Rhea," Jake said. "Don't think about it now—we got out, that's the main thing. I probably should have had the electrical wiring checked—it was an old house."

He reached over and squeezed her hand. "I'll turn up the heat. Soon as we get home, you can shed those wet clothes and jump into a hot bath."

JAKE FLIPPED ON the cruise control as a precaution against speeding. His adrenaline was still surging. When he had awakened in the smoke-filled house his first thought had been for his wife's safety. He'd crawled beneath the pall of choking fumes to her bedroom, and not finding her there, had dashed into the bathroom and soaked a towel with water. Holding it over his head, he stumbled from room to room calling her name, his fear for her so great that he ignored his bursting lungs.

When he had searched the entire house he remembered that Huxley was with them, but there was no sign of the dog either. Praying that the Doberman had awakened Rhea and that they'd both got out, Jake had at last left the blazing house.

His relief when Rhea came up the beach stairs to him was so great that for an instant nothing mattered but that she was alive and unhurt—and that they were holding each other close. And when she clung to him, he was sure she felt the same way.

MEG WAS STILL too dazed to fully appreciate the size and splendor of the estate to which they drove. She was vaguely aware of traveling along a private road, pausing as automatic gates slid open, then proceeding along a wide, curving driveway lined by shadowed trees. The driveway ended in a well-lit circle, in front of a house that to Meg's eyes was surely as large as a city block.

They climbed stone steps, flanked by enormous urns containing flowers and shrubs, to a wide terrace. Jake unlocked a magnificent carved oak door, and Meg found herself in a vast marble-floored entry hall.

Almost immediately a silver-haired man clad in pajamas and a dressing gown appeared magically and hurried to greet them. Jake said, ''It's all right, Mason, go back to bed. We'll take care of ourselves.''

Jake kept his arm around her shoulders as they climbed a graceful central staircase together and entered a spacious bedroom. The room appeared to be furnished with genuine eighteenth- and nineteenth-century pieces, and Meg caught a glimpse of separate dressing rooms through half-open doors.

Still in a state of shock, she was on the point of confessing to her deception, but hesitated when she remembered the gas cans in the rental car. What if Rhea had died in the burning house? Meg breathed a silent prayer that that hadn't happened; reason told her that the fire must have started just as Rhea reached the house, so in all probability she had never gone inside. But what if she had, and Jake had been unable to find her in the smoke? If Rhea were dead, Meg could be accused of murder.

She decided to hold off telling Jake her story until she could contact Mike Aragon to confirm it. She would have to get hold of him somehow, and quickly.

"Shall I fix you a drink?" Jake asked.

"No—thanks," Meg said hastily. "I'll just jump into the tub and then go to bed."

Jake looked at her for a moment, then asked, "Do you want me to stay with you, or would you prefer to be alone?"

Meg bit her lip. "Jake, I—"

His expression seemed carefully blank. "I'll sleep in one of the guest rooms. Good night."

The bedroom seemed enormous, empty and lonely, after he left. Determining that Jake and Rhea each had a dressing room with adjoining bathrooms and huge walk-in closets, Meg went into Rhea's bathroom, peeled off her wet clothes and filled the tub.

Clad in one of Rhea's filmy nightgowns and a matching peignoir, Meg walked over to the bedside table and looked at the telephone. She had to call Mike, but what if Jake were to pick up and overhear? She didn't want him to learn the truth that way. Jake was already suspicious about her calls.

There was also a good possibility that Mike wouldn't

answer his phone in the middle of the night. Still, she had to at least leave a message, tell him what happened.

She picked up the phone, listened to the dial tone for a moment, then tapped in his number.

To her surprise, Mike answered on the first ring.

"Mike—"

"Meg! I'm glad you called. I was going to come and see you and give you a complete report in the morning, but I think the sooner you know about your husband, the better. I'm sorry, Meg, brace yourself—"

"Hal? You've found Hal?" Meg asked faintly.

"Meg, I'm real sorry. He's dead. He was heavily in debt to loan sharks—in addition to the legitimate loans you've been paying off. He panicked, took off for Mexico with fake ID—apparently fell asleep at the wheel about seventy miles south of the border and crashed over a cliff. He was killed instantly."

Meg collapsed weakly to the bed.

"Meg, did you hear? You've been a widow for almost a year. His body was never claimed—you were never notified because the Mexican police didn't have his real name. I'll bring the complete report from the Ensenada *policia* over to your place in the morning. Now that you're all done with the Chastains—"

Meg found her voice at last. "I'm not at my place, Mike. I'm at the Chastain's main house and I've no idea where it is. You see, the beach house burned…"

She related in swift, fragmented whispers the events of the evening.

When she finished, Mike said, "Okay. Stay put. Don't tell Jake anything yet until I can find out what happened to Rhea. Where did she leave that rental car?"

"About three blocks south—no, north of the house on the Pacific Coast Highway. Mike, I should tell you something else. After Jake left London, a man was murdered in his hotel suite. I should have told you before.''

''Yes, you should have. Look, I'll get back to you as soon as I can. When I call I'll tell the butler I'm an art dealer and you ordered a sculpture from me. The lady of the house is apparently an antique and art collector.''

Meg put down the phone and drew a deep, heart-stabbing breath. Hal was dead. Hal had been running from loan sharks...from her.

Knowing sleep would evade her now, she wandered about the room, only vaguely aware of the beautiful antiques, marble statuary and paintings, although her attention was caught by a portrait of Rhea above an Italian marble fireplace. Her own likeness seemed to gaze down upon her mockingly. Shivering, Meg turned away.

She considered checking the medicine cabinet in the bathroom for sleeping pills, but decided against it. She couldn't afford to fall into a drugged slumber until she knew Rhea was safe.

A Queen Anne writing desk stood in the window alcove, and she pictured Rhea sitting there, reading her mail, penning notes. Did Rhea keep a diary? That thought tantalized.

Meg opened the top drawer. There were several invitations to various events, a couple of clothing bills that caused her to blink, an elaborate birthday card still in its envelope. From the postmark, Rhea's birthday was close to her own; the card had been mailed about a week before Meg's birthday.

She was still thinking about this coincidence when she noticed a paperback book at the bottom of the drawer. Curious as to Rhea's reading habits, Meg picked up the book and a folded sheet of paper slipped out from between the pages.

Unfolding the paper, she saw that she was holding a

letter from an adoption agency in Atlanta, Georgia. The letter was dated six months earlier.

A muffled drum seemed to beat in her ear as she read.

Dear Mrs. Chastain:

In response to your latest call, we wish to advise you that we have learned that your biological mother died five years ago. Therefore we cannot comply with your request to put you in touch with her. However, it might be possible for you to locate your twin sister, as due to her deformity she was placed in State foster care for approximately two years before being adopted.

The letter fluttered from Meg's fingers to the floor.

Twin sister. Deformity… Meg had been born with a club-foot. The postmark on Rhea's birthday card had been close to her own birthdate. Meg's parents had originally come from Georgia…

But she hadn't been adopted. *Or had she?*

Meg's parents had been a kind and loving older couple who had passed away before she was out of her teens. People had always commented on the fact that they were so dark and Meg was so fair. Was it possible that they had adopted her but never told her?

She had never seen her birth certificate; her mother claimed it had been lost. They had used a baptismal certificate to enroll her in school.

She remembered then that she had not been baptised until she was two years old.

Picking up the letter from the adoption agency again, Meg reread, *she was placed in State foster care for approximately two years before being adopted.*

It all fit, even without the added evidence of their identical looks.

Feeling suddenly weak, Meg walked unsteadily to the bed and sat down.

Rhea is my twin sister.

Rhea had been adopted at birth, but evidently her adoptive mother had not wanted to take on the responsibility of twins, especially one with medical problems. So Meg must have been placed in foster care.

Thinking about her parents, Meg was forced to admit that they had really been too old to have a baby, but perhaps eligible to adopt a two-year-old with a clubfoot. She remembered how diligently they had taken her to orthopedic surgeons and physical therapists, and spent hours manipulating her Achilles tendon.

Recalling Jake's comment about Rhea's abusive childhood, Meg wondered which twin, ultimately, had been more fortunate.

Most perturbing was the fact that Rhea had obviously tracked her down but hadn't told her they were sisters. Reconstructing how this had probably happened, it seemed obvious that after Rhea married the wealthy Jake Chastain, she'd had the time and money to search for her biological mother and had learned for the first time that she had a twin. It must have been a lie that someone had seen Meg at a wedding and noticed her resemblance to Rhea.

Since she had hired Mike as a go-between, and also kept him in the dark as to their true relationship, it seemed clear that Rhea had more in mind than being reunited with her twin. But what?

Meg remembered the fire at the beach house. Had she just discovered that she had a twin only to lose her?

IN A NEARBY GUEST ROOM, Jake paced the floor restlessly. It had taken all of his willpower to leave his wife alone in their bedroom. He had stood outside the door for several minutes, tempted to return to her.

Hadn't she looked at him in a way that surely said more clearly than words that she wanted to be with him tonight?

He was reaching for the doorknob when he heard the faint sound of her voice, speaking in low, urgent whispers.

Jake froze. She had called somebody. Somebody who was waiting for her call and who wanted to talk to her, despite the lateness of the hour.

Cursing himself for being a fool to believe Rhea had really changed, Jake had turned away.

Now he forced himself to face the truth about his wife. She didn't want a divorce, probably because of the prenuptial agreement. How fortuitous that Huxley had needed to go outside just before the fire broke out. Even if he discounted that coincidence, what about the fact that a man had been killed in the London hotel suite where he should have been sleeping?

Jake's blood ran cold. *Was Rhea trying to kill him?*

Surely she wouldn't go that far. Besides, how would she have had the contacts to hire a hit man in London? She had been in St. Maarten at the time. But then Jake remembered that Sloan had been released from prison a couple of weeks ago. Rhea had always been manipulated by her adoptive brother and he was a career criminal. Still, he was on parole. He couldn't have gone to London either.

Jake told himself that he was being paranoid. The beach house fire had to be due to faulty electrical wiring, and Roland was probably followed to his London suite and murdered for some other reason. But the rationalizations did little to ease Jake's suspicions and doubts.

He knew he was reluctant to believe the worst because of Rhea's new persona. Even if she had been putting on an act the past few days to keep him from contacting divorce lawyers, some perverse and reckless part of him wanted to enjoy having a dream wife for a little longer.

But that didn't mean trusting her. The first thing he had to do was find out who she had been surreptitiously calling.

Chapter Eleven

Meg awoke to find Huxley licking her face and a flustered maid at the door trying in vain to coax the Doberman out of the room. Seeing that Meg was awake, the maid said, "Oh, I'm sorry, Mrs. Chastain. I don't know how he got the door open. I let him out of the kitchen and he came flying up here and scratched at the door—"

"That's all right," Meg said, stroking Huxley's silky head and turning her face to avoid both his slurping tongue and the full impact of dog breath. Glancing at the clock on her nightstand, she was surprised to see that she had slept until nearly nine.

She cleared her throat. "Is Mr. Chastain downstairs?"

"No, ma'am. He left real early. I think he gave Mr. Mason a message for you. Shall I take the dog back to the kitchen?"

"No. He can stay."

"Can I bring you anything?"

Meg hesitated. "Just my usual."

The maid nodded. Evidently this was an acceptable response.

Meg had just finished dressing when there was a knock on the door, and a voice called, "It's Guadalupe, Mrs. Chastain."

"Yes, come in," Meg called.

The maid carried a tray holding a glass of tomato juice. Meg would have preferred orange juice and coffee, but took a sip and discovered it was a Bloody Mary. She put it down.

Guadalupe, an exceptionally pretty young woman with dark curly hair and friendly brown eyes, said sympathetically, "You look so tired, Mrs. Chastain. Are you sure you wouldn't like to sleep a little longer?" Her English, although slightly accented, was perfect.

Immediately drawn to her, especially in view of the butler's apparent disdain, Meg answered with a smile, "I'm fine, really, thank you...Guadalupe."

"Can I get you anything else, ma'am? Would you like me to go and get the message Mr. Chastain left for you?"

"No, thank you. I'm ready to go downstairs now."

The minute Guadalupe departed, Meg realized she should have taken her up on the offer to bring Jake's message to her. Meg had no idea which of the many doors opening to the central hall led to Mason's domain.

Huxley bounded ahead of her and made a beeline for the far side of the hall. Meg was about to follow when a clipped accent behind her exclaimed, "Ah, Mrs. Chastain, good morning."

She turned to see the butler emerging from a nearby room. "Your husband asked me to tell you he was going to see if anything could be salvaged from the beach house, then would probably go to his office for a while. He'll call you later."

"Thank you," Meg murmured. She had dressed in linen slacks and a white shirt she had found in Rhea's closet, and felt that if she could fool Jake into believing she was Rhea, she should not be receiving a suspicious look from his butler. But Mason's expression seemed questioning, to say the least.

"Mr. Chastain said we were not to awaken you," Mason continued. "A Mr. Michael Gumm called a little while ago. He said you'd ordered a sculpture from his gallery. I wrote down his number."

He handed her a message slip.

Meg raced back upstairs to call Mike. She supposed the real Rhea would have stepped into a ground floor room to use the phone, but since Meg might have found herself in a closet, the bedroom phone seemed safer. Huxley stayed with her.

"Michael *Gumm?*" Meg said, when Mike answered his phone.

"Short for gumshoe," Mike explained. "Are you alone?"

"Yes. Jake's gone to check the damage at the beach house."

"It's a total loss. First of all—no human remains were found in the ruins. That's the good news. The bad news is that the fire was deliberately set."

"Oh, no…Mike, that rented car—"

"Don't worry, I removed the gas cans."

"How did you get into the trunk?"

"Picked the lock. Did you handle any of those cans?"

"Yes, all of them. I picked them up and shook them to see if they were empty—they were."

She heard him sigh. "So your fingerprints are all over them. I was careful not to add mine, and probably whoever put them in the car wiped theirs off, too. Okay, Meg, it's time to 'fess up to the whole masquerade. We have to turn those cans over to the arson squad. I think Rhea is trying to kill her husband."

Meg gasped. "I can't believe that! You must be wrong. Surely there's an explanation for all of this."

"How do you explain her showing up last night just before the beach house was torched, and leaving the gas cans in a car you were about to use? Come on, Meg, we've both been had. Do you want to tell Jake before we go to the cops? I'll come over to back up your story."

"Mike, not so fast. There's something else you need to know. I found a letter from an adoption agency last night. I think…Rhea and I are twins."

When he didn't respond, she added, "*Sisters,* Mike. Blood-related. Biological, *identical twins.*" She told him of the letter's contents.

Mike whistled softly. "Well, this puts a whole new slant on things."

"I have to talk to her. I have to find out for sure. You know, all of my life I've had a sense of something missing, a part of myself that just wasn't there. I loved my parents but I never felt truly connected to them. To have a sister, a twin, would be a dream come true."

"Yeah, well, don't get too overjoyed yet. She might look like you, but from what I've observed, you two don't share anything beyond your physical attributes. Think about something else—if she knew you were sisters, why didn't she tell you? That alone smacks of some nefarious scheme."

"Please, Mike, at least let me find out for sure."

"What's the name of the agency, and who signed the letter? Maybe I can get some more information."

"The Verity Agency of Atlanta, and the letter was signed by a Mona Verity."

"A private agency. Good. Look, I think we'd better continue this conversation somewhere other than over the phone. I checked on your location—you're on a private road about a mile from the highway. Can you walk down there and I'll pick you up?''

''Yes, I'll tell Mason I'm taking Huxley for a walk— What was that? Did you hear a click on the line?''

''No. But don't say anything else. Give me about an hour. I want to make a couple of calls.''

''YOU DIDN'T MENTION that Huxley is a Doberman,'' Mike said with understandable apprehension.

''Don't be deceived by appearances—'' Meg began.

Mike raised an eyebrow and ran his eyes over her appraisingly. ''I must try to remember that.''

''Touché.'' Meg kept a firm grip on Huxley's leash as she urged him into the back of Mike's car. Huxley sniffed Mike's neck suspiciously.

Mike looked over his shoulder. ''Hi, boy. How's it goin'? Hux-ley, that's some ridiculous name—''

Huxley bared his teeth.

''Hey, boy, good boy, good dog, I didn't mean it.''

''I'd better sit in the back seat with him,'' Meg said.

''Sounds like a plan.''

Mike drove through rolling hills where multimillion-dollar homes nestled in walled estates. He said, ''I called that adoption agency. I also did a fast check on a couple of databases—which I probably should have done before I took this case.''

''What did you find out?''

''Rhea and Sloan were both adopted, eight years apart, by a pair of psychiatrists named Pensby. Rhea's mother went to the agency while she was pregnant, and the Pensbys paid all her medical and living expenses, plus a lump sum for turning over her newborn. To everyone's surprise, she delivered identical twins, one of whom was born with a clubfoot. The Pensbys decided they only wanted one of the babies.''

"The perfect child," Meg said.

"That's a matter of opinion. Perfect is as perfect does. Anyway, seven or eight years later, the Pensbys divorced. Neither of them wanted the kids so they returned them to the agency, who then turned them over to the state.''

"But I thought once a child was adopted, it was forever.''

"It seems one of the best-kept dirty little secrets of the adoption process is the number of children deemed ''difficult'' or ''disruptive'' who are returned to even state-licensed agencies, often after years with adoptive parents.''

Meg shook her head in disbelief. ''My parents were wonderful.'' She sighed. ''But they never told me I was adopted.''

"You were luckier than Rhea. She was bounced from one foster home to another. Sloan was in his teens and already in trouble with the law at the time of the divorce. He ended up in a juvenile detention camp. I guess he managed to keep track of Rhea, because at the time of his arrest they were both in San Francisco, which incidentally was where Rhea met Jake…after her brother was incarcerated.''

"And my parents relocated to Los Angeles when I was six," Meg mused. ''What did Sloan do?''

"Two years, for aggravated assault, drug dealing and sundry other felonies. He also had a record in several southern states before he headed west. He's one bad dude. Look, Meg, I've a good friend on the force. Why don't I drive us over to talk to him.''

"I must talk to Rhea first. Perhaps Sloan is the one who rented the car and set the house on fire. Perhaps Rhea knows nothing about it. I have to give her the benefit of the doubt, Mike. She's my flesh and blood—a sister I longed for all my life. A part of me must have known about her, and I'm sure she feels the same way. Just give us a chance to straighten this out. You know, things aren't always as they appear on the surface.''

"Meg, for Pete's sake. A man was killed in the hotel suite in London where everyone believed Jake was sleeping, but he'd secretly flown to St. Maarten to surprise his wife, only his wife wasn't there. A look-alike, hired by his wife, was there. What if he'd been killed in London? Rhea would have had an iron-clad alibi. She was in St. Maarten opening a new hotel.''

"But you and I know that *I* was there, not Rhea.''

"And we in turn believed Rhea was in San Francisco with her terminally ill brother. My guess is that Rhea was in London, with murder on her mind. I'm also wondering what might have happened if her plan had succeeded. Since we knew about the switch, would you and I then have had unfortunate accidents?''

Shocked, Meg said, "That's pretty wild conjecture.''

"Yeah, well here's some more. When the London plan goes wrong and after Jake returns to California with you in tow, a new plan evolves. How about killing Jake and giving the cops a suspect—you, Meg.''

"What?'' Meg asked faintly. "But—''

"The arson fire at the beach house,'' he went on, "was a second attempt on Jake's life. She got you out of there so there would only be one body, because Mrs. Jake Chastain had to survive in order to inherit his estate.''

Meg said slowly, "The gasoline cans in the rental car...''

"I think it occurred to Rhea—or more likely, Sloan—that instead of using you as an alibi, a better plan would be to pin the blame on you. Rich twin, poor twin. Poor twin tries to kill rich twin so she can take her place. Hell, there was even a much-publicized case in Orange County where one twin tried to kill her sister so she could assume her identity. She didn't succeed, but she was convicted of conspiracy and attempt to commit murder.''

''But how would they explain Jake's death if it was Rhea I was supposed to be plotting to kill?''

''Okay, how's this for a scenario? Evil twin attempts to kill good twin by setting the house on fire, believing she is alone in the house, but she manages to get out in time and Jake dies in the flames instead. Terrified widow Rhea then goes to the police and points a finger at you. Hence the gas cans in the car, which, by the way, was rented in your name.''

Her mind reeling, Meg asked, ''Where is the car now?''

''I returned it to the agency, which means I've already tampered with evidence and probably obstructed justice.''

''Mike, this is horrible. Why on earth would Rhea do this?''

''Prenuptial agreement. If there's a divorce, Rhea gets very little in the way of a settlement. However, as a widow she would control all the Chastain holdings. Or more likely, Sloan would.''

''But this is all just a theory. We really don't know anything for certain. I have to meet my sister again, and talk to her. Please don't turn those gas cans over to the police until I do.''

Mike pulled over to the side of the road and slammed on the brakes. He turned to her, his face a study in exasperation.

''She's dangerous, Meg. I've never met a more accomplished liar. I'm as cynical as most people in my profession, but I believed every word she told me. And we won't even discuss Sloan. Besides, we don't even know where Rhea is.''

''When she finds out Jake is still alive, I'm sure she'll

surface again. Besides, sooner or later she has to resume her own identity—she must realize the longer I'm in the picture the more likely it is Jake will recognize I'm not his wife. Just give me a few hours to wait for her to contact me. If we go to the police now, we have no evidence to offer, except the fact that I impersonated her. How can we explain those cans of gasoline in a car rented in my name? Please, Mike, before I get arrested as an imposter and an arsonist, at least give me a chance to find out what's going on.''

Huxley nuzzled Meg and whined softly.

''I don't like it,'' Mike muttered at length. ''But I'll take you back to the Chastain place. Are you going to tell Jake?''

''Not until I talk to Rhea. Mike, I told Carrie—my caterer boss—I'd call her when I got back to L.A., but I'm supposed to be at the theater today. Will you do me a favor and call the manager for me—tell him I can't make today's matinee?''

''Sure. But one way or another, we go to the cops today. Call me as soon as you hear from Rhea. If I don't hear from you, I'll be at the house to pick you up at six tonight.''

MASON GREETED HER return with a suspicious sneer. ''That was quite a lengthy walk, Mrs. Chastain. You've really changed your attitude toward dogs, haven't you?''

''Will you give him some water, please,'' Meg asked, her request sounding more timorous than she would have preferred. ''Were there any calls for me?''

''Your husband rang. He asked me to tell you he'll be home for lunch. He asked that you instruct Cook as to what to serve.''

''Thank you.'' Meg looked around uneasily, wondering which of the many doors led to the kitchen. She couldn't admit to being an imposter to anyone yet, not until she'd confessed to Jake and talked to Rhea.

She handed Huxley's leash to the butler and slowly ascended the stairs, watching to see which door they exited. Mason probably would take the Doberman to the kitchen to get him some water.

In the master bedroom Meg sat down weakly at the Queen Anne desk. A second telephone, an elaborate antique, sat atop the desk, and she stared at it, willing Rhea to call.

Numb from the revelations of the last twenty-four hours, Meg tried to sort out her thoughts. Remembering her brief encounter on the shadowy beach with her twin, Meg couldn't believe she had envied her. Meg's adoptive parents had loved and cared for her until the day they died, and she still missed them and grieved for them, grateful that she had so many happy memories to help assuage her grief. What a contrast to Rhea's ghastly childhood.

But unlike Meg, Rhea had married a wonderful man. Meg sighed deeply, knowing she was still in denial about Hal's defection and death. That was something she would have to deal with soon, but for now, if Mike's theories about Rhea and Sloan were accurate, there were even more distressing facts to be faced. Not to mention the danger in which she had placed both Jake and herself.

The phone rang so suddenly that it startled her. She grabbed the receiver. "Hello."

"You must have been close to the phone." Jake's voice came over the line, sounding tired and tense. "Were you waiting for a call?" The question had an edge to it.

Meg said, "No...I mean only from you. Is the house a complete loss?"

"Yes," Jake answered shortly. "You know, your voice sounds even more different over the phone."

Ignoring the comment, Meg asked, "What time will you be home?"

"Well, that's what I'm calling about. Jess paged me. She's being discharged from the hospital today. She bullied her doctors into letting her go, but with Carmelita in Mexico I can't take Jess home because she absolutely refuses to have anyone else in her house. Rhea, would you mind if my mother came and stayed with us for a few days?"

"Of course not," Meg said immediately.

"Good. We'll be there in about an hour. Have Mason prepare her room." He paused. "Thanks, Rhea."

Meg put down the phone. The presence of Jake's mother would be an added complication, especially in view of the disclosures about Rhea that Meg might be forced to make. But she'd worry about that later.

Huxley had evidently escaped from Mason's custody; he was sitting outside the bedroom door. He stood up, wagging his tail.

Meg patted his head and scratched his ear. "I don't know how Jess is going to react to finding out you aren't a one-woman dog."

HE HAD DISABLED the smoke alarms during his visit the previous afternoon while the woman was there alone. That evening, he'd doused the entire house with gasoline, yet incredibly, Chastain had escaped the fire. He must sleep like a cat. Twice now their plans had gone awry. Third time had to be the charm. They couldn't afford another fiasco.

Chapter Twelve

Jessica Chastain's perfectly arched eyebrows lifted in surprise.

Amused by his mother's astonishment, Jake leaned back in his chair and studied his wife's reaction to the butler's comment.

Mason stood, ramrod straight, at Rhea's elbow. Jake noted that she flushed as she stammered, "I really... didn't..."

Mason said stiffly, "I'm sorry, madam, I felt Cook would have wanted you to take credit for the luncheon. It was not my intention to cause you embarrassment."

Jess, her arm in a cast, had insisted upon having lunch with them downstairs, rather than in the bedroom prepared for her, despite Jake's protest that she should be resting in bed. They were in the sunny breakfast room where a wall of windows overlooked velvet lawns, banks of flowers and a decorative pond framed by willows. Rhea kept glancing at the view, almost as if she were seeing it for the first time.

Jessica said, "You've been hiding your light under a bushel, Rhea. Even if you only *suggested* that grilled vegetable pizza and incredible salad, rather than having a hand in preparing them as Mason indicated, then I'm wondering why you waited eighteen months before displaying your culinary skills.''

Rhea looked from Jessica to Jake, her blush deepening and her eyes pleading. Seeing her discomfort and grateful she hadn't responded to his mother with some caustic remark, Jake said, ''Jess, you're pale as a ghost. It's time for you to rest. Come on, I'll take you up to your room.''

''Darling, you have a lot of work to do,'' his mother said, a sly gleam in her eye. ''Rhea will take me, won't you, dear?''

''Yes, of course.'' His wife jumped to her feet, as Jake helped his mother from her chair. His suspicions deepened. The old Rhea would have ignored the request. In fact the old Rhea probably would have had other plans for lunch and certainly wouldn't have prepared it. Convinced now that she had an ulterior motive for her sudden change of heart, Jake decided he'd better monitor her activities closely, and watch his own back.

He took his mother's arm firmly and slid it through his. ''We'll both go with you. You're not too steady on your feet yet.''

The butler faded into the background. Meg was certain Mason was suspicious of her, and had deliberately announced that she had prepared the meal in an attempt to expose her.

Falling into place at Jessica's other side, Meg walked with them through the entry hall toward the staircase. Halfway across, Mason reappeared, carrying a cordless phone. ''There's a call for you, madam. It's Mrs. Wells. Are you home?''

Uncertain what to do, Meg looked at Jake. He said, ''Go ahead and talk to her. I'll take care of Jess.''

They continued on their way, as Meg stood holding the

phone. She heard Jessica whisper, "She's up to something, Jake. This is not natural, it's all an act."

"I'll attribute that remark to your present state of health, Jess, and pretend you didn't make it," Jake shot back, sotto voce.

At Meg's side, Mason murmured, "Perhaps madam would like to take her call in the study?"

Meg turned to look at him. *He knows I have no idea where the study is,* she thought. *Why doesn't he say something to Jake?*

Ignoring the suggestion, she flicked on the phone's talk button and strolled toward the front doors, sure at least if she went outside she would avoid wandering into a closet. "Hello?"

"Rhea? I just heard about the beach house," a strange female voice said. "I didn't know you were back from St. Maarten and I was really surprised that you and Jake were even using the house—what is going on?"

"Jake's mother had an accident. We flew back to take care of her," Meg said. "The beach house is closer to the hospital."

Mrs. Wells, evidently a friend of Rhea, gasped audibly.

Meg added, "She's going to be all right. In fact she's out of the hospital and here with us."

"Good grief! Are you going out of your mind?"

Not knowing how to respond, Meg asked, "How did you hear about the beach house?"

"On my car radio. Anything concerning Jake is news. You know, Rhea, your voice sounds…strange."

"I think I'm coming down with a cold," Meg said quickly.

"Well, I have to tell you I just ran into Cecily Morgan and she swears she saw you coming out of the Ritz-Carlton this morning. She said you were getting either into or out of a Porsche with a big muscular fellow with a shaved head. Rhea, darling, what *are* you up to? You're not being naughty, are you?''

"Cecily was mistaken," Meg said as calmly as she could. "Did she tell you what *she* was doing at the Ritz-Carlton this morning?"

Laughter bubbled over the phone line.

Meg said, "Do you mind if I call you back later? I've got a million things to do."

"Oh, all right. Shall we get together for cocktails?"

"I'll call you," Meg said.

Standing on the wide terrace looking out on park-like grounds, Meg wondered why Rhea could not be happy in such a setting. Obviously, she had everything she could possibly need or want, and Jake had certainly indulged her penchant for acquiring antiques, judging by the way the bedroom and breakfast rooms were furnished. Meg hadn't seen much of the rest of the house, but it wasn't difficult to imagine Rhea had spent a fortune on it.

The only possible explanation was that Rhea simply didn't love Jake. And that, to Meg, was more baffling than anything else. Even if she didn't love him, how could she hate him enough to want to kill him? Mike had to be wrong about her. Surely Sloan must be engineering the plot, and Rhea was either unaware of it or being controlled by him in some way.

Meg heard the door open behind her and turned to see Jake crossing the terrace.

"Jess is in bed," he said, "no doubt dreaming about gourmet food. Why did you never mention you could cook like that?"

"Jake, I need to explain—" She broke off as the phone in her hand rang.

He remained standing beside her, and she saw an angry

glint appear in his dark eyes. "I suppose you don't want
to answer that until I leave. I'll use the study phone to call
the insurance company." He turned on his heel and strode
away.

Meg pressed the talk-button in time to hear Mason picking up on another line.

A muffled female voice asked for Rhea.

"I'll take the call, Mason," Meg said, wondering if he
had recognized that the real Mrs. Jake Chastain was on the
other end.

Meg waited until Jake reentered the house and she heard
a click indicating Mason had hung up. Then she whispered,
"Rhea, is that you?"

"Where were you? I tried to call you this morning."

"I took the dog for a walk."

"Are you nuts? I'd never do that."

"What happened last night?" Meg demanded.

"I'll explain everything as soon as we can get together.
But the first thing we have to do is switch places."

"I agree, and as soon as possible. I'm sure your husband
suspects—"

"Look, I can't just show up there, so you've got to get
away from the house. I've got an idea how we can change
places without Jake suspecting. Our favorite restaurant is a
little Greek place on the cliff over Moonlight Cove. Get
him to take you to dinner there tonight. I'll be in the ladies'
room at eight. Just continue to be me until then, please."

The line went dead.

I'll explain everything. Surely that included the fact that
they were twins, Meg thought. They shared the same
womb; how could Rhea be capable of plotting to destroy
her? Or of killing her own husband? It was unthinkable.
Mike had to be wrong about Rhea.

Mike! He'd be showing up here by six and she had to

play the part of Rhea until eight. She'd have to call and delay him.

A gardener pruning roses a short distance from the house glanced in her direction then moved away quickly, but not before Meg caught a glimpse of his face beneath the brim of a straw hat pulled low over his brow and, as he walked away, saw the stringy ponytail of blond hair hanging down his back. She was sure he was the same man she had seen in St. Maarten, only then he'd worn a waiter's white jacket.

She turned and walked back to the house. Rhea must have sent the man to keep an eye on her. Meg supposed it would have been a natural precaution, to be sure she didn't do anything inappropriate. But the waiter/gardener had the wily expression of a ferret and the covert movements of a felon, and Meg wondered if Rhea had checked his background before hiring him. His presence explained how Rhea knew Meg's whereabouts.

The entry hall was deserted. Meg tiptoed to the nearest door, opened it and found herself looking into a beautifully furnished drawing room. Meg knew a little about antiques and recognized that some of the pieces were priceless. The next door revealed what was apparently a music room, with a grand piano on a dais. Her third try took her to a well-stocked library.

Closing the door, she looked around. Where was Jake's study? She was about to check the remaining doors when a maid appeared, carrying a vase of fresh flowers.

Meg had an inspiration. "Mr. Chastain is in his study. Would you tell him I'll be in the library when he's finished with his business?"

"Yes, ma'am."

Meg opened the library door and would have lingered long enough to see where the maid went, but the woman had paused to put the flowers on a side table and glanced at her curiously.

In the library Meg randomly selected a volume without checking the title, and took it to an enormous leather sofa. A telephone sat temptingly on a nearby table, and she wondered if she dare call Mike. A grandfather clock stood in one corner of the library and it chimed suddenly, reminding her that time was passing.

She was about to reach for the phone, when Jake appeared. He regarded her with mild amusement. "You're determined to keep me guessing, aren't you? This is the first time you've been in here since you ordered umpteen yards of assorted books."

"I just thought—" Meg began.

His long strides closed the distance between them and he sat next to her, so close that she could feel the heat of his arm through his shirtsleeve.

Unconsciously, Meg drew away.

Jake snapped, "Why do you shrink from me?"

"I'm sorry. I didn't mean to—I guess I'm a little jumpy."

He stared at her for a moment, then reached over and took the book from her hands.

"De Maupassant? I wouldn't have thought he would have appealed to you." He returned the book to her.

Meg read the book's title. *Fort Comme La Mort.*

Jake was watching her closely. "As strong as death."

"What?"

"I translated the title for you."

"Oh."

"What's going on, Rhea? I'd have put your jumpiness and unusual behavior down to the fire or to Jess being here…but you were acting differently in St. Maarten, too."

"I didn't even look at the title of the book," Meg said. "I picked one at random."

"And I presume you intended to read it?" he asked mockingly.

"Actually Proust is my favorite French author," Meg answered.

Jake laughed. "You continue to amaze me with how fast you can think."

Especially when I respond to you truthfully, as myself, Meg thought. She shrugged. "Have to keep you on your toes."

She became aware that he had slid his arm along the back of the sofa, not quite touching her. He said, "You were going to explain something to me."

"Oh, I was going to ask if we can go to that little Greek restaurant on Moonlight Cove for dinner tonight. I thought perhaps it would be easier to discuss our problems in a neutral setting. Do you think Jessica would mind if we went out?"

His dark gaze studied her, searching for answers to questions he evidently decided not to ask. At length he said, "I'm sure she won't. She was pretty well wiped out when I took her upstairs. Now tell me about that delicious lunch."

"It wasn't...I really didn't..."

"And by the way," he went on smoothly, "the chef at the Hotel Rhea on St. Maarten informed me that you didn't just suggest that picnic lunch we took to the beach—you prepared most of it yourself."

"I...wanted to surprise you," Meg said hesitantly. After all, it had been established that Rhea enjoyed good food, was even something of a food critic. "I've been studying cooking."

"You got very good, very fast," he commented.

"Not really," Meg said. "It didn't happen overnight. But I do have a natural aptitude. I just didn't tell you what I was doing."

Let Rhea explain this one, Meg thought. After all, she shouldn't have left me in this predicament.

"I'm truly impressed. I misjudged you, Rhea. I thought all these months you were involved solely with pampering yourself and engaging in more frivolous pursuits."

He rose to his feet again. "Well, I'll leave you in de Maupassant's capable hands. I have to go back to the Dana Point project for a while. Will you make the reservations for dinner?"

Meg nodded, wishing she'd asked Rhea the name of the restaurant. It probably wasn't listed as "our favorite little Greek place on Moonlight Cove."

She waited until she was sure Jake had left, then went up to their bedroom. Perhaps Rhea had an address book in her desk.

Before going through the desk drawers, Meg called Mike, got his machine, and left a message that they were going out for dinner and that she had arranged to meet the party in question at the restaurant. She promised to call him again later with more details. She wasn't certain, but she thought she heard another faint click on the line before she finished leaving her message.

Well, if someone was monitoring her calls, it couldn't be helped. She had to make them. She'd just say as little as possible. A call to the theater confirmed that Mike had let them know she wouldn't be in that day. The manager informed her that she needn't bother coming back: she'd been replaced. Meg sighed deeply, wondering how much worse things could get. Without the job at the theater, it would be difficult to make ends meet, let alone pay off her debts, on what her part-time catering job paid her.

A search of Rhea's desk did not produce an address book, and Meg was about to go downstairs and seek out Jake's study in order to look for the restaurant number, when there was a knock on the bedroom door and Mason appeared.

"Excuse me, madam, but Mrs. Chastain asks that you go to her."

For a split second Meg pictured Rhea waiting for her, until she remembered Jessica in the guest room. Why hadn't the butler said Mrs. Chastain *senior?* He wore a faint smirk, and Meg thought, *He definitely suspects and thinks I'm going to give myself away.*

"I'll go right away— Oh, and Mason, Mr. Chastain and I will be going out to dinner. Call and make reservations for us at the little Greek place on Moonlight Cove, will you?"

There was a moment's hesitation and Meg held her breath. Then Mason said, "Certainly, madam. What time?"

"7:30—no, 7:45."

"Very good, madam."

Huxley was sprawled at the foot of Jessica's bed and he roused himself to greet Meg with so much enthusiasm that Jessica scowled and said, "Damn it, Rhea, for months you made us lock him up on the rare occasion you accompanied Jake when he dropped by my house, and heaven forbid I even bring him over here. Now look at him, slobbering all over you—and you encouraging him."

Meg scratched Huxley's ear. "I was afraid of him. When I finally got up the courage to make the first friendly gesture, he responded. Jessica, I'm sorry I was such an idiot."

Jessica didn't appear to be mollified. "You're up to something, Rhea. You know it and I know it. You may have pulled the wool over Jake's eyes, but not mine. You've convinced him you've reformed, haven't you?"

"I don't think this conversation is appropriate—" Meg began.

"Scant weeks ago he told me you two were not going to make a go of your marriage," Jessica said, her dark eyes blazing. "What happened? Did you figure out what you were giving up? The prestige of being Mrs. Jake Chastain, not to mention *the money?*"

"Jake and I are trying to work things out. I'd rather not discuss our problems when he isn't here."

"I don't know what you're up to, Rhea, but I know this—you are not the same woman who went to open the Caribbean hotel, and I don't want to see my son hurt when you revert back to your true self. So just be warned, I'm watching you. And I'll do whatever I need to do."

Chapter Thirteen

As soon as Meg entered the restaurant she wondered why Rhea had selected such a small, intimate setting. How would she be able to slip unnoticed into the restroom? Especially since the beaming proprietor who ushered them to a choice table evidently knew Jake, and presumably Rhea.

Hoping her twin would be heavily disguised, Meg took her seat and unfolded her napkin. She was vaguely aware of Jake choosing wine and discussing the menu.

Glancing at her watch she saw that it was exactly 7:45.

Meg wore a simple black dress that she had unearthed among Rhea's endless pantsuits. Jake's dark eyes had briefly lost their suspicious glint and expressed approval. If he noticed that she had not added jewelry, he didn't mention it. Wearing Rhea's clothes was a necessity, Meg felt, but wearing her jewelry seemed presumptuous. She would have to remind Rhea to remove any jewelry she was wearing before changing into the black dress and slipping on the black hose that Meg had tucked into one of Rhea's beaded evening bags.

When Jake suggested that Niklos, the proprietor, make their selections, Meg murmured her agreement. Looking around, she saw that every table was occupied and that there was a liberal ratio of waiters and busboys. Perhaps Rhea would arrive unnoticed in the bustle.

Another nagging worry refused to go away. Concerned that Mike might not have picked up her message and could show up at the house at six as he'd said he would, Meg had again called him. She'd let the phone ring at least twenty times, but Mike hadn't answered, nor had his message machine picked up as it had earlier—which seemed odd.

"You haven't tried your wine," said Jake.

Meg took a sip and nodded. "Very good."

He watched her with hooded eyes. "Are you ready to discuss our plans for the future?"

"No—I mean, could we have dinner first?"

"Do you want a divorce, Rhea, or a reconciliation?"

Meg squirmed, but the look on his face told her he wasn't going to let her off the hook.

He said, "I can't believe I'm even suggesting the possibility of a reconciliation, but I've never seen anybody change so much, so quickly, as you have. I hardly know you anymore, Rhea. When I remember how it was between us before St. Maarten, and how it's been the past few days…well, let's just say that before St. Maarten I never would have considered reconciling. So that's why I ask, do you want a divorce or…"

Recklessly, Meg answered, "A reconciliation."

She saw him let out his breath slowly. "You realize there will be conditions? Sloan is out of your life, for one thing. As are any men friends you've been sneaking around to see."

"Yes, of course." Meg knew she was answering as herself, but couldn't seem to stop.

He swirled the wine in his glass, not looking at her. "It's going to take a while for me to trust you again, Rhea."

"Yes, I know that."

"Have I ever given you any reason to doubt me?"

How could she possibly know? Meg glanced at her watch. *Please, Rhea, don't be late.* She said, "No, why?"

"Then why are you dealing with a private detective? Were you hoping to get some dirt on me?"

Meg almost dropped her wineglass. "No! Honestly—"

"Before you make the mistake of denying it, I know you've been calling a PI named Michael Aragon."

When in doubt, tell the truth. Or at least part of it. "Jake, I've been trying to trace my biological mother. That's why I've been dealing with Aragon."

Relief flooded his face. "Has he found her?"

"No…I'll tell you all about it later, when we're home. It's a bit complicated."

Jake nodded, but he was looking at her in that probing way that made her wonder what other doubts he was harboring.

He leaned forward. "While we're clearing the air, let's talk about Capri."

She gulped some wine, more than she intended. "Jake…I don't want to talk about Capri."

"No more stalling," he said sharply. "Let's talk now about what happened in Capri."

Meg stared at him helplessly. She looked at her watch again: 7:50. *Please, Rhea, be here!*

Jake leaned back, regarding her in a way that made her feel like an insect pinned to a board.

Desperate to maintain the masquerade until Rhea arrived, Meg said, "Capri…was also a lovely island."

"Do you remember what we talked about in the Gardens of Augustus?"

She nodded and glanced away nervously, trying to think

of a way to change the subject before she gave herself away.

But his eyes drew her back to him. "I can see it now—the flowers and ancient stonework, the sheer cliffs and the brightly painted boats in the Marina Piccola. The sea was cobalt blue that day and you...do you remember what you said?"

Standing up abruptly, Meg said, "Excuse me. I have to go to the rest room."

Picking up the beaded evening bag, Meg made her way through the closely placed tables. She felt Jake's eyes follow her.

She found the ladies' room door opposite to the restaurant entrance, which relieved some of her anxiety. Rhea could probably have slipped in and quickly vanished into the rest room.

The room was empty. There were three washbasins and three stalls. Pink-and-gray tile, a vase containing pink carnations. Meg sniffed the flowers; they were real. She stood waiting, resisting the urge to check the time again.

Two women, chatting and giggling, came into the room. Meg hastily slipped into the nearest stall. She stayed there until she heard them leave; it was now after eight.

Five minutes later Meg decided she would have to go back to the table and make another excuse to return to the rest room later. Spilled wine, perhaps.

Jake rose and pulled out her chair for her. He made no comment about her lengthy absence, but when they were seated he said, "Capri, remember?"

"Jake, why can't we forget the past?"

"Those who forget history are doomed to repeat it."

Wishing she could read what was behind his enigmatic gaze, Meg didn't respond. He looked both handsome and slightly sinister tonight. He wore a dark silk shirt and charcoal-gray suit, and women in the restaurant glanced repeatedly in his direction. He seemed oblivious as he fixed his gaze on Meg.

Mercifully, at that moment, their first course arrived. Meg ate, but had no idea what she was eating. Jake evidently decided to let the subject of their visit to Capri drop. She wondered what could have happened there. She would have to remember to tell Rhea how persistently he spoke of Capri.

Jake raised his glass. "Shall we toast new beginnings?"

They touched wineglasses.

He said, "You haven't demanded any conciliations from me. Surely you have some?"

"I'll compile a list later."

The tension easing, he grinned.

At 8:30 she nudged her wineglass and managed to spill a little into her lap, then quickly excused herself.

The ladies' room was again vacant. After ten minutes she had no choice but to return to Jake.

He said, "That weekend in Capri had been perfect, right up until the moment you disappeared."

Meg bit her lip. "Did it ever occur to you that perhaps I needed to be alone for a little while?"

A sudden gleam in his eyes disconcerted her, but he didn't bring up the weekend in Capri again.

Somehow Meg got through the meal, refused dessert and suggested they leave. "I'll just wash my hands while you take care of the check," she said, and made a final run for the rest room.

An elderly woman was washing her hands. Meg stood beside her, rummaging through her purse, and covertly examining the other woman's reflection in the mirror, wondering if Rhea could have disguised herself to that extent. The woman glanced at her, smiled and departed.

More minutes dragged by.

So Rhea wasn't coming after all.

Jake was waiting at the door, and they went outside. Clouds were obscuring the stars and the moon hadn't risen.

The parking lot, a narrow strip curling around the edge of the cliff, was almost full and dimly lit. The subdued lighting suggested that the proprietor wanted patrons to admire the distant lights across the bay rather than the rows of parked cars. The small family-owned restaurant did not use valet parking.

Afterward Meg wasn't sure what caught her attention—an alien sound, the shadow that suddenly rose up over the hood of a car scant feet away from them, or perhaps a split-second reflection of light on the barrel of a raised gun.

She screamed, "Jake! Look out!" at the same instant that he grabbed her and flung her to the ground.

As she went down, her head struck a concrete curb, stars exploded and then she was spinning into a black void.

WHEN MEG OPENED her eyes, she was lying on a hospital bed and Jake was sitting beside her, massaging her hand. She could hear the bustle of activity beyond a curtain around the bed and realized she was in a hospital. Her head throbbed and she had trouble focusing her eyes.

Jake gave her a reassuring smile that didn't quite disguise the worry in his eyes. "You've a nasty bump on your temple and the doctors want you to stay overnight, in case you have a concussion. I'm sorry I didn't see that chunk of concrete when I pushed you down."

"Are you all right? You weren't hurt?" Her voice was hoarse.

"No, I wasn't hit. Although as close as the shooter was, I don't know how he missed. Unfortunately, he got away."

Meg explored her forehead, her tentative touch connecting with what felt like a golf-ball-size lump. "You didn't see who it was?"

"No."

She was assailed by a wave of acute weariness and closed her eyes.

Jake's voice, sounding far away, said, "I'll stay with you. I'm going to have to wake you up every couple of hours to make sure you aren't unconscious..."

SITTING BESIDE his wife's hospital bed, Jake gently stroked her hair and silently fumed over his failure to protect her. When he'd gathered her limp body into his arms, unsure if she had been struck by one of the bullets fired at them, he had felt an agonizing fear like none he had ever known.

Racing to the hospital, he had prayed as he had never prayed before, making extravagant bargains with the Almighty, *Let Rhea live, please let her live, and I'll do anything...even give her up, if I have to...*

The harried E.R. doctor had quickly assured him that she had not been shot, but looked at him dubiously and commented, "Nasty blow to the head, concussion maybe. What happened?"

Jake knew that if he disclosed what had really happened, he would be facing reporters before morning. He hadn't seen the shooter, nor even the shooter's car, and both would be long gone. A police report seemed pointless. He would have his own security people look into it, possibly check on disgruntled ex-employees, although in these days of random violence the would-be assassin could have been a complete stranger.

He told the doctor that she had tripped in a poorly lit parking lot and struck her head, which was more or less true.

Rhea stirred and moaned softly, and he whispered, "I'm here. You're safe now. Everything's going to be fine."

When her breathing indicated that she was resting peacefully, he bent over and kissed her cheek lightly. Then he picked up her hand and drew it to his lips.

Oh, Rhea, if only you hadn't been playing a part these past few days…if only you'd been play-acting all those previous months. If only we'd met for the first time in St. Maarten. Could a leopard really change its spots? How he wanted to believe in miracles. But the shooting tonight changed everything. Just what was she involved in?

And why had his mentioning Capri make her look like a deer caught in headlights? She acted as if she couldn't remember being there.

He looked at her bandaged brow, the seed of an idea growing. Perhaps she really *didn't* remember? Was it possible she'd suffered some sort of memory loss? Or was he clutching at straws?

THE FOLLOWING MORNING, Jake, unshaven and grim-faced, checked Meg out of the hospital.

Meg, who had a fierce headache and felt queasy, decided she would confess her deception the moment they were alone. But as they emerged from the hospital, a Rolls-Royce driven by Mason glided to a stop.

Jake opened the rear door. "Mason will take you home, Rhea. I'll see you after a while."

"But…can't you come, too? You've been up all night."

"I've a few things to do. I'll try to get back in time for lunch, but don't count on it. And Rhea…"

"Yes?"

"Better not mention last night's incident to Jess."

He closed the door, and Mason pulled away. Meg had never ridden in a Rolls before and wished she felt better so she could truly appreciate the superb comfort of a car that seemed to float soundlessly above the road.

She stared at the back of the butler's head. His silver hair was as sleek as a steel helmet. He didn't speak until after the Rolls was parked in front of the house and he came around to open her door.

"Perhaps if madam is still feeling unsteady she would care to take my arm?"

"I'm fine," Meg began, then she caught sight of a familiar figure lurking near the terrace. "Mason, that gardener over there—the one with the blond ponytail—what's his name?"

He followed the direction of her glance. "Why, madam, that's the man you hired yourself a few weeks ago. Have you forgotten?"

"I've forgotten his name," Meg said.

"I've heard the head gardener call him Rick, madam. Did you wish to speak with him?"

"No. Go ahead and put the car in the garage. I can get myself into the house."

Once inside, Meg went straight up to the bedroom and called Mike. Again he didn't pick up, nor did his machine.

She drummed her fingers on the desk. Where *was* he?

It seemed that Mike's evaluation of the situation had been correct, after all, although Meg hated to admit it. Rhea had lured them into an ambush last night. Now Meg wanted the private investigator at her side to answer Jake's questions when she told of their deception.

Meg was still wearing the black cocktail dress from the previous evening, so decided to shower and change. After her shower she slipped on pants and shirt, then called Mike again, with the same result.

Recalling that his card had listed a Santa Ana address, she decided to drive over to his office. If Jake showed up while she was gone, it couldn't be helped. She needed Mike to back up her story.

She had memorized his phone number, but couldn't recall his address. His card was in the handbag she'd been using before switching to the beaded purse the previous evening, and she had left it on a closet shelf.

The handbag felt heavier than she remembered it being. Snapping it open, she stared disbelievingly.

A small handgun nestled amid the familiar objects.

Her heart pounding, Meg let the bag slip from her fingers. It landed with a soft thud, and she reflexively drew back.

Having no knowledge of guns, Meg didn't know how to check to see if it was loaded. In either case, she didn't dare leave it behind. Picking up the bag, she carefully slipped the strap over her shoulder and went downstairs.

Mason was crossing the hall, and she said to him, "Will you get a car out of the garage for me, please? Not the Rolls."

He hesitated. "I believe Mr. Chastain mentioned you should take it easy today, madam."

"I won't need you to drive. Please bring a car to the front door."

Mason frowned, obviously reluctant to disregard Jake's instructions.

She stared him down. The weight of the bag on her shoulder seemed unbearable. She would not have asked him to bring a car had she known where the car keys were kept.

"Your Mercedes, madam?" the butler inquired at length.

"Yes, please get it immediately."

Mason finally did as he was asked, and minutes later brought a cream Mercedes from the garage, and parking it—the engine running and keys in the ignition—in front of the house. She could feel Rick the gardener watching her climb into the car and drive away.

Meg drove carefully, observing the speed limit. Glancing at the bag on the seat beside her, she hoped she wouldn't attract the attention of any cruising squad cars. She didn't know much about guns, but she did know it was against the law to carry a concealed weapon.

She had expected the address in Santa Ana to be an office building, but found herself in an older residential neighborhood hemmed in on all sides by freeways.

So, Mike operated out of his house, which proved to be a twenties-style stucco bungalow set back from the street by a wide lawn and shaded by mature trees. She could see a couple of newspapers on the front porch, and the mailbox was overflowing.

For a moment she sat in the car, staring at the house, a sick premonition immobilizing her.

Finally she picked up her bag and got out of the car. She stepped over the newspapers and rang the doorbell.

Waiting, she wished she'd enquired as to the name of his friend on the force. Could Mike have been abruptly summoned out of town? If so, why hadn't he let her know? Why had his answering machine been turned off?

The front door remained closed, but as she pressed her ear close, she could hear a ragtime tune playing inside. Perhaps Mike hadn't heard the doorbell? Could he be asleep inside?

She walked around to the rear of the house, and found herself in a forest of trees. The back door was almost obscured by an orange tree laden with fruit. There was a glass panel in the door, and she peered through it.

Meg's heart leapt into her mouth and ice flowed through her veins. She gripped the door to try to keep the world from spinning away from her.

The slightly grimy glass panel offered a clear view of a kitchen, and she could see Mike's body, sprawled on his back on the floor, his eyes wide and staring, and a dark stain surrounding his head.

There was no doubt that he was dead.

Chapter Fourteen

Heart pounding, Meg stared in horror at the motionless body of the investigator, a part of her willing him to get up and walk to the door even as rational thought told her Mike would never walk anywhere again.

Oh, dear God, no, please no! Had she uttered the words aloud? She jammed her fist against her teeth to keep from screaming.

She felt rooted to the spot, unable to tear her eyes away, despite waves of shock-induced nausea washing over her. She realized that she was panting, as if she'd been running, and forced herself to wrench her gaze from the blood-spattered room.

Turning away, she leaned back weakly against the kitchen door.

Her first instinct was to run to a neighbor's house and call 911. But then she remembered the gun in her purse. That pool of dark blood under Mike's head could have come from blunt-force trauma, but it also could have come from a bullet. What if she were carrying the gun that had killed the investigator?

Meg scarcely remembered jumping into the car and driving away. The image of Mike's body with his staring eyes eclipsed everything else. She had liked Mike, he'd been honest and decent, in spite of the clandestine nature of his profession.

She felt adrift, unsure what to do or where to go. There was a cellular phone in the car and she thought of calling the police, but then they would trace her call, and how could she possibly explain her part in this to them? Especially since she hadn't yet told Jake.

Her head ached and her thoughts were a confused jumble of impressions from two very different lives that had converged with tragic consequences.

Mike had been the only one able to confirm her story, but all she had from him was a receipt for a retainer hiring him to locate her missing husband.

Perhaps he had a file detailing the case? Still in a state of shock, Meg wasn't sure if that would be a good thing or not. What had Mike suggested—about a bad twin wanting to take the good twin's place? That story now sounded more plausible than hers.

When Meg's racing thoughts took her back to the previous night's shooting at the restaurant, she decided that before she did anything else she had to make a full confession to Jake.

She headed for his house.

JAKE WAS PACING back and forth on the terrace when she arrived. He ran to the car and opened her door.

Sweeping her into his arms, he said, "You shouldn't be driving yourself. Why didn't you let Mason take you wherever you wanted to go? I've been going out of my mind worrying about you. Where were you?"

She looked up at him helplessly, unsure where to begin.

He gripped her shoulders and held her at arm's length, staring at her. "*Who* are you?"

Out of the corner of her eye she could see Rick the gar-

dener peering from behind one of the bushes. "Not here,"
Meg said. "Let's go inside."

Jake kept his arm around her, almost as if he were afraid
she would slip away again. He led her to a ground-floor
room that was obviously his study.

Meg had a quick impression of a handsome mahogany
desk, several leather wing chairs, bookcases, a computer.
She sank into the nearest chair.

"Would you like something to drink?" Jake asked.

"A glass of water, please."

Jake pressed a button on the paneled wall behind the
desk and a small bar, complete with sink and refrigerator,
appeared.

Meg tried to collect her thoughts, as Jake dropped ice
cubes into a glass and filled it with water. Handing her the
glass, he perched on the edge of his desk, regarding her
with genuine concern.

"Rhea, I know the blow to your head last night probably
added to your confusion, but I'm convinced something else
happened to you after I left for London. Ever since I surprised you in St. Maarten, you've been acting almost like
someone in a state of fugue."

"Jake, let me explain—"

"Before you do, I'm going to ask you to be honest and
truthful. We both know you haven't always been. Tell me,
are you aware of your apparent lapses of memory lately?"

"I haven't lost my memory."

"No? Then why did you pretend you couldn't remember
that weekend in Capri? Rhea, that was the only stress-free
time we've spent together since we were married. But every
time I tried to recapture the mood when we were in St.
Maarten, you withdrew. I'll admit to a little deception last
night when I asked why you disappeared in Capri, just to
test my theory that perhaps you're suffering some slight

amnesia...Rhea, you never disappeared. We were together every minute. But you don't remember, do you?''

Meg drew a deep breath. ''No, I don't...because I was never in Capri with you. Jake, I'm so sorry—if I'd known what was going to happen I never would have agreed to this masquerade.''

His dark eyes narrowed. ''What are you talking about?''

''I'm not your wife. I'm not Rhea. I'm her twin sister. My name is Meg Lindley.''

Conflicting emotions registered on Jake's face, culminating in one of disbelief.

''Twin? A nice story, Rhea, but you don't have a twin. I checked on your background pretty thoroughly before we were married. I'm not proud of being suspicious, but the corporate lawyers insisted. Sloan is your only sibling and you aren't even blood-related to him. You were both adopted by the Pensbys.''

Meg said quickly, ''After she married you, Rhea decided to search for her biological mother. Apparently she didn't tell you. When she learned about me, she didn't tell me either. I didn't find out until I came here and discovered a letter from the adoption agency...Jake, you have to let me start at the beginning.''

JAKE WAS SILENT for several interminable minutes when Meg finished speaking. She had told him everything except her horrific discovery that morning, hoping that he would accept her story before she had to tell him that she had no one to back it up, and worse, that Mike was probably dead because she had agreed to impersonate Rhea.

At length Jake asked, ''Do you have any idea where Rhea is now?''

Meg shook her head. Then she remembered something. ''But when Rhea's friend Mrs. Wells called, she said she had run into another friend who claimed to have seen her at the Ritz-Carlton.''

"In Laguna Niguel?"

"Yes. I believe so."

"But you haven't heard from Rhea since yesterday, when she told you she'd be at the Greek restaurant?"

"No. But I have a feeling she hired a gardener to keep an eye on us. He might know how to get in touch with her." She told him about Rick.

Jake walked over to the window and stood looking out, his back to her. Meg longed to go to him and put her arms around him.

"Jake," she said, "I haven't told you the worst part of this. I went to Mike's house this morning because he didn't answer his phone." She broke off, the horror returning, overwhelming her.

Biting her lip, she whispered, "He's dead."

Jake spun around, walked back to her and stood looking down at her. "How? When? You do realize how convenient this sounds?"

Meg pressed her fingers to her throbbing head. "I don't know how or when, but I think he was murdered. I could see him through the kitchen window, lying on the floor. There was blood…and before I left I found this…"

She opened her handbag and took out the handgun. "I swear to you, it isn't mine."

Jake took it from her and examined it. She looked away.

He said, "It's a .25 automatic. Good size for a woman to carry. I don't know who it belongs to or how it got into your purse, but I'd say it's been fired recently."

"Do you…do you think it's the gun that killed the private detective?"

"No," Jake answered thoughtfully. "I think it was probably the gun that was used to shoot at us last night. I think

Aragon's take on the situation has some merit. Rhea—or more likely Sloan—wants me dead and they're setting you up to take the blame. Since they only stand to gain if I'm dead, I'm the target.''

Meg realized that she was trembling. She clasped her hands together and tried to breathe normally.

Jake said, ''I should have foreseen there'd be trouble when Sloan was paroled. From what I've learned about their background, those two have had an unhealthy symbiotic relationship for years. He was in prison when I met Rhea, and for a little while she was free of his influence. When I first met her, she bore no resemblance to the lying, cheating woman I asked for a divorce. But, of course, I have no way of knowing when she was acting and when she was showing her true colors. I could never anticipate her mood from one day to the next.''

''Jake, you do believe I've told you the truth? I never would have agreed to be Rhea's stand-in in St. Maarten if I'd known you were going to be there.''

His dark stare was unfathomable. ''Yes, I can see that must have been an unpleasant surprise for you.''

''Well, fortunately you were a gentleman,'' Meg demurred. ''Jake, what are we going to do?''

''Proving a conspiracy is going to be pretty difficult. All we can prove right now is that you are here impersonating my wife.'' He paused. ''We *can* prove that, can't we?''

''You're still not sure that I'm not Rhea, are you?''

He sighed. ''Perhaps because I wanted—so much—for you to be the woman I married. Rhea—''

''Meg—my name is Meg.''

''Perhaps I'd better continue to call you Rhea. We need to keep this to ourselves for the time being.''

''What about your mother? Don't you think we should tell her?''

"No. We'd have to tell her the whole story, and I don't want to worry her. I'll see if I can persuade her to go back to her own house with one of the maids until Carmelita gets back."

Disconcerted by the way he was looking at her, Meg said, "To answer your question, yes, I can prove who I am."

"Some time soon I'd like to hear all about Meg Lindley...but right now we need to find out if the PI's body has been discovered yet and whether the police have connected Rhea and you through him."

"But how can we do that without admitting I saw his body and didn't report it? And what if Mike still had those gas cans he took from the rental car? Jake, I realize that all of this is a shock to you, but I'm in a terrible predicament, too."

"I know some people who can discreetly get me some inside information. But it looks as though Sloan wanted me to die in the fire and you to be accused of arson. When that didn't work, he tried to shoot me last night. Maybe he thought he'd hit me and so had his inside man plant the gun in your purse. We spent the night at the hospital, so they probably figured I was dead and you were hurt. What would you say our first concern should be?"

"That there will probably be another attempt on your life with me set up to be the accused. Jake, maybe I should go home and resume my life as Meg Lindley. If I'm not here, their plan won't work."

"Too late for that. I'm sure Rhea has witnesses who can testify to the fact that you went to St. Maarten in her place and have been impersonating her ever since."

"Having decided I'd like to take her place permanently," Meg added, "but somehow ended up killing you instead of her."

He nodded. "Even if you weren't here, they could still pin it on you. Rhea got you out of the beach house before they set it afire because they need you alive. For now, I'd like you to stay where I can keep an eye on you—if you will."

"Yes, of course. It's the least I can do. I will have to make some calls to explain my absence to a few people."

"Your employers and the creditors you mentioned? You said you have no family."

"That's right."

"Sure, you can call them later. But right now why don't you go and rest, while I find out what I can about Aragon."

"I can't possibly rest. If you don't mind, I'd like to go to the kitchen and cook something."

For the first time the lines of strain on Jake's face eased slightly. "If only I'd met you two years ago."

Meg dared not meet his gaze.

JAKE'S COOK, a stern-faced middle-aged woman whose features were somewhat softened by pretty auburn hair, managed to conceal her surprise when Meg, with Jake at her side, announced she would take care of dinner—and no, she didn't need any help. Jake promptly suggested that the cook take the afternoon off, to which she happily agreed.

He murmured to Meg, "Let the kitchen maids stay with you, okay? That bump on your head still looks substantial, and I don't want you passing out again."

"I'm fine, really. I'll feel better if I keep busy."

"All right, but I'd feel better if you were lying down with an ice pack. I'll go speak to Jess now. Then I'll deal with that other matter and let you know what I find out."

He lingered for a moment, staring at her, then squeezed her shoulder gently in wordless reassurance.

JAKE FOUND the ponytailed gardener hanging around one of the toolsheds and grabbed his arm, spinning him around.

"Okay, Rick, tell me where my wife is."

The man's mouth sagged and his eyes bulged with fear. "She...she's in the house."

Jake slammed him back against the shed, none too gently. "The woman who hired you—*that* Mrs. Chastain— where did you last see her?"

"Here—I saw her here—this is where she hired me."

Jake's hand went to the man's skinny throat, and he yelped with fright. "I don't know what you're talking about, I swear to God. Your wife's in the house."

Grabbing the man's ponytail, Jake yanked his head back and stared into his eyes. He saw only fear there, so released him. "Come on, I'm going to escort you off the premises."

Marching the gardener down the driveway, Jake's mind methodically organized a plan of action.

HE NEVER SHOULD have trusted Rick to do the job with a .25, but they needed a compact weapon that a woman would be likely to use. Maybe they were lucky Rick had missed. Somebody might have seen him put the gun in the woman's hand. At least he had the presence of mind to wipe it off and plant it in her purse. If the cops recovered any bullets, they could match them up to her gun.

The only reason he'd sent Rick was because he'd had to take care of Aragon. But next time would be different. He'd do the job himself.

First they had to disappear. Wigs, shapeless clothes, flea-bag motels, a different car.

Chastain would be looking for them now.

Chapter Fifteen

Meg found a well-stocked pantry, freezers full of meat, and refrigerator crispers packed with fresh vegetables. She was looking forward to performing familiar tasks. Cooking would give her a sense of normalcy, at least for a little while. It would also give her time to think.

A young kitchen maid was scrubbing the already gleaming counters, and Meg was glad when Guadalupe, the friendly maid, joined her.

Guadalupe said respectfully, "We'll not bother you, Mrs. Chastain, you just let us know if you need anything."

"Thank you, Guadalupe. You know, I haven't had lunch. Perhaps you could make me a sandwich and a pot of tea? I'd like a couple of aspirin too, if you can find some." Meg hoped the latter would help ease her headache, if not her heart-pounding tension.

Guadalupe was swiftly efficient as well as being very attractive, and Meg wondered why she didn't aspire to a better job than waiting on the idle rich. A steaming pot of tea and a cold roast beef sandwich, along with a small salad, appeared like magic. Guadalupe also brought the aspirin. Meg took a bite of the sandwich and then swallowed two aspirin.

The maid lingered for a moment. "Maybe you'd like me

to call somebody for you? You know, tell them you were hurt? Sometimes you need family more than a husband.''

Surprised by the depth of Guadalupe's concern, Meg said, ''Thank you, but I'm fine.'' She supposed the maid must wonder about a husband who brought his wife to the kitchen to cook dinner so soon after her brush with death. Guadalupe seemed hesitant to leave, but finally nodded and moved to another part of the room. She glanced frequently in Meg's direction.

Climbing onto a stool beside a butcher-block counter, Meg sipped her tea and was sorting a bunch of fresh herbs when the kitchen door opened and Jessica appeared, her expression angry. Huxley loped in after her and nuzzled Meg's ankle. He was always most interested in her right foot, which seemed to confirm the widely held view that animals sense human hurts and injuries.

''So, you want me to leave my son's house, do you?''

Meg said carefully, ''Jake felt you'd be more comfortable in your own home.''

''Oh? And this is the same Jake who insisted I *come* here?'' Jessica enquired sarcastically. ''Don't blame Jake, I know who wants to get rid of me. What happened, Rhea? Did that bump on your head turn you back into the jealous, self-centered gold digger you were before you decided to turn on the charm?''

''Jessica, I don't want you to leave, but Jake thinks—''

''What really happened last night, Rhea? Jake said you took a tumble in a dark parking lot, and he spent the night at the hospital with you. But there was more to it than that, wasn't there? I always know when he isn't telling me the whole truth.''

''That's exactly what happened. It was clumsy of me,'' Meg answered quietly. It was obvious that Jessica had been out to get Rhea for a long time and, despite everything, Meg felt she had to defend her absent twin.

As if sensing all was not well between the two women, the Doberman flopped down and rolled over onto his back.

Jessica exclaimed, "Oh, Huxley, do get up. Mommie can't get down there to scratch your belly with her arm in a cast."

Glad of the diversion, Meg murmured, "Allow me," and jumped down to rub Huxley's stomach while he squirmed and grinned foolishly. After indulging himself for a moment, he sat up and sniffed Meg's forehead, careful not to actually touch the bump, then sympathetically licked her hand.

Jessica watched for a moment, then said grudgingly, "I do wish you'd stay in character, Rhea."

Meg looked up at her and replied sincerely, "I wish we could be friends."

Jessica gave a short sardonic chuckle. "Now I know you're up to something. Too late to make amends, Rhea. Too many ugly scenes under the bridge."

"But it's never too late to start over," Meg said. Huxley kissed her ear. Meg looked up at Jessica hopefully.

"Friends, indeed! Look at us. My arm is encased in plaster, and you've got a purple goose egg on your forehead. We look like we've gone ten rounds with each other."

Meg smiled in spite of her tension.

She had forgotten the presence of Guadalupe and the other maid, who had discreetly withdrawn into the adjacent pantry, although Meg now noted they had left the door open.

"Jake said you're cooking," Jessica commented. "Must I leave before dinner?"

"No, of course not."

"Good. I must say, of all the tangents you've been on

since you married my son, this cooking bit is a welcome change. I've always admired the culinary arts. I feel the best cooks are artists in every sense of the word, so as a fellow artist, I commend you. As a woman and a daughter-in-law, you leave a whole lot to be desired—but maybe as fellow artists, we could find some common ground to meet on, Rhea. What do you say?''

"I'd like that very much,'' Meg answered sincerely.

Jessica gave her a thin smile. ''Just keep in mind that if I find out you're cheating on my son, I'll probably kill you.''

Before Meg could react, Jessica said, ''Come on, Huxley, stop groveling at her feet and let's go get some fresh air.''

"You're going outside?'' Meg asked, alarm bells sounding.

Jessica arched an eyebrow in mock surprise. ''That's usually where one finds fresh air.''

Meg thought of the sinister Rick, prowling around the grounds, and wanted to beg Jake's mother to stay safely inside the house. But she couldn't think of a way to do so without arousing her suspicions. She could only hope that Jake had now had time to remove the man from the premises.

As soon as Jessica and Huxley disappeared, Meg headed for Jake's study. She knocked and entered.

He was on the phone. ''...so the place had been ransacked?'' He paused, then said, ''Try to find out what the police have found in his files, will you?''

Waving Meg to a chair, he continued, ''No, it's just that my wife used him to locate her birth mother. Yes, she was adopted. Okay, good. Call me as soon as you have anything.''

He looked at Meg. ''Everything all right?''

"Your mother took Huxley outside. I'm concerned about that gardener I told you about."

"Rick's gone. I personally supervised his packing up and leaving before I talked to Jess. I couldn't get any information out of him about Rhea's whereabouts. He put on a big act, insisting that my wife was right here in the house. You, in other words. I'll have one of my people check the Ritz-Carlton."

Meg said, "Your mother thinks I want her to leave."

"Don't worry about it. I called Carmelita and she's flying home tomorrow. Jess will be fine."

"I hadn't realized just how rancorous the relationship between Rhea and your mother was."

"My mother never trusted her," Jake said shortly.

"Were you able to find out anything about Mike Aragon?"

"The police are there now. I reported a possible homicide."

Meg gasped. "You implicated me? You told the police I found the body?"

"I told them my wife had seen the body through a window. I had to. Neighbors probably saw you and may have a description of the car, maybe even a license plate. We don't want to be caught in any lies. I just said the PI had been working for you, didn't return calls, and you drove over to speak to him in person. That *is* the truth, isn't it?

"Except for the fact that I'm not your wife. Will the police want to interview me?"

"No. I told them you're distraught and have been sedated. That you didn't enter the house and that your only connection to Aragon was that he was tracing your biological family. Fortunately I have a few friends in law enforcement and if necessary I'll call in a couple of favors and keep you out of the murder investigation, at least until we can locate Rhea. Of course, we'll have to wait and see what they turn up about you and Rhea in Aragon's files.''

''Jake...what about the gun?''

''It's in a safe place.''

''Last night at the restaurant, did you file a police report?''

''No. I didn't wait around. I drove you straight to the hospital. I'm not sure anyone else saw or heard anything. There was no one else in the parking lot, and between the sound of the surf, the traffic on the Coast Highway and the noise inside the restaurant, a couple of shots from a small-caliber gun could have gone unnoticed. I'd prefer not to talk to the police until we have some idea of what Sloan is planning.''

''Is there any way we can find out if the police found those gas cans at Mike's place?''

''I have a friend in the D.A.'s office. Maybe he can get some information for us.''

The phone rang and Jake picked it up. Meg quietly left the study.

BACK IN THE KITCHEN Meg realized that she had been running on adrenaline, and, suddenly weary, she decided on a simple dinner of roasted chicken and a delicately flavored risotto. She gladly accepted Guadalupe's help, but was taken aback when the maid waited until they were alone and then whispered, ''There are places women can go...you know, when husbands beat you.''

Shocked, Meg exclaimed, ''Mr. Chastain didn't beat me! I fell in a poorly lit parking lot and hit my head.''

Guadalupe didn't look convinced, and Meg recalled Rhea's claim that Jake could be violent. Meg wondered uneasily if he, like herself, was also putting on an act. No, she decided immediately, she couldn't be that wrong about him—and besides, Rhea was a confirmed liar. Still, how well did Meg know Jake Chastain, really? After such a short acquaintanceship, how could she be sure what kind of man he was?

That evening Jessica pronounced the meal delicious and coyly suggested she might stay on for a few more days.

Jake said, "Rhea and I have to go away on business for a couple of days, Jess. You'll be better off at home—you can take Mason with you as well as a maid."

"Mason! Absolutely not. He intimidates the heck out of me."

Meg smiled in sympathy. She felt the same way about the butler.

Jake said, "Well, Carmelita will be back late tomorrow. As I said, Rhea and I have to leave. You don't want to stay on here alone, do you?"

Jessica sighed. "Oh, all right." She slipped a piece of chicken under the table to Huxley, and both Jake and Meg pretended they hadn't noticed.

Meg's head was throbbing again and she longed to crawl into bed.

Mason appeared, carrying a telephone. "I'm sorry to disturb you, sir, but a gentleman insists you told him to interrupt no matter what you were doing. He wouldn't give his name."

Jake took the phone, listened for a moment, then said, "Hold on." To his mother and Meg he said, "Finish your dinner, I'll take this call in my study."

IT WAS LATE that evening before Meg was able to speak privately with Jake again. He'd driven Jessica, Huxley and one of his more mature maids back to his mother's house, then taken several more calls in his study.

Meg had soaked in a warm tub and, exhausted, slipped

on one of Rhea's nightgowns and crawled into bed. She awakened to find Jake gently stroking her hair.

"I would have knocked," he said, "but one of the staff might have seen me. I don't want to give rise to any rumors that we're breaking up, in case a gossip columnist gets wind of it. I don't usually knock on doors in my own home and I'd like to keep things as normal as possible. I thought you'd like to know what I found out about Aragon."

Meg sat up, instantly awake.

Jake said, "He was killed execution style, two shots to the head. No forced entry, suggesting he knew his killer. The place had been ransacked and several items are missing, all pointing to robbery. But needless to say, the police are also interested in his list of clients."

"What about his files? Did they find anything?"

"They think he kept all of his records on a computer, but it was one of the items stolen. All the police know about our connection to him is what I told them—that my wife asked him to trace her biological family."

Meg was all at once aware that one of the straps of the satin nightgown she wore had slipped from her shoulder. She had left a bedside lamp on when she got into bed, intending only to rest rather than to sleep, and now realized she was showing a great deal of cleavage.

Jake seemed to have read her mind. Maintaining his carefully detached expression, he picked up the satin robe she had left lying at the foot of the bed and handed it to her.

"Are you too tired to talk?"

Slipping on the robe, she got out of bed. "I slept for a while, I feel better. Perhaps we could sit over there?" She indicated the fireplace, flanked by twin sofas.

A ghost of a smile plucked at Jake's mouth. "Yes. I'd better keep my distance."

They took opposite sofas. Rhea's portrait above the mantelpiece looked down on them with a contemptuous smirk.

Jake said, "I never offered my condolences on the loss of your husband."

"Thank you. To be honest, I lost Hal long before he disappeared. But it's hard to believe he's dead."

"What was he like?"

"Too handsome, too talented, too impatient to wait for the success that surely would have come to him in time. Like many great chefs, he was something of a showman and needed constant reassurance from an adoring audience. I guess my adoration wasn't enough for him after our restaurant went under."

In this dimly lit, intimate setting, it was easy for Meg to ask, "What about Rhea? The Rhea you fell in love with, I mean, before her brother got out of prison."

He shrugged ruefully. "I don't believe I ever was in love with her. 'Marry in haste'—what's the rest of the quote?— 'repent at leisure'? I didn't really know her. We were swept away by passion, and perhaps I gave her too much, too quickly. Sudden wealth is difficult for some people to handle, especially for someone who'd spent most of her life on the edge of poverty. Jess thinks I saw myself as some sort of Svengali, but I didn't try to make Rhea over, she was already well along the way to transforming herself when I met her."

"What did she do—for a living, I mean?" Meg asked.

"She was an inveterate job-hopper. Never stayed long in any one place apparently. Waitress, clerk, sometimes model. She's bright enough to do or be anything she chooses, but the term 'instant gratification' was coined for Rhea."

"When we were in St. Maarten, you mentioned that she'd had an abusive childhood."

"Yes. One foster home after another, deprivation, beatings and I suspect sexual abuse, although she never admitted it. I'll be truthful, I was a bachelor for a long time and perhaps more in love with the idea of marriage and family, when I met Rhea, than with her. I so desperately wanted her to be my soul mate that I overlooked a lot of warning signals. I knew before the honeymoon was over that I'd made a mistake."

"But you stayed married—for eighteen months. There must have been some love between you."

"I'd made a commitment and I didn't want to admit I'd been wrong. My feelings for her soon proved to be an illusion. There's no love without fidelity."

How true that was, Meg thought, remembering Hal's transgressions.

Jake let out a long breath, as though he'd been bottling it up for some time. "Shortly before I flew to Paris, one of my business acquaintances informed me that she was cheating on me. I didn't bother to confirm whether or not it was true, because I'd suspected it for months. I asked for a divorce. She suggested we wait until after the St. Maarten hotel opening and my European trip before discussing it. And then, there you were…I thought dreams did come true, after all."

"I wish I could have known her years ago," Meg said with genuine regret. "If only we could have grown up together. We would have had each other, and maybe she wouldn't have been influenced by Sloan." She added, "Perhaps it isn't too late. Perhaps she's being manipulated by Sloan and isn't guilty of—"

Jake shook his head. "Don't nurture any false hopes, Meg."

It was the first time he had called her by her real name, and she was unprepared for the impact it had on her.

"I have people searching for her," he added. "People I can trust. I'm hoping we can find her before she does anything foolish." He stared at Meg for a moment. "You really are identical."

"My hair isn't this color naturally," Meg said, "and I don't usually wear it this short."

"Rhea's hair was shoulder length and honey colored when I first met her."

Like mine used to be, Meg thought. "Jake, surely you must have had some inkling that I wasn't Rhea. There had to be some differences."

In the half light she could see a small smile playing about his mouth. "I wondered about your fingernails. Rhea favored talons, but she knew I didn't care for fake nails and I rationalized you got rid of them to please me."

"Mike evidently forgot the nails in my makeover. All I got was a manicure. Didn't you become suspicious when I couldn't do the tango?"

"Ah, yes, the tango," he murmured, and didn't elaborate.

They were silent for a moment. Meg said awkwardly, "Perhaps we ought to turn in."

He stood up. "I'll be in a guest room two doors down the landing from this one if you need me—or if you think of anything else that might help us find Rhea."

At the door he turned and looked back at her. "There was something else that seemed out of character."

"Yes?"

"When we kissed…you seemed to mean it."

Meg was glad the dim light hid her flaming cheeks.

Chapter Sixteen

The vegetables in Meg's dream were enough to set the pulse of any cook fluttering: eggplants dressed in purple satin, rosy beets, deep green kale, gnarled celery roots. An abundance of the riches of the earth. But then a shadow fell across her work area, a raised arm holding a cleaver that glistened with blood.

She awoke with a silent scream trapped in her throat.

The room was dark, but she was certain the bedroom door had just closed with a faint click.

Snapping on the bedside lamp, she leapt out of bed and ran to the door, flung it open and looked out.

The landing was deserted.

Perhaps she had imagined that someone opened her door. Or maybe it was Jake, checking on her? He said he was sleeping in a guest room two doors away. He could have returned to it in the time it took her to reach the bedroom door.

What am I doing here? Meg thought, experiencing a sudden longing for her own modest rented house. She had been drawn into a web of intrigue that had ensnared her before she realized there was no escape route.

She switched on all the lights in the bedroom, wishing the night away. It was a little after four a.m.

Looking around, she tried to determine if someone had crept in and disturbed anything while she slept. Everything seemed to be in place.

I've got to do something, she told herself. *I can't just sit around and wait for something to happen.*

Her gaze rested on the desk, where Rhea had concealed the letter from the adoption agency inside a paperback book. Had she hidden anything else that might offer some clue as to her plans—or better still, her whereabouts?

Knowing she would be unable to get back to sleep, Meg decided to shower and dress and then make a thorough search, not just of the desk, but of the entire room.

She didn't have to look far. Opening the top drawer of the desk she saw an envelope that had not been there when she found the letter from the adoption agency. Unlike the letter, the envelope was in plain view. It was marked, *Open if anything happens to Jake or Rhea.*

Meg tore it open. Inside were photocopied pages from either a diary or a journal.

With mounting indignation she read:

Spoke to Meg today. She wants to take my place in St. Maarten. She says since Jake will be in Europe, no one will be any the wiser and it would be a lark. I'm uneasy about her and wonder if I made a mistake in agreeing to meet her. She complains about how rough her life is and how I have everything she ever wanted.

Meg gasped as she flipped to the next page and read on.

I'm terrified of what Meg is going to do. She has made herself over to look exactly like me. Hair, clothes, everything. I believe she wants to be me. She refuses to meet Jake, or any of my friends. She says it will be more fun to keep our relationship secret so we can switch places whenever we please. She says if I tell Jake about her he will think I'm crazy, because she will simply vanish, and since neither she nor I knew we had an identical twin until just a few weeks ago, nobody will believe me. It's all too weird and scary.

The third page was torn in half, the top portion missing.

…and I thought if I let her go to St. Maarten that would satisfy her, but now she's masquerading as me here at home and refuses to leave. She showed me a gun and threatened to kill Jake's mother unless I stay away. I don't know what to do. If I go to the police, it would be Meg's word against mine, and she is with Jake, in our home. I'm now on the outside. What do they say—possession is nine-points of the law? Besides, I can't put Jessica in danger. Meg Lindley— God help me, my twin sister—is a psychopath.

Meg reread the entries. Her throat constricted. Since the pages were photocopied, there would be an original diary somewhere. The copies had been left because Rhea wanted her to know about the diary. The message to Meg was obvious: *If you go to the police, it will be your word against mine.*

With Mike dead, Meg had no doubt Rhea's story would sound plausible. Worse, would Rhea's account of their relationship be believed by Jake? Meg desperately wanted Jake to trust and believe in her.

But outweighing every other consideration was Rhea's not-so-veiled threat against Jessica. Whether or not Jake would be inclined to believe Rhea's account of their relationship, he had to be told that he must protect his mother.

Gathering up the pages, Meg made her way to his room. Another thought hammering at the back of her mind was that although Rick had been dismissed, someone had entered the bedroom and planted those diary pages in the desk.

She knocked on Jake's door. There was no response. She knocked again, louder, then opened the door.

His bed had been slept in, but there was no sign of Jake. Suppressing a stab of fear, she hurried downstairs.

She saw with relief that there was a glimmer of light under his study door.

He called, "Come in," in response to her knock.

Jake was seated at his desk, his computer screen lit up and the phone in his hand. Seeing her, he put down the phone.

"You're up early. Are you all right?"

"Yes. Well, no. Jake, do you have a security system here?"

"Yes, a very good one. Why?"

"Someone got into the bedroom last night and left this." She handed him the envelope.

He caught his breath. "It's Rhea's handwriting."

Slipping the photocopies from the envelope, he read the diary entries and then looked up at her. She tried unsuccessfully to read his expression.

Meg said quickly, "I swear to you that none of that is true. It all happened the way I told you. Mike Aragon came to me and asked me to stand in for your wife while she visited her dying brother."

"Speaking of whom," Jake said grimly, "I called his parole officer in San Francisco. Sloan hasn't reported to him."

"Jake...do you think they might hurt your mother?"

"No, I think it's part of an elaborate scheme to set you

up. But I won't take any chances. I'll persuade Jess and Carmelita to go on a convalescent trip and assign one of my security people to go along with them.''

"Jake, you do believe that I'm not trying to…that I don't want to…" Meg floundered, feeling herself color.

The study was dark except for the pale glow of the computer screen and a single desk lamp. A gray dawn sent tentative fingers creeping around the window shutters. Jake's obsidian-dark gaze seemed to pierce her mind, finding thoughts she dare not admit even to herself.

He finished for her. "Do I believe you want to take Rhea's place as my wife?"

Meg felt her color deepen. "Well, the diary entries…"

Jake stood up and walked around the desk. "No, I believe what you told me. If you'd had any romantic designs on me, I certainly gave you plenty of opportunities to explore them. You kept me very much at arm's length most of the time.''

"You're a married man," Meg murmured. "And until a couple of days ago, I believed I was a married woman.''

"And now that you know you are a widow, and you're aware that my wife and I were virtually separated before you came along…?"

Meg cleared her throat. "We can't have this conversation, Jake.''

He said softly, "I suppose I'm hoping you feel some spark of interest in me. For myself, I see a woman who physically is a duplicate of the woman whose beauty captivated me, but whose character repulsed me. But you know, Meg, even now I find it hard to believe you and Rhea are blood-related, because you have none of her flaws.''

Meg looked away from his questing dark eyes, willing

herself to remember that she had brought chaos into his life. At length she sighed. "I have plenty of flaws, Jake."

"I wish you'd exhibit some. Right now you seem to be the woman of my dreams."

"How about my impersonating your wife? For a price?"

"You thought it would be a harmless masquerade and we'd never meet—and the price included Aragon finding your missing husband. A saint would have been tempted."

Meg was silent, fearing anything she said might give away her feelings.

After a moment Jake said, "I'm sorry. I didn't mean to make you feel uncomfortable. Now, before you decide to run out on me, how about fixing a fast breakfast while I call Jess?"

"Isn't it a little early to wake her?"

"Good point. I'll drive over to Laguna and pick her up. I can be more persuasive face-to-face."

"So I've noticed," Meg murmured.

He followed her into the kitchen. None of the servants were up yet, and Meg found the empty room and Jake's presence beside her curiously intimate. She opened cabinet doors, looking for a coffeepot.

"Jake, you said you have a good security system, and yet someone got into the bedroom."

"Yes, I've been thinking about that." He went to the refrigerator and took out a pitcher of orange juice.

"How long has Mason been with you?" Meg asked. "I think he's known from the beginning that I'm not Rhea."

"Mason's been with me for years, since long before I married Rhea. Perhaps he was more perceptive than everyone else. As for the rest of the staff, Mason always runs a thorough background check before hiring anybody. Still, it's an unfortunate truism that anybody can be bought."

He brought her a glass of orange juice and watched as

she put on the coffee, then took some eggs from the refrigerator. "I can whip up an omelet in nothing flat. Will that do?"

"Great. Excuse me if I stare. I've never been around a woman who cooks. Jess never did, and neither did Rhea."

Somewhat flustered, Meg broke the eggs into a bowl. "If we weren't in a rush I could make something more interesting."

Jake said, "I hope I can look forward to that sometime. You know, I'm thinking that maybe we need to circle the wagons a little tighter."

"What do you mean?"

"This is a big house—sprawling grounds, all kinds of servants, gardeners, pool maintenance and other service people, coming and going. Even with the security system, it would be fairly easy for an assassin to get in. Especially since Rhea knows how to circumvent the security system. Perhaps we'd be better off somewhere else until I can track her and Sloan down."

"Do you have somewhere in mind?"

"Yes. After we eat and while I drive over to Laguna, pack a few things and have Mason pack a bag for me. Just tell him I'm going to do an on-site construction inspection and will need boots and clothes suitable for rugged terrain. Since it would be too much of a stretch of anyone's imagination to believe Rhea would accompany me on that kind of a trip, tell him you're going to visit a friend. If Rhea has a spy in the house, this will get the word to her that we're in two different locations. Since they need to know where both of us are for their plan to succeed, it might just make them show themselves, as they try to find us."

"*Will* we be in two different places?" Meg asked.

"No. I want you near me."

THE LUGGAGE Mike had provided for Meg's trip to St. Maarten was still in the vast walk-in closet off the master bedroom, and Meg decided to use it again. Presumably the rest of Rhea's luggage was stored away somewhere.

She surveyed the rows of color-matched outfits and shelves containing accessories. She would have preferred to use only the clothes provided for the trip to St. Maarten, which had been purchased for her, but a maid had unpacked her bags and taken those items away for laundering and dry cleaning. They had not yet been returned. Besides, since Jake had specified boots and rugged terrain, the tropical items would hardly be suitable.

It seemed incredible to Meg that only a couple of days earlier she and Jake had been basking in the sunshine of a Caribbean island. A wave of unbearable guilt washed over her as she remembered Mike taking her to the airport. No matter what Jake said, nothing would convince her that Mike's murder was not connected to her masquerade.

She found a couple of pairs of designer jeans that looked new. There were also a denim jacket and some lightweight sweaters tucked away on a shelf at the back of the closet. She took one pair of jeans, the jacket, a shirt and a sweater. Surely they would be able to find Rhea in a couple of days, and this nightmare would be over.

If only she had access to her own running shoes. Rhea wore a size smaller and so the only shoes Meg could wear were the kidskin flats, beach sandals and the evening shoes Mike had provided after she gave him her shoe size.

Perhaps she could persuade Jake to stop by her house so that she could pick up her own clothes and shoes. How she would love to be Meg Lindley again, if only for a little while, to escape this feeling of having lost herself. Her own things would surely help.

Snapping open the carry-on bag she had taken to St.

Maarten, Meg packed the jeans and sweater and was about to stuff some toilet articles into an outside pocket of the bag when she saw two sheets of paper, stapled together.

Knowing the bag had been completely unpacked, Meg's heart began to thump again as she examined the two sheets of paper. The top page was a carbon copy of an application to buy a firearm, stating that the applicant had no history of mental illness or any criminal record.

The applicant was Margaret Lindley, and Meg's address, phone number, and all of her personal information was given.

But it was the second sheet that sent a wave of fear racing icily along Meg's veins. It was an invoice from a gun shop, dated the day before she left for St. Maarten, recording the purchase of a Smith & Wesson .22 caliber pistol.

Not the .25 automatic I found in my purse.

There was a second gun registered in her name.

Chapter Seventeen

Meg was surprised when Jake returned with Huxley, but she was glad to see the Doberman. Huxley greeted her like a long lost friend, almost knocking her down in his enthusiasm.

Jake had changed into jeans, a sweater and a denim jacket. Despite the unaccustomed garb, he still managed to look as if he'd stepped from the pages of *GQ*. "Are you ready to go?"

Meg nodded, indicating the two overnight bags packed and waiting. The gun application and invoice in her pocket rustled as she moved.

Jake looked at the kidskin flats she wore. "There should be some tennis or exercise shoes somewhere."

"They're a size too small," Meg said. "I can't wear anything tight on my right foot. I thought we could stop by my house and get a pair of my own."

"I don't want to risk being tailed. I guess those flats will have to do."

Mason awaited them at the front doors. "Did you wish me to drive you to the airport, sir? Madam didn't instruct me to call to have the Cessna readied, so I presume you are using commercial flights?"

"We're not flying," Jake answered. "I'm taking the Jeep, and I'll drive my wife to her friend's place."

"And if I need to get in touch with you, sir?"

Jake looked at him sharply. "Call my office, as usual."

Huxley trotted obediently behind them, sniffed the Jeep, and then jumped onto the back seat. Meg asked, "Did you tell anyone in your office where you'll be?"

"No. For the moment, I don't trust anybody."

Meg slid into the passenger seat. Between the seats there were several boxes, on top of which Jake placed their bags. She noticed a hard hat on the seat and mentally tried it on Jake, who was revealing facets of himself that she hadn't expected.

Huxley trampled a small circle on the back seat until he was satisfied it was acceptable, then lay down, placing his head on his forepaws and relaxing.

She asked, "How did your mother react to going away— and being separated from Huxley?"

"Not well," Jake answered. "But regulations prohibit dogs where she's going. I told her I'm dealing with a deranged employee and expect to have him in custody in a couple of days. I put her on my private plane with my most trusted security man. Carmelita will join them later today."

Meg resisted the impulse to look back at the gracious house as they drove away. Jake hadn't mentioned where Jessica was going, and the omission made Meg wonder if he still had doubts about her. If he did, she reasoned, who could blame him?

She said, "Have I told you how very sorry I am that I've caused you all this turmoil?"

He glanced sideways at her. "The turmoil began eighteen months ago when I married Rhea."

"Jake…I found something else when I was packing."

She told him of the gun application and invoice. "I suppose Rhea must have posed as me. She would have had all my personal information from Mike. The signature on the application doesn't look like mine, but I'm sure the dealer, a gun shop in L.A. near where I live, would identify me as the buyer.''

"Well, we knew about the gun," Jake said.

"Actually, no, we didn't know about *this* gun. It's a different one. Didn't you say the gun I found in my handbag was a .25 automatic? The invoice is for a Smith & Wesson .22-caliber pistol.''

"Another ladies' weapon," Jake commented.

At the end of the private road he turned east, toward the mountains. Meg didn't ask their destination. Huxley snored softly in the back seat, his tail thumping occasionally as he enjoyed his dreams.

The two-lane highway snaked through the foothills, at times passing under canopies formed by the interwoven branches of ancient live oaks. Jake glanced frequently in the rearview mirror. There was little traffic in the late morning on a weekday, but Meg assumed he was checking to be sure they weren't followed.

As they climbed to the higher elevations, the live oaks gave way to pines and the air grew cooler.

Jake reached for his cellular phone. He didn't identify himself to the recipient of his call, but merely asked, "Any word? What about Sloan? Check with his parole officer again, although he was in violation when I called. Uh-huh, yeah. What about the murder investigation?''

He listened without comment for several minutes, then said, "I'll be in touch."

Meg waited, but he didn't fill her in on what, if anything, he had learned. At length she said, "Are you going to tell me where we're going?''

"I bought some land up here a few years ago. It borders

on the National Forest. I didn't get around to developing it and probably never will. I figure I've given the world more than enough high-priced hotels and resorts and there's no way man could improve on nature up here.''

His approval rating in Meg's mind notched upward again. She said, ''So you weren't kidding about the rough terrain?''

''This particular piece of land has an abandoned campground on it. A landslide obliterated the road leading to it, but some of the cabins are still standing.''

This explained the choice of the four-wheel-drive Jeep for the journey, Meg thought, as he turned the wheel and they bumped over a rutted dirt trail that soon disappeared into a shallow stream. After crossing the stream they zigzagged between trees and outcroppings of rock.

Meg felt an urge to drop breadcrumbs out of the Jeep window, in case she needed to find her way back.

''This seems remote,'' Jake remarked, ''but we're less than two hours from town.''

''Yes, I realize that,'' Meg said. ''But I wonder if in hiding out here we're just postponing a showdown.''

''If my people haven't located Rhea and Sloan in the next twenty-four hours, then I'll go back home and stake myself out to lure them to me. You, my dear Meg, will join Jess on the island until this is all over.''

''The island?''

''Off the coast of Baja.''

''Which you own.''

''Actually, no. The Mexican government doesn't allow foreigners to own their land. But neither Sloan nor any of his cronies would be allowed to land, even if they knew about the island—which they don't, because Rhea doesn't know about it. There's no way to get in by boat and I do control the airstrip, since I built it.''

"I always wondered how the other half lives," Meg murmured.

In the back seat Huxley awoke and sat up, sniffing the fragrant pine-scented air appreciatively.

Jake glanced over his shoulder at the Doberman. "He couldn't go to the island, because it's being turned into a bird sanctuary. In fact, in a few more months, we won't be able to fly in."

The remains of a rustic wood sign, tottering on rotting posts, came into view. Meg could make out most of the letters burned into the wood: Tall Pines Family Campground. Ten RV spaces with full hookups, six cabins, twenty tent campsites.

Jake said, "I'm thinking of rebuilding the access road, then renovating the place and turning it into a camp for abused and neglected kids. What do you think?"

I think I love you, but it's a forbidden love. Aloud, Meg answered, "It's a wonderful idea. Kids would love it up here."

Jake drove past crumbling concrete pads designed for recreational vehicles, and grassy tent sites shaded by tall trees, then came to a row of redwood cabins. He stopped in front of the last one, which, unlike the others, still had its front door and window shutters intact. There was a fire ring in front of the cabin with a barbecue grill. A redwood picnic table stood nearby, its surface covered with a thick mat of pine needles.

Huxley leapt out excitedly to explore these alien surroundings, spotted a squirrel and chased it up a tree, then began to mark his territory.

Jake offered his hand to help Meg down from the Jeep, an old-fashioned courtesy she accepted gratefully. She was unprepared for the impact of his warm grip, or for the way he continued to hold her hand after she was on the ground, his dark eyes expressing feelings so intense that her heart fluttered against her ribs like a caged bird.

They stood like that, staring at one another, transfixed by a force more powerful than reason or propriety. It seemed to Meg that the world fell away, swept aside by the ancient imperative that had driven man and woman since the beginning of time.

For one giddy, euphoric second Meg thought that perhaps there would be a way for Jake to love her, for her to love him.

Then Jake said huskily, ''Meg, what if we were to—''

Huxley pushed between them, a pinecone in his mouth. The Doberman's presence instantly brought back into focus the other players in this drama. Recovering her senses, she said quickly, ''No, don't say it. Jake, please don't say anything we'll both regret.''

Jake raised her fingers to his lips and kissed them. He said ruefully, ''Why is it that all the qualities in you I so admire are also obstacles to getting close to you?''

She sighed deeply. ''We don't have the right, Jake, and probably never will. Shall we unload the Jeep?''

Reluctantly he released her hand. He had to put his shoulder to the cabin door to get it open, then he led the way inside and opened the shutters. The window glass had long ago disappeared.

Meg brushed aside dangling cobwebs and looked around. A Franklin stove stood in one corner. There were two chairs, and a table with three legs. The fourth leg lay on the floor. A sink stood alone, bereft of drain board. A second, smaller room, visible through a missing interior door, appeared to contain bunk beds. Meg could see another door that probably led to a bathroom, the condition of which she didn't dare imagine.

Jake said, ''Not exactly the Hotel Rhea on St. Maarten,

but last time I checked, the plumbing was working. I'll get a fire going after I've unloaded the Jeep. It gets cold up here at night this time of year.''

He went back outside. Meg found a broom propped in one corner and routed the cobwebs, then began to sweep the floor. Jake returned with two cardboard boxes, Huxley at his heels. In short order he unloaded a pair of sleeping bags, a box of cleaning materials and cooking utensils, and a small ice chest. Then he brought in a toolbox and proceeded to reattach the table leg.

Meg observed this activity with some astonishment, but then he surprised her still further by producing an axe and going outside to chop firewood.

Meg filled a bowl with water for Huxley. The sink was by the window, and she saw Jake strip off his shirt before placing a log on the stump of a tree. She watched, transfixed, as he swung the axe over his head, the muscles of his deeply tanned back rippling. The blade flashed through the air and cleanly split the log.

As he worked, his skin began to glisten with sweat. Meg had seen Jake's powerful shoulders and well-developed biceps on the beach in St. Maarten, but she had not felt then as she did now. Perhaps she had been too nervous about her deception to be fully aware of his masculine appeal, which now hit her like a thunderbolt. Realizing she was breathing unevenly, she forced herself to move away from the window.

When Jake returned, his arms loaded with firewood, Meg was glad to see his shirt was back on. Her cheeks still flamed at the unbridled lust she had felt. She had attempted to counteract the wild direction her thoughts had taken her by furiously scrubbing the sink and tabletop. When Jake reappeared, she was unpacking trail mixes, jerky, dehydrated meals in packets, coffee, cereal, some canned goods, bread, apples. Opening the ice chest she found steaks, juice, a carton of stay-fresh milk.

Jake said, "I picked that stuff up on the way back from taking Jess to the airport. It's been a while since I did any camping, so I hope I haven't forgotten anything. The water comes from a deep well and is safe to use."

He raked ancient ashes from the stove, cut up one of the cardboard boxes for kindling, and placed the smallest logs on top. The fire flared to life.

Meg said, "I'm impressed. I wouldn't have thought you'd ever been camping in your life."

He smiled. "You'd be surprised." Straightening up, he said, "I'll bring in the dog food."

Huxley wagged his tail and licked his lips in anticipation.

WHEN THE CABIN was habitable they made sandwiches for lunch, and after Meg reassured Jake that she could handle walking in the less than ideal shoes, they went for a short hike.

When he took her hand to help her negotiate stepping-stones across a narrow stream, she managed to hide the way his touch resonated throughout her entire body, but when they had to clamber over an outcropping of rock and Jake seized her around the waist to lower her to the ground, Meg was sure her composure would desert her. She dared not let herself look into his eyes.

How could she possibly spend the night alone with this man, here in this wildly beautiful and isolated place, and keep from succumbing to a yearning that wiped out all rational thought? She pulled away from him, and stumbled down the trail after Huxley.

That evening Jake lit a fire in the barbecue ring outside the cabin and expertly broiled the steaks, while Meg opened a can of beans and reconstituted a package of pasta with sauce. They took the chairs outside and dined by the fire as stars began to pierce the night sky.

Meg felt a pleasant languor. The afternoon of exercise and fresh air had at least temporarily relieved her tension. Up here, on top of the world, it seemed nothing could touch them. For a little while she could pretend they were two ordinary people escaping workaday routines and enjoying each other's company.

The moon rose and the pines became silhouettes moving restlessly, like dark dancers. Nocturnal animals began to stir.

They ate in companionable silence, then gave the steak bones to Huxley, who buried one and then settled down to gnaw the other.

A wisp of a cloud drifted like gray chiffon across the moon, and in the diminished light Jake stirred the remnants of the campfire so that it flickered to life again.

He asked, "When we resolve this mess we've drawn you into, will you consider a position in my organization?"

"Food-related? Similar to what you suggested in St. Maarten?"

"Yes, but perhaps on a wider scale. I thought then I was asking Rhea to take time away from her more hedonistic pursuits."

"Jake, please don't feel you owe me—"

"I've built my entire organization on the premise that the only surefire way to success is to hire the best people for the job. I don't make this offer based on anything other than your qualifications."

Meg silently wondered how she would handle dealing with Jake as an employer. As much as she needed and wanted the job, she knew she cared too much for this man to be near him and still contain her emotions.

She said, "Let's deal with the present before we talk about the future, shall we?"

"If that position doesn't interest you," Jake said with elaborate nonchalance, "perhaps we could discuss another, more personal one?"

There was no mistaking the meaning of his words. His tone, the way he was looking at her—both spelled danger.

Needing to steer him out of those perilous waters, Meg spoke quickly, "You know that's out of the question."

She heard him sigh. The fire crackled, and a coyote howled somewhere in the night.

At length Jake said, "I feel I've been searching for you all my life."

Meg did not dare turn to look at him. She stared at the blazing logs and changed the subject. "My father—the man who adopted me—was a lawyer. He was in his fifties and didn't really relate to me the way other fathers did to their children. Oh, it wasn't a bad thing—he just treated me as if I were a not-too-bright miniature adult. His idea of a bedtime story was to tell me about obscure points of law or precedent-setting cases. He was particularly interested in the origins of our laws, in what we retained and what we ignored of English common law."

"He hoped you'd follow in his footsteps?"

"I think he knew that wasn't going to happen the first time my mother showed me how to make a soufflé," Meg answered. "But to get back to English common law, did you know that it prohibited a man from marrying his divorced wife's sister?"

"Interesting," Jake commented. "And designed no doubt to encourage a man who fell in love with his sister-in-law to kill his wife instead?"

"I hadn't thought of that. I suppose I'm remembering

this now to remind myself that you are married to my sister and therefore any relationship between us is forbidden.''

''Unless I kill her?'' Jake suggested lightly.

''Please don't joke about that. Perhaps I got it mixed up—and he isn't supposed to marry his deceased wife's sister. But in either case, the law recognized both the temptation and the consequences.''

''Well, I don't believe English common law applies in our divorce courts, so the subject of the impropriety of any relationship between you and me doesn't arise.''

''Doesn't it?'' Meg murmured.

''My marriage to your twin is over, Meg. It was over before you came into my life. This latest horror she's perpetrating merely tells me I waited too long to deal with the biggest mistake of my life.''

''Jake, please don't condemn Rhea before you know she's guilty of anything more than allowing herself to be manipulated by Sloan.''

''Don't *you* be blinded by some misplaced sense of family loyalty. Sloan may be directing Rhea's actions, but she *is* making choices. She knows she could have come to me for protection from him. When he was paroled, I begged her to cut all ties to him. She's with him now because that's where she wants to be.''

Meg didn't answer. Her lighthearted mood vanished and it seemed the surrounding forest sighed warnings of forbidden passion and lost love.

Rising to her feet, Meg said, ''All at once I'm very tired.''

''You can take the bedroom, such as it is. I'll put my sleeping bag on the floor in front of the stove.''

They stood for an awkward moment, acutely aware of the whispering pines and the vastness of the sky, and, above all, of one another and the yearning they dare not express.

Jake suddenly slipped his arm around her waist and pulled her to him—and kissed her with a hunger that took her breath away.

She felt her knees buckle, and when he released her a moment later she was too stunned to speak, even if she had not been breathless and unsteady on her feet.

Jake shrugged. "Sometimes it's hell trying to be a gentleman."

Wordlessly, Meg walked into the cabin.

Chapter Eighteen

Guadalupe had reported that Chastain and his "wife" had gone away for a couple of days, but no one knew where. The maid was worried Jake planned to harm "Rhea," which meant she'd bought the "concerned brother" story.

Okay, so they had a couple of days to come up with a final, foolproof plan. While they were away, Rhea could resume being Mrs. Chastain and set it up.

JAKE HAD NOT followed Meg into the cabin.

She lay awake in the cocoon of her sleeping bag, listening to the murmur of a night breeze in the pines, thinking about the way he had kissed her. Unable to think of anything else.

Her mind's eye saw again his sweat-glistened torso, muscles rippling, as he effortlessly swung the axe to split the logs, and in her imagination she was nestled close to those firm pectorals, his arms around her, and he was kissing her again, hungrily, endlessly. She sighed. If only...*if only he were not married to my twin.*

Eventually, she drifted off to sleep.

In her dreams she floated languorously through a montage of sparkling waterfalls, verdant meadows and rustling forests. For a little while she felt utter serenity. Then all at once she saw the dark horizon looming ahead and she struggled to turn back. But it was too late, she was hurtling toward the darkness.

Opening her eyes, Meg brought the spartan room slowly into focus. The dream faded as the wonderful aroma of coffee and frying bacon drifted into the cabin. She wriggled out of her sleeping bag and opened the window shutters. Fingers of sunshine were probing the trees, and nearby a bird sweetly sang his morning song.

Meg was pulling a sweater over her head when she heard Jake answer a call on his cell phone.

"Yes? What? Okay, send a man up there."

There was a pause. "No. Have Taylor handle all the other calls. I'm taking a day off."

Shivering in the morning chill, Meg went outside and inhaled the brisk mountain air. Huxley, looking unkempt, puppyish and slightly giddy, bounded over to greet her. She patted his head and tickled his ears.

Jake looked up from his position at the frying pan and said, "Morning, Meg. How do you like your eggs? I know you're a nutritionist, but I don't want to hear about cholesterol today."

Meg smiled, any residual tension from last night's kiss and the disturbing ending to her dream forgotten. "Over easy. What can I do?"

"Coffee's ready. You can cut some bread. You want it fried?"

"Why not? Let's go for broke on the cholesterol."

"A woman after my own heart."

Meg washed her hands; the water was ice-cold. Then she poured coffee into two substantial-looking mugs and handed one to Jake.

He said, "Just had a call from one of my security people. They haven't located Sloan or Rhea, but our friend Rick was spotted back in their old haunts in San Francisco, so he's flying up there. How did you sleep?''

"Like a baby. How about you?"

"Not bad…once I managed to fall asleep. I spent a long time last night thinking about my options.''

Meg took a sip of her coffee before asking, "Did you reach any conclusions?''

"Mainly, I reinforced a decision I made some time ago. I'm going to divorce Rhea. My attorneys drew up a prenuptial agreement, but I'll give her anything she wants. She can have it all, if that's what she's after. I started from scratch before and I can do it again. Now, let's eat before the food gets cold.''

JAKE WATCHED MEG as she and Huxley slid delightedly down a grassy bank toward a mountain stream. How she reveled in simple pleasures, how graceful she was even in rough-and-tumble play. And oh, God, how he wanted her! He had lain awake most of the night, acutely aware of her presence in the cabin, of their isolation, of his longing for her. But most of all, of an urgent need to protect her.

Why had a perverse fate brought Rhea into his life first? In his mind the solution was simple: a quick, clean divorce giving Rhea whatever she wanted. But Meg had made it clear that she was bound by a code of honor she would never break, no matter how she felt about him, and whether or not he and Rhea ended their loveless marriage.

Jake, who had always believed there was a solution to every problem, could not see any way he would ever be able to overcome Meg's misguided sense of loyalty to her psychologically damaged sister. And unless he could do that, he knew he would never be able to persuade her that they were meant to be together.

All he could do was cherish these fleeting moments

they would be together, and make damn sure no harm ever came to her.

How had the hours slipped away so quickly? Meg wondered as the sun disappeared behind the mountain, and Jake set about building another campfire.

What a perfect day it had been. Even better than the time they had spent together on St. Maarten, because now they could be honest with each other. No more pretending to be something she was not. Some of the guilt she felt about deceiving him dissipated—until she remembered poor Mike.

Jake had tried to allay that guilt. "We still don't know that Aragon's death was in any way connected to you and Rhea. He was a licensed investigator and knew the risks his profession posed. He might have stumbled into something other than Rhea's machinations."

"But after the fire, he knew we were involved in something more deadly than a harmless masquerade. He wanted to take me to the police then, but I persuaded him to wait until I told you what was going on."

"You didn't put a gun to his head and stop him. He could have gone to the police himself. Stop blaming yourself, Meg."

Meg couldn't think of a reasonable argument and so let the subject drop.

They acted like two people in the early stages of an important love affair, eager to know everything about each other, amazed that out of all the millions of people on earth they had managed to come together. He told Meg of his early struggles, his failures and successes; she told him of hers.

But in speaking of the past they avoided speculating about the future, and Meg knew in her heart there could never be a mutual one for them. If she had been a stranger, instead of his wife's sister...if she had not come into his life under a cloud of deceit... These were powerful obstacles she could see no way of overcoming. Still, for a few hours, it was nice to pretend.

They explored their surroundings, found a stream and skimmed pebbles, waded in the chilly water, threw sticks for Huxley, laughed at the Doberman's sheer delight in running free.

When the campfire flared to life Meg surveyed the dehydrated dinners and asked, "What would you like, beef Stroganoff or—"

The cell phone intruded. Jake muttered an epithet. He flipped on the phone, listened, and then drew in his breath sharply. "Damn. Yes, stay with her. I'll be there in about two hours."

He looked at Meg. "We'll have to hit the road." He began to douse the fire.

"Have they found Rhea?" Meg asked.

"No. But Jess decided she was bored on the island and missed Huxley too much. She's on her way back home."

JAKE DROVE BACK to the coast in tight-lipped silence, and Meg knew he was worried about his mother.

"Is Jessica en route, or has she already arrived?" Meg asked.

"They're probably arriving back at her house just about now. Dan O'Rourke, my local security chief, is with her, and so is Carmelita. Jess is probably safe there, but I wish she'd stayed on the island."

"We'll soon have Huxley back with her, too. I'm sure he's a good watchdog."

Jake looked dubious. Huxley laid his head on Meg's

shoulder and sighed, perhaps sensing the implied lack of confidence.

"By the way," Jake said, "Dan O'Rourke doesn't know my wife is missing. I brought in a couple of people from my San Francisco operation to search for her. I figured the fewer people who know the whole story, the better, since we don't know the identity of Rhea's spy. Besides, I didn't want Dan to slip up and let Jess know what's going on."

It was dark when they reached Laguna Beach. They drove up the serpentine road to the top of the hill. The summit offered a view of twinkling lights strung around the bay like a necklace of precious gems. The Doberman sat up and barked excitedly as he recognized his surroundings.

As they parked the Jeep, a shadow detached itself from the wooden deck. Jake called, "Hi, Dan! Everything okay?"

"Yes, sir. I was just admiring the view."

Jake chuckled. "And no doubt escaping the women."

"Well…"

Dan O'Rourke was tall, lean, and looked as though he were fashioned from coiled sinew. He opened Meg's door. "'Evening, Mrs. Chastain."

She was momentarily startled by the greeting, but managed to murmur, "'Evening, Dan."

"How's my mother?" Jake asked as they climbed the wooden steps to the deck.

"Getting a little annoyed about that cast on her arm because she can't paint. And she's not a good candidate for living on a small island. But otherwise, fine."

"Sounds about right. Look, Dan, I think you'd better stay here for a couple of days."

"Sure, no problem. There's a maid's room over the garage. I can see all approaches to the house from there, including the canyon to the rear."

Jake rang the doorbell, but Huxley's shrill bark was louder.

Carmelita opened the door. ''...so we hope you won't be mad at us, Mr. Jake, but the señora she misses her own place and you know she never did pick up any Spanish even though she had me there to do her talking, but you know how she is...''

Meg followed Jake and Huxley into a large room that seemed to extend, by means of a wall of windows, to the deck beyond, giving an indoor/outdoor effect that was enhanced by wicker and bentwood furniture with bright chintz pillows, and a profusion of plants.

The walls of the high-ceilinged room were covered with paintings: oils, watercolors—everything from pensive portraits and single sprays of delicate flowers to entire gardens rendered in exquisite color. Unframed canvasses were propped against the walls. An easel holding a half-finished seascape stood near the window, next to a paint-spattered table laden with artists' paraphernalia. From the size and location of the room, Meg guessed Jessica had converted the living room into a studio.

The artist herself reclined on a chaise longue, a book propped against her cast. Huxley skittered across the parquet floor and laid his head on her lap.

Jessica's nostrils clenched. ''Good grief! What have you done to my dog? He smells like a raccoon, or some other feral beast.''

Jake bent to kiss his mother. ''He's been in the woods and relished every minute of a short break from his usual routine. Now explain to me why you couldn't do the same thing?''

Ignoring the comment, Jessica looked at Meg. ''Your wife is limping again. You surely didn't drag her to the woods, too, did you?''

Wondering if she should also kiss Jessica's cheek, or if the gesture would be completely out of character for Rhea, Meg decided to keep her distance and trust the fussing Doberman to cover any lapse. She said, "We really did have a wonderful time. I'm sorry Huxley is a little ripe. I'd be happy to bathe him for you."

Meg realized her mistake when Jess and Carmelita stared at her in openmouthed astonishment.

Jake chuckled. "Let's not get carried away here, Rhea. Old Hux will be fine until he can go to the groomer tomorrow."

Jessica continued to stare at Meg for what seemed an interminable amount of time. At length she turned to Jake. "You are going to take your human watchdog home with you, aren't you? I really don't like him lurking. You can take your maid, too—she's up in her room. Carmelita and I will be fine on our own."

"No, I think Dan and the maid will remain, Jess. We still haven't found that disgruntled employee I told you about."

"That girl up there is useless," Carmelita complained. "She just gets in my way."

Meg asked, "How is your sister, Carmelita?"

"Hmph...that one! She just wanted me down there in Guadalajara to wait on her hand and foot. She weren't that sick. Jessica needs me more, with her busted arm."

"Do you have everything you need here?" Jake asked.

"Of course," his mother answered. "Find your deranged employee quickly, Jake, so Carmelita and Huxley and I can call our souls our own again."

Jake and Meg took their leave. When they were again in the Jeep driving down the hill, Meg said, "I think your mother knows I'm not Rhea."

"She may suspect, but she can't possibly know. Although, when you offered to bathe the Doberman, I thought she was going to ask you to rip off your face mask.''

"I'm going to hate having to tell her I deceived her."

Jake sighed. "Me too."

They left the Coast Highway and drove through San Juan Capistrano, then turned off on the private road that led to the enclave of multimillion-dollar estates.

The ornamental wrought-iron gates at Jake's house were operated by a remote control, but although he pushed the button several times, nothing happened. He shrugged. "Battery in the remote must be dead." He got out of the Jeep to open the gates.

The long driveway curved twice and then formed a circle in front of the house. As the house came into view he braked sharply.

"Something's wrong."

Meg looked at the house. There was no glimmer of light anywhere. All of the windows were dark. The terrace lights were out; there was no light over the front doors; and the concealed lighting that usually illuminated the grounds and driveway was missing.

"No wonder the gates wouldn't open. The fuses must have blown," Jake said. "Can't be a power outage, because the lights on the road were on. But why hasn't Mason or somebody taken care of this?"

He drove past the house to the detached eight-car garage, got out of the Jeep and raised one of the doors by hand, then returned to the car and drove inside.

"After I've taken care of the fuse switches, we can enter the house from here. Will you turn off the headlights after I find the fuse box?"

Meg remained in the Jeep as he went to the nearest wall and raised a metal lid, then began to flip up a row of switches. An overhead garage light came on. She turned off the Jeep's headlights and got out.

"I can't imagine what Mason and the staff are doing in there in the dark, or why the security system going out didn't alert the police," Jake said as he led the way to an interior door.

Meg clutched his arm. "Jake, you don't think…could this be an ambush?"

He hesitated, one hand on the door handle. "Why don't you wait here while I check it out?"

Meg shivered. "I'd rather stay with you, if you don't mind. I don't suppose you have a weapon of any kind, do you?"

"Not on me," Jake muttered.

Opening the door, he stepped inside, and Meg followed. They were in a long corridor. Jake led the way to a door at the far end of the corridor, pulled it ajar and listened.

Silence.

He pushed the door wide-open, and Meg saw that they were in the kitchen. Lights had come on, but there was no sign of activity, no sound. Not only that, but Meg noticed at once that all of the surfaces—counters, tables, chopping blocks—had been cleared. There was no sign of any food, and even spice racks and canisters had been removed. The total effect suggested a vacant house.

Meg whispered, "Could they all have gone to bed?"

Jake glanced at a clock on the wall. "At ten past ten? Hardly."

"I don't suppose anyone left a note attached to the refrigerator with a magnet?" Meg suggested in an attempt at levity.

Jake walked over to an intercom panel on one of the walls, pushed a button and said, "Mason? Are you there?"

After a few seconds he tried several of the other buttons. There was no response.

He looked at Meg. "Did you ever read the story of a ship found drifting at sea where the whole crew had vanished without a trace?"

"Yes, it was the *Marie Celeste,* I believe," Meg said.

"I have a feeling we're going to find the same situation here, except I don't see any half-finished meals. I'll check the rest of the house."

"I'll go with you."

Jake flooded the house with light as they walked from room to room. Silence, complete and eerie, accompanied them.

It seemed obvious that the entire house was deserted, from the servants' wing to the family quarters. After they finished checking the bedrooms they walked back down the stairs.

"There's just the main dining room left—might as well look there, too, I guess," Jake said. "Maybe Mason and the others will all pop out and yell, 'Surprise!'"

He opened double doors, and Meg gasped at the size of the room, which she hadn't seen before. Beneath glittering crystal chandeliers, a long table was flanked by beautifully carved antique chairs. Massive sideboards stood laden with gleaming silver and gold dishes, a gigantic Renaissance tapestry adorned one wall, and on another she saw a Renoir and a Cézanne. There were two enormous fireplaces, side tables holding priceless-looking vases and statuettes, even sanctuary benches and monks' leaning chairs that surely had once graced ancient cathedrals.

But the vast room—almost the size of an auditorium—was deserted.

Seeing Meg's reaction, Jake said drily, "Rhea wanted to turn this place into another Hearst castle—she admired how he looted most of the cities of Europe for the treasures he used to furnish that monstrosity up the coast. I gave her free rein, and in retrospect, realized I hadn't paid enough attention to her grandiose decorating ideas.''

''It's…awesome,'' Meg managed to say.

''Personally, I don't care for antiques, but Rhea seemed to get such pleasure from acquiring all this stuff…'' His voice trailed away as he stood for a moment, contemplating the furnishings that Meg estimated had to be worth a king's ransom.

She cleared her throat awkwardly. ''She has very good taste.''

Jake smiled. ''Do you always find something positive to say?''

''Not always,'' Meg said. ''Where do you suppose Mason and all the others have gone?''

''More to the point, *why* have they gone?'' Jake mused. ''Come on, let's go back to Mason's study. He'll have home phone numbers for the staff.''

Back in the servants' wing they entered a paneled room filled with modern office furniture, including a computer and fax machine. Jake went to the desk and reached for a card index, then picked up the phone.

There was evidently no answer at the first couple of numbers he called, then on the third, he said, ''*¿Eduardo? ¿Hola, como está?*'' Reverting to English, he continued, ''This is Jake Chastain. I'm at the house. Where is everybody?''

After a pause Jake said, ''I see. Yes, all right. Tell me, do you know how to get hold of Mason? No, don't bother, call him in the morning. Tell him to round up the rest of the staff and come back tomorrow. It's all a misunderstanding.''

Replacing the receiver, Jake looked at Meg and said

grimly, "It seems Rhea arrived early this afternoon and told everybody she had found an infestation of insects and was going to have the house fumigated. She ordered them all to leave, and to stay away until she sent for them. She also called the security company and told them to deactivate the system because fogging the house with pesticide would set it off."

Meg swallowed. "Jake...I think we ought to get out of here."

Chapter Nineteen

"Damn it, I'm not going to be run out of my own house," Jake said. "But I am going to call Dan and have him get somebody over here to drive you to a hotel for the night."

"No," Meg said quickly. "I'd rather stay here with you. I couldn't stand not knowing what's going on. Do you mind?"

"I'd be glad of the company, if you're sure you want to stay. I don't know what Rhea's up to, but the first thing I'm going to do is call the security company and reactivate the system. Then I'll check all the doors and windows. Believe me, nobody is going to get in here unannounced."

"How about I go to the kitchen and make dinner?" Meg said. "We never did get any."

Jake smiled. "The way to a man's heart..."

"Don't go there," Meg cautioned. "My only motive is my own hunger."

Meg again felt like the proverbial kid in the candy store, having the well-equipped kitchen and super-stocked pantry to herself. Before leaving, the staff had put away all exposed food items, in anticipation of fumigation, and had tightly sealed the cabinets in the pantry. Rhea must have been very convincing. It was difficult to imagine what her motivation for such action could have been.

Meg prepared an appetizer of prawns with white-bean-and-pimiento salad, and because of the lateness of the hour decided to forgo any nightmare-inducing serious protein in favor of a main course of penne with wild mushrooms and a sauce of her own invention.

By the time Jake came to see how she was progressing, she was putting little chocolate pecan tarts in the oven. The fudgy tartlets had been quick and easy to make in a food processor and would bake in fifteen minutes.

"Could we eat in here?" Meg asked, indicating a large scrubbed wood table where the kitchen staff probably had their meals. "I need to keep an eye on the oven."

"Sure. I'll set the table."

Meg didn't let on that she was surprised he knew exactly where to find cutlery and dishes. She just checked to see if the penne was done.

When she took the appetizers to the table she found Jake had set out a bottle of champagne. She turned the bottle and whistled softly under her breath. "This is serious bubbly, Jake…a 1990 vintage Moët et Chandon's flagship Cuvée Dom Pérignon. I'm impressed, but I don't think you should open it. We need to keep our wits about us."

"I've double-checked every possible means of entering the house, Meg, and the security system is activated. The smoke alarms and sprinkler systems are all in order. Short of installing a moat and drawbridge, there's not much else I can do to keep out intruders."

"I wasn't referring to the danger from intruders," Meg murmured pointedly.

His dark eyes gleamed. "Ah, I see. How about just one glass?" He produced two flutes.

"Not for me," Meg said firmly, hoping he couldn't read her mind. *I don't trust myself with you, and how can you be so oblivious to how attractive you are? I want to un-button your shirt and run my hands all over your chest.*

She turned away quickly as her thoughts brought hot color to her face.

Jake sighed and removed the bottle and glasses. "What will you have to drink? Cider, milk, juice, tea?"

"I've a pitcher of ice water ready. I thought I'd make hot chocolate with dessert, in view of how late it is."

They sat down to eat beneath the glaring kitchen lights in the eerie silence of the deserted house. Jake watched her intently. "This feels right, Meg. You and me, together." His hand slid across the table and covered hers. The gesture was so tender that she wanted to weep.

He said, "Someday I'd like to bring the champagne and candlelight and dine on food you've prepared."

"Jake," Meg said, steeling herself to withstand the warmth of his touch, "when this little drama is concluded, we have to go our separate ways. In fact, I think if your people haven't found Rhea and Sloan by tomorrow, I should go home then."

"Despite the fact that if we separate and I get hit, you may be framed?"

"We don't know for sure that's what they're planning. But even if it is, they'd have to be certain I didn't have an iron-clad alibi for the time of the hit. Since I work long hours, with lots of other people, that would be tricky."

"And do you sleep with lots of other people, or would you be alone at night?"

"Well…"

"I can't keep you with me against your will, Meg, but if you must go back to your own life, at least let me send a man I can trust with you, and put you up in a hotel."

Meg blinked away a vision of herself showing up to cater

a wedding or bar mitzvah with a bodyguard in tow. "No, that's out of the question."

She rose to take the tartlets out of the oven, and Jake sniffed the aroma appreciatively.

When she sat down again, he said, "The condemned man ate a hearty meal."

"Please don't joke about it."

"Sorry. The food is terrific, by the way. Thank you."

Meg had lost her appetite. He was right, there was an aching sense of finality about the meal.

"I thought rich people had bodyguards," she said after a while.

"I've never felt the need for one."

"Before now, you mean. Jake, will you please hire one? If anything happens to you, I won't be able to live with myself."

He leaned forward. "Would it matter to you that much?"

"Yes, it would."

"How much, Meg? Tell me."

"No, we can't talk about this. Not now. Not ever. Just—please hire someone to watch your back."

It was a little after eleven when they stacked the dishes in the sink. Jake asked, "Are you tired? Do you want to turn in, or could we spend another hour together?"

"I think I'm too wound up to sleep yet," Meg answered.

"Then I have the ideal solution. Come with me."

He took her to the room she had dubbed the "music room," and proceeded to roll up a beautiful Persian rug, revealing a hardwood floor. At the touch of his finger, the room was filled with the slow and sensual music of the tango. Turning, he extended his hand to her.

"Jake, you know I can't—"

"Yes, you can. I'm going to teach you."

She hesitated, and he said, "If you think I'm suggesting

we dance just so I'll have an excuse to hold you in my arms..."

Meg walked toward him; he took her right hand in his and slipped his arm around her waist. When they were in position he grinned and finished the thought. "...you're probably right."

Before she could respond, he went on, "I'm going to lead by guiding you with this hand, and by subtle pressure on your back with my other hand. You're going to start with your right foot—two long, slow steps backward, then two short quick steps to the side. Listen to the music, pause when the music pauses. Above all, *relax*. Now listen...two, three, four..."

"I don't think I can—"

To Meg's surprise, she found that she could.

Jake held her close, his lead firm and sure, and the music seemed to speak to her. She forgot about her feet and gave herself up to the magic of being held in Jake's arms, moving with him in strange and exotic ways to the hypnotic beat of the tango.

When the music ended Meg found herself bent backward over Jake's arm, his face close to hers, his mouth a breath away. The question in his dark eyes was unmistakable, and the pressure of his hands sent a warm tingling radiating throughout her body.

Every instinct she possessed fought to override rational thought. Oh, how she wanted to be swept away by passion, to put aside every constraint, every qualm. But she had never been one to break the rules, and she knew that if she made love to Jake, she would never be able to forgive herself. Or him.

His lips brushed hers lightly.

"No..." Meg whispered, "Don't..."

"I'm falling in love with you, Meg. With *you*, not simply

with your beauty, but with your essence, your decency and honesty.''

She managed to pull away. ''I haven't been honest with you, Jake. I deceived you. I pretended to be your wife.''

''You thought you'd agreed to a harmless weekend masquerade and that you and I would never meet. Instead you were caught in the jaws of a trap that kept clicking tighter around you. Meg, tell me you feel some attraction toward me. Tell me I'm not imagining this electricity we're generating.''

''I can't tell you that. I don't have the right.'' *You're my sister's husband.*

She turned and ran from the room, stumbling in her haste to get up the stairs to the bedroom so she could be alone and away from the greatest temptation she had ever faced.

The music followed her and she realized the entire house was wired for sound. She covered her ears to shut out the insistent siren call of the tango, and wished she could close her mind to the memory of being in Jake's arms.

She didn't lock the bedroom door. She knew there was no need.

Above the fireplace, regarding her mockingly, was Rhea's portrait.

WHEN MEG WENT downstairs the following morning she heard Jake's forceful voice addressing someone outside.

''No, you are not going to tent the house. I'm the owner and I'm telling you that I have not authorized fumigation. Now take your men and your equipment, and leave. Send me a bill for your time and trouble.''

Meg went into the kitchen and was about to reach for the coffeemaker when the phone rang. Since she was alone in the house, she picked it up and said, ''Hello?''

A strange male voice, speaking barely above a whisper, said, "Meg Lindley?"

The phone almost slipped from her hand. "Who is this?"

"Aragon."

Meg felt a chill ripple down her spine. "Mike?"

"His brother. Listen carefully. I've just checked Mike's stuff and found something you'd better see. Don't tell anybody I called—especially not Chastain. If you do, you could be in big trouble. Can you meet me this evening? Eight sharp. Alone. Just you. I see anybody else, I'm gone."

"I'm leaving here today. Besides, you're just a voice on the phone," Meg said. "Why should I believe—"

"Meet me at the same coffee shop where you met my brother when he first approached you about the gig in St. Maarten. The fact that I know where that is proves I'm not lying. Remember, *come alone and don't tell Chastain.* Your life depends on it."

There was a click and the line went dead.

Meg was still holding the phone when Jake came into the house. For a moment his eyes locked with hers, searching for something he evidently didn't find.

"Hope that commotion outside didn't wake you," he said. "My dear wife evidently thought it would be amusing to send in a whole crew of exterminators. Was that Mason on the phone?"

Making a split-second decision, Meg decided to keep quiet about the identity of the caller. She had all day to think about whether or not to meet him in Los Angeles. The big question was, what had Mike's brother found? He knew her name, knew where she and Mike had gone to talk that night. Mike had been murdered. His effects would probably be given to his next of kin. Could he have left something incriminating? Against her? *Against Jake?*

"Did you just go somewhere?" Jake asked.

She said, "No, it wasn't Mason on the phone. It was a wrong number. Have you had breakfast?"

He hesitated for a moment before answering, and she wondered if her lie had been obvious. Then he said, "You do realize how much I'm going to miss you if you decide to leave?"

"Speaking of which," Meg said carefully, "I really do need to check on my house and my job with the caterer. I'll rent a car and drive up to L.A."

"I'll take you."

"No—thanks. I'd rather go on my own."

"Please reconsider having one of my security people go with you then."

"I have to go alone. My neighbors and my boss would wonder why I need a bodyguard. I have to resume my former life, Jake. I have to get back to normal."

Jake's brow puckered into a worried frown. "I can't order you, of course, but—"

"It's settled then," Meg said quickly.

He sighed deeply. "If you say so. I'll probably spend the day at my office. I'll give you the number of my direct private line."

"I'm not going to promise to call you, Jake. But I hope you'll call me when you find Rhea. I so want to talk to her."

HOW SHABBY THE OLD neighborhood looked. The barred windows and unkempt lawns seemed even more grim after the lush grounds of the Chastain estate. To add to the gloom, the first rainstorm of the season was brewing, bringing dark clouds creeping over the rooftops.

Meg parked the rented car on the crumbling blacktop driveway and unlocked the front door of her house, which seemed to have shrunk considerably during the last few days. It seemed incredible that only a week ago she had never heard of the Chastains.

A small heap of letters lay inside the door, delivered through the mail slot. She scooped them up without examining them—knowing they'd consist of bills and junk mail—then went straight to the phone and flipped the message-retrieval button.

There were two frantic pleas from Carrie Hooper, the caterer for whom Meg worked: *"Puh-leeze, Meg, call me! I've got back-to-back parties next weekend. Help! I need you."* Then, *"Meg, where are you? You said you'd be back by now. Call me!"*

There was also a call from the theater manager, sheepishly asking her to call him: her replacement hadn't worked out.

Dropping the bundle of mail on the telephone stand, Meg called Carrie, who was a friend as well as an employer, fielded her questions about her mysterious trip and promised to be available for the catering jobs the following weekend.

She decided to ignore the call from the theater for a couple of days. Walking home alone late at night was not an option until Rhea and Sloan were found. She still had virtually all of the advance Mike had given her, but she couldn't afford to keep the rental car so she'd be doing a lot of walking.

Catching a glimpse of herself in the mottled mirror on the wall above the phone stand, Meg decided the first order of business was obvious—change out of Rhea's clothes. Then she could tackle the layer of dust that had settled everywhere during her absence.

She tried to avoid thinking about Jake, but it was impossible. She wasn't prepared for the pain brought by contemplating never seeing him again.

Somehow she got through the afternoon. She cleaned the house, drove to the supermarket and bought some groceries. The sky had turned leaden and a light rain had started to fall. She decided to keep the car until the following day, in order to be able to drive to her rendezvous with Mike Aragon's brother that evening.

The nagging worry about what he'd found in Mike's effects remained with her. The gasoline cans? But how would he have connected them to her? No, it had to be something else. A file on her, probably. Meg hoped she wouldn't be dealing with a blackmailer.

At seven-thirty she regretfully took off her well-worn and comfortable tennis shoes. She had missed her own shoes more than anything else during the last few days, and her Achilles tendon was reminding her of that fact. As she slipped on a pair of boots in deference to the rain, she remembered, with a sudden pang, dancing the tango with Jake. How unbearably sweet those moments had been.

The rain was heavier now, beating a tattoo against the windows, and the wind was rising. She pulled on a hooded jacket before going out to the car.

By the time she pulled into the parking lot in front of the coffee shop, sheets of rain were blowing almost horizontally on a cold wind. There were only a couple of parked cars, and the sidewalk was devoid of pedestrians.

Pulling up the hood of her jacket, she raced into the coffee shop. She didn't notice the black sedan, its headlights dimmed, that pulled in behind her. The driver didn't get out of the car.

A quick check of the nearly empty coffee shop revealed no one who could possibly be Mike Aragon's brother. The only patrons braving the storm were an elderly couple, a single woman, and a pair of teenagers engrossed in each other—none of whom did more than glance in her direction.

Seated beside the window, Meg sipped tea and peered into the rainswept darkness, but could see nothing beyond the blurred amber glow of the streetlights.

She waited for over an hour before deciding Aragon, or whoever he was, wasn't coming. She paid for her coffee and left.

A blast of cold wet air took her breath away and she bent her head into the wind as she ran for the car.

She had the keys in her hand, but another car had parked close on the driver's side and she had to squeeze between the two cars.

One minute she was fumbling with the car keys, and the next second something rough and smothering went over her head and she was being dragged across the wet pavement.

She tried to scream as she was lifted off her feet, but the rough material pressing against her mouth made an effective gag.

Wincing as her ankle struck sharp metal, she struggled and tried to kick her assailant, but he was too strong. She was pushed down into a cramped space that smelled of rancid oil and gasoline fumes. Some unseen cover slammed shut with a vibrating metallic thud.

Shocked by the suddenness of the abduction, it took a minute for her to realize that she was in the trunk of a car—a car that was screeching off into the night.

Chapter Twenty

Meg gingerly felt around her in the darkness, seeking something to use as a weapon when the kidnapper came for her. There was nothing. No jack, no tire iron.

Too late, she realized her mistake. The caller on the phone who had set her up wasn't Mike's brother. The investigator probably didn't even have a brother. That voice on the phone who knew about her first meeting with him, and the masquerade in St. Maarten, had undoubtedly been Sloan or one of his thugs.

Remembering the brawny arms that had forced her into the trunk, Meg was sure that it was Sloan who was now driving the car, and with whom she'd have to deal when they reached their destination.

Frantically she pounded with her fists on the unyielding metal, but as her panic subsided, she knew no one would hear her while the car was still moving, especially during the heavy rain.

Where was he taking her?

She had always been a little claustrophobic, and being confined in the cramped space was sheer torture. She drew several deep breaths, trying to calm herself so that she could think clearly and reconstruct what she knew, and perhaps then anticipate what might happen.

If, as Mike had theorized, and Rhea's journal suggested, Sloan and Rhea planned to kill Jake and place the blame on Rhea's "jealous" twin, then it seemed logical to assume that they had no intention of harming her. They needed her alive to take the fall.

But if their story was going to be that Meg wanted to take her twin's place, they would have to concoct a plausible explanation as to why she had killed Jake instead of Rhea. Unless…they intended to kill both Jake and her and try to make it look like an accident? But that might pose too many logistical problems. Besides, they'd gone to a lot of trouble to register guns in her name, which surely meant they intended to shoot Jake and accuse her of the murder.

The car abruptly started up a curving incline, sending her sliding to the side of the trunk. She winced as her head slammed into cold metal.

Then they were traveling on a smooth surface at a higher rate of speed. She thought, we came up an on-ramp and now we're on a freeway—probably going south, toward Jake's estate.

Sloan had assumed, correctly, she thought, that she'd be more likely to meet a stranger in familiar surroundings, like the local coffee shop where she'd met Mike, than anywhere else. But why kidnap her? Perhaps they needed to keep her out of sight for a while as they set up their plan, but to have her available to face arrest. They also needed to keep her separate from Jake…*in order for Rhea to return to him?*

Meg felt an icy chill. What if Rhea showed up at the house, pretending to be her? Would Jake's guard be down? What if he didn't recognize Rhea? *Was that how she intended to get close enough to kill him?*

That possibility made Meg pound on the trunk again and

scream for help. It was several minutes before she forced herself to stop and try to think what their plan might be.

The fact that Rhea had managed to get all the household staff to leave indicated that the house was the chosen site.

Meg shivered, imagining herself waking up with a gun in her hand, Jake dead beside her and the police bursting in to arrest her.

Rhea and Sloan had already fabricated a formidable amount of evidence against her: the journals in which Rhea wrote that she was afraid of her and suspected she wanted to take her place; the guns purchased in Meg's name; the fact that she had fortuitously left the beach house just before it was torched; not to mention the gasoline cans they had probably retrieved from Mike's house.

In the final showdown, it would be Rhea's word against hers as to how Jake had died, and even Meg had to admit Rhea's story would sound more believable than hers. Especially with Mike dead.

How easy it would be to present her as the poor twin, struggling with mountains of debt, deserted by her own husband, working long hours merely to stay alive, then briefly tasting incredible luxury and coveting the life-style of the rich twin.

Meg pounded on the trunk again.

It was hopeless. No one would be able to hear.

Nor was there any way to get the trunk open with her bare hands.

What if she could find the wires connected to the tail-lights and yank them out? Perhaps a passing highway patrol would pull the car over. Then maybe her screams and pounding would be heard.

She scrabbled with her hands in the darkness.

Minutes later her searching fingers found several wires. She pulled and twisted, desperation giving her strength.

One of the wires came loose. Had that been enough to eliminate the taillight? She worked feverishly on the other wires, to be sure.

But the car continued on its way, its missing taillights apparently unnoticed. Perhaps the highway patrol were busy with accidents due to the rain. It was a given that Californians drove poorly in the rain, especially the first rain of the season when water settled on the film of oil coating the freeways, causing cars to hydroplane if drivers didn't slow down.

Breathing heavily, Meg relaxed for a minute, striving to think of some other way to get out of the car. When Sloan raised the cover of the trunk, there would be no escaping him. He was too strong; he would overpower her in seconds.

She had not carried a handbag to the coffee shop, and all she had in her jacket pocket were her keys and a wallet with her driver's license. The keys weren't much of a weapon, but they were all she had. Perhaps she could rake his face with them and at least distract him long enough to get away.

Attempting to ease herself into a less uncomfortable position, she moved backward and her shoulder connected with something that gave slightly. Squirming sideways, she pushed the rear of the trunk with her hands, wondering if she was touching the back seat of the car. She knew some back seats folded down in order to extend the trunk and create more cargo space.

Hope flared. There was no way to raise the lid of the trunk to get out into the open, but perhaps she could break through to the back seat and get into the car itself? She would then be faced with jumping from a moving car...but anything was better than lying there, helplessly waiting for Sloan to come and get her.

But although she shoved with all her might against the back of the trunk, the dividing panel remained stubbornly in place, keeping her trapped.

I can't give up, she thought. *If I do, they'll kill Jake.*

Chapter Twenty-One

Rhea smiled as Jake came through the bedroom door.

His face lit up with pure joy and he breathed reverently, "*Meg!* You came back. Thank God."

Rhea managed to keep her smile intact.

So, he had fallen for the little caterer, just as she suspected.

Damn him. Damn them both. Sloan was right. The two of them had been laughing at her behind her back. Well, they'd see who had the last laugh.

Rhea rose to her feet, and Jake came to her and wrapped his arms around her.

They stood in a close embrace. Rhea didn't speak, relishing the moment.

She had been looking forward to turning the tables on her twin. Meg had been living it up as Mrs. Jake Chastain, impersonating her, and now Rhea was going to be Meg Lindley for a little while and destroy whatever illusions Jake had about her.

Rhea had been infuriated when Guadalupe, whom Sloan had bribed to spy on Jake and Meg, reported how cozy the two of them were. Why, her twin had even cooked for him! Not to mention sleeping in their bed and whatever else she had done there. The *nerve* of her. And all the while playing the part of the unsophisticated innocent, whose moral code would not allow her to sleep with a married man.

Sloan had not told Guadalupe that the woman she was spying on was an imposter. He had conned the maid into believing that he was concerned that Jake might be mistreating his sister. The fewer people who knew they were dealing with twins, the better. But when Guadalupe called to report that Mr. and Mrs. Chastain were obviously very much in love, it was Rhea who had answered the phone, identifying herself as Sloan's wife. She had been enraged.

Sloan had been concerned about Rhea's state of mind as they put the final stages of their plan into action. He had warned her to be careful not to let Jake know that she was Rhea—not to get any ideas about taunting him.

"Babe, he's going to be dead tomorrow and your twin's going to be in jail. What the hell difference does it make what they've been doing these past few days? You've got to keep your cool."

"I'd like him to suffer before he dies. How dare he? He knows she's my twin, but she's still there. He's playing with us—but don't worry, I won't tip my hand." She certainly wouldn't tell Sloan that she had no intention of passing up her one chance to avenge herself.

Sloan had instructed her not to show up at the house until just before he arrived with Meg, but Rhea had ignored him. She had been waiting for Jake for over an hour, and although Sloan was due back from L.A. within the next half hour, she was counting on the heavy rain to delay his arrival.

The plan was for Sloan to leave Meg in the trunk of the car, enter the house through the garage and stay out of sight until Rhea put a bullet in Jake's chest. *Don't aim for his head—you might miss. Keep the gun out of sight until you're close enough to shoot him in the heart.*

Sloan would then bring in Meg and put the gun in her hand. He would hold Meg while Rhea called 911, hysterically telling the cops that her twin had tried to shoot her but that her gallant husband had jumped in front of her and taken the bullet himself.

Her story would be that Meg had come to the house, confronted her with the gun and told her that she was going to assume the role of Mrs. Jake Chastain permanently—no one would ever look for or find the body of her twin. With the real Mrs. Jake Chastain out of the way and Mike Aragon dead, there was no one who knew of the existence of an identical twin.

Sloan had rehearsed Rhea repeatedly. "Remember, Jake arrives home unexpectedly, Meg shoots at you but hits him. I've come to make sure you're okay, I'm worried about you, you've been acting scared lately. I'm downstairs. I come running and grab her, hold her while you call 911. It's our word against hers—her gun, her fingerprints on the gun. It's foolproof, babe, so long as you can make Jake believe you're *her* until I get there."

Rhea had argued that it would be better for Sloan to do the shooting; he was accustomed to handling weapons and would be less likely to miss.

But Sloan had overridden her objections. "We don't know what Jake might do if he sees me. But if you can make him believe you're Meg Lindley, you'll be able to get close to him and let him have it before he knows what you're going to do."

"But what if I miss?" Rhea had fretted.

"I'll be through that bedroom door the second I hear a shot. I'll have my own piece to do the job if you've missed. But you won't miss. Don't worry about it. It's a done deal. Just keep your head. Don't forget to deactivate the security system, and turn on the music."

If Rhea had had any qualms about killing her husband before, all doubts vanished the moment Jake addressed her as Meg, his eyes lighting up with love in a way they never had for Rhea.

Now, as Jake tenderly embraced her, Rhea raised her face to his and smiled seductively. "I couldn't stay away from you," she whispered. She slipped her arms around him, pressing her body close to his.

For an instant she was certain that he was going to kiss her, but he hesitated, gazing with piercing intensity into her eyes.

She lowered her gaze quickly. Surely he hadn't guessed? She had rehearsed several opening gambits, trying to come up with things her twin might say to him. Meg had been gone all day, back to her miserable little life in L.A.

The tango music still played softly in the background. The entire house was wired for sound, and when she'd arrived, Rhea had found the last CDs played had been tangos. It was safe to assume the tango had been played during Meg Lindley's sojourn. The music was also necessary for their plan.

Rhea said softly, "It was horrible in L.A. I missed you so much, Jake."

He was still staring at her in that odd way, although he hadn't withdrawn from her.

"I know how much you love the tango, Jake," she added, looking at him from beneath a fringe of lustrous eyelashes. "Would you like to dance with me…or we could make love…"

When he didn't respond, she slipped one hand around the back of his neck, pulled his head toward her and kissed him. She squirmed even closer, pressing her breasts against his chest, and her free hand dropped to his thigh.

In the past, Jake had always been swift to respond sexually, but now his mouth was closed and unyielding and his arms dropped away from her. He released her so abruptly that she lost her balance and sat down heavily on the bed.

Taking a step backward, he stared at her. "So you've finally come back."

"Why, Jake, you know I was in L.A. all day."

"Cut it out, Rhea. I know who you are."

She gave a sly smile. "How can you be sure?"

"I'm sure. Where's Sloan? Lurking in a closet?"

"Darling, I know my twin and I had you confused, but honestly, you're talking to Meg. Shall I prove it? Ask me any question about Meg and her life."

"I don't have to. You're Rhea."

She laughed. "Okay. I'm Rhea. My twin and I really had you going, didn't we? What a joke on you, Mr. Big Shot. Meg and I giggled ourselves silly over how she fooled you."

For a split second, doubt flickered in his eyes, quickly masked, but not before she had seen it and experienced a little flush of triumph.

He said, "Actually I'm glad you came back, Rhea. We can talk about the divorce."

"Oh, sure, we'll get to that later. But don't you want to hear what Meg thinks about you? Oh, my, she's quite the actress. She told me she really had to play the part when you touched her. Seems your masculine charms didn't work on her, sweetie. She said her skin crawled when you put your hands on her. But I understand she managed to hide her revulsion. She said she really turned you on. Of course, I taught her a few tricks—"

"Shut your filthy mouth," Jake snapped.

He turned from her and strode into his dressing room. Seconds later he appeared with an overnight bag.

"I'll go to a hotel. You'd better get Mason and the staff back. Tomorrow we'll meet with the lawyers. I'll let you know what time."

He began to pack the overnight bag.

Rhea watched him with narrowed eyes. Maybe she couldn't wait for Sloan to arrive....

The Smith & Wesson .22 she had bought using Meg's ID was hidden in a lingerie drawer in her dressing room, along with the gloves she would put on before picking up the gun.

All she had to do was walk in there and get the gun. He wasn't even looking at her. She could walk right up to him, then put a bullet in his heart.

But Sloan wasn't here yet, and that was a deviation from the plan that worried her.

She had to stall Jake, somehow.

"Jake...I'm sorry, I really am. I know how much heartache I've caused you. Please, could we just talk for a little while? Don't go yet."

He kept his back turned to her. "What is there to talk about, Rhea? It's over. It was over before the honeymoon ended. What's the point of dragging out this charade? I won't hold you to the prenuptial agreement, if that's what you're worried about."

Yeah, right, Rhea thought. *That's what you say now. But wait until your lawyers get to you.*

Aloud she said, "Just tell me one thing. Were you truly fooled by my twin?"

That made him turn and look at her. "I was truly fooled by you, Rhea. If anybody is an accomplished actress, it's you. I thought I'd found a woman of integrity."

"I do love you, you know, Jake, in my own way...it's just that you're so...demanding."

"Demanding loyalty and fidelity, you mean?"

He had stopped packing.

She asked, "How did you know it was me tonight?"

He studied her for a moment and his expression told her more clearly than words that any feelings he'd ever had for her were gone.

Finally he said, "It was the eyes that gave you away. Meg's eyes are the most expressive I've ever seen—filled with hope and compassion, as well as the certain belief that there is goodness and love in the world. Yours, Rhea, are dead eyes. I don't know what happened to you that left you little more than an empty shell...but I think whatever made you what you are is irreparable. There's no joy in you, Rhea, and all the possessions in the world will never fill up that hollow place in your soul."

Rhea glanced at the antique china clock on her bed table. If she could just keep him talking for a few more minutes... Once Sloan was in the house he would signal her by going to the central controls and turning off the music.

As soon as the music stops, Jake...as soon as the tango ends...you're a dead man.

Chapter Twenty-Two

The car in which Meg was trapped had left the freeway and started along a winding road, hitting a pothole that must have opened up in the heavy rain, and jarring every bone in her body. Speeding now, the car lurched, and her right foot jammed into a corner of the trunk.

Sensing that the journey was coming to an end, and desperate to escape, Meg ignored the pain in her foot and braced herself into an excruciatingly cramped position in order to kick with both feet at the panel separating the trunk from the back seat of the car.

Suddenly she felt the panel give. Scrambling onto her side, she pushed with both hands, and a moment later the back seat folded down with what sounded to her ears like a resounding thud. She held her breath, hoping the driver hadn't heard the sound above the beat of the rap music playing on the radio.

The car didn't slow down.

It was difficult to move around in the cramped space, but she managed to ease herself into a position from which she could peer into the car.

She could see the interior lights and even the bulky shape of the driver, who seemed frighteningly close. He didn't look back, so evidently hadn't heard the back seat fold down. With wind and rain lashing the night, and the car bouncing so much on the rougher road surface, he probably thought any sounds were the wheels hitting potholes.

Then all at once the car was again on a smooth surface and slowing down. The radio was switched off. Through the wash of rainwater and slashing windshield wipers she could make out the shape of ornamental gates sliding back, then the car moved forward again.

Before she could slip through the opening onto the back seat, she heard the faint *whir* of a garage door opening and the windshield was flooded with light.

Startled, she drew back into the trunk as the car came to a complete stop. Meg wanted to weep with frustration. Just a few seconds more and she could have been in the back seat, yanking open the door and leaping to freedom.

She pulled her keys from her jacket pocket. The keys were a puny weapon, but she wasn't going to give in without a fight. She lay still, waiting for him to come for her.

But the trunk did not open. She heard footsteps outside, then silence. He had gone into the house.

Meg slithered through the opening into the back seat of the car and cautiously raised her head.

The car was parked in the Chastain garage, and the door leading into the house was open. Sloan must have gone in that way.

Had Mason and the others returned? Or was Jake still alone? Was he even here, or was Sloan setting up an ambush?

Meg opened the car door as quietly as she was able, and got out of the car. She looked around. There were at least half a dozen cars in the garage, including the Jeep.

From inside the house, muted but distinct, came the unmistakable music of the tango.

Seconds later, the music stopped.

Meg was about to step through the door into the house when she heard a woman's voice, screaming obscenities, then, distinctly, *"Sloan, get him! He's on the stairs!"*

In that split second Meg remembered the fuse box was inches from where she stood. She grabbed the cover, raised it, and flipped all the switches.

The house was plunged into darkness.

Almost simultaneously a shot reverberated throughout the house, echoing across the marble-floored entry hall.

There was a second explosion, the sound of shattering glass.

A man's voice yelled, "Rhea—where the hell are you? What happened to the freakin' lights? Damn. Did I get him? Which way did he go?"

Her heart thumping madly, Meg stepped through the door and felt her way along the dark corridor, trying to fix in her mind the layout of the house. At the end of the corridor a door opened into the kitchen, a room she knew well.

It seemed obvious that the staff had not returned. Jake was here alone and they were trying to kill him.

Thinking of the two shots she had just heard, she prayed. *Please, God, don't let him be dead.*

She was in the kitchen now; she could feel a granite countertop. Her fingers explored the surface until she came to wood. This was the butcher-block chopping surface, and below it a drawer contained carving knives. Sliding open the drawer, her fingers closed around the largest of the knives.

There was an ominous silence in the rest of the house. Then there were several thuds. Something crashed to the floor.

Meg's heart leapt into her throat.

Where was the phone? Could she reach it and make a

call in the dark? She remembered a wall phone near the work area. Clutching the knife, she felt her way along the countertop.

With the phone in her hand, she laid down the knife. Her fingers were shaking. *Careful now,* she told herself, *you have to find 911 in the dark…think!*

She concentrated on visualizing a phone. Weren't there usually nine buttons? No, twelve. The first would be one and the last on the third row would be nine. The bottom row usually consisted of pound and star signs.

The clicks of the phone seemed frighteningly loud as she pressed what she hoped were the right buttons.…

Then, with relief, she heard the emergency dispatcher on the line and she frantically whispered that shots had been fired at the Chastain estate.

At the same time she heard the hollow ring of footsteps on marble. She grabbed the knife again. But the footsteps were not coming in her direction.

Feeling her way to the door, she slipped into the hall.

A muffled curse, then a crash followed by a series of thumps, came from the direction of the staircase.

Two shadows, more dense than the surrounding darkness, were grappling at the foot of the stairs.

Sloan and Jake. Thank God, Jake was still alive!

Gripping the knife, she attempted to move toward them in the smothering darkness, but suddenly collided with a statuette on a display stand.

Startled, she dropped the knife and heard it go skittering away from her across the marble floor.

Her eyes were becoming accustomed to the darkness and she could see that Jake was locked in a deadly struggle with Sloan. Another shot rang out, and in the brief flash she saw that Jake had forced Sloan's arm upward and that the gun had fired toward the ceiling, high above them.

But a second later Jake lost his footing and fell heavily against the stairs.

Sloan stepped back to take aim.

Meg was never sure, afterward, where she found the strength. She grabbed the statuette from the stand and swung it with all her might at Sloan's back.

He grunted with surprise and pain and swung around, firing the gun again. Meg felt the bullet whiz past her ear, and something shattered behind her.

The diversion gave Jake time to get to his feet and he again closed with Sloan, smashing his fist into Sloan's jaw. But Sloan didn't go down.

Meg moved uncertainly around the edges of the fray, wanting to help, terrified the gun would go off again, uncertain what to do.

Listening to the sickening sounds—crunching flesh and bone, heavy breathing, gasps of pain—she worried that although the two men were approximately the same height, Sloan outweighed Jake by at least fifty pounds.

She tried to determine which of the two was close to her and again raised the statuette, praying she would not strike Jake. The floor underfoot was slippery and she found it hard to keep her balance.

Then both men crashed to the floor, and the gun exploded again. In the brief flash Meg saw that Sloan lay at her feet; Jake had fallen back against the stairs.

She smashed the statuette down onto Sloan's head. He moaned, but didn't get up.

For an instant the only sound in the darkness was that of labored breathing. Then Jake spoke, his voice ragged, breathless. "Rhea…?"

"It's me—Meg. I've called 911."

"Can you find your way to the fuse boxes in the garage? I've got to get his gun before he comes to his senses."

"Yes, I think so. But where is Rhea?"

"Upstairs, I think."

"She might have a gun."

"I'll be careful."

Now he sounded as if he were speaking from the bottom of a well. Meg thought, *He's hurt.* "Are you all right? Jake, I don't want to leave you."

"I'm fine. Get the lights."

His voice sounded far from fine, but she inched her way across the hall in the darkness, and felt along a wall until she found the kitchen door. It seemed to take forever to make her way back along the corridor to the garage.

Before she reached the fuse boxes, she heard the welcome sound of sirens shrieking toward the house.

The squad cars—three of them—pulled up in front of the house as Meg switched the lights on again. She walked out toward the police, her hands in the air.

Two uniformed officers jumped from the cars and raced toward her, guns drawn.

"I c-called you," she stammered breathlessly. "There's a man inside with a gun...but I think he's unconscious."

All at once, it seemed surreal: the flashing lights of the police cars, the officers surrounding the house, and her own voice shakily directing them to the marble-floored hall.

"Are you hurt, miss?" one of the officers asked her.

She shook her head, then saw that he was looking down at her boots. They were spattered with blood.

"Why don't you sit in the back of the patrol car while we check on the house?" the officer said, taking her arm gently but firmly and leading her to the closest black-and-white.

Seated in the back seat of the patrol car, Meg suddenly began to shake violently. Everything seemed to be happening now in slow motion.

An ambulance came wailing up the driveway.

Another police car arrived—this one bringing detectives in plain clothes.

A uniformed officer returned to her. "You say your name is Margaret Lindley?"

She nodded.

"We're going to drive you down to the station. We'll need a statement from you."

"But Jake—Mr. Chastain… May I speak to him first?"

"We need your statement, miss."

Too dazed to argue, Meg leaned back in her seat. Her right foot throbbed. It was an old, familiar pain, and for once she welcomed it.

As the patrol car she was in pulled away from the house, she saw officers stringing yellow crime-scene tape across the driveway. The significance of that struck her like a physical blow.

There had been a homicide.

Chapter Twenty-Three

"Please," Meg begged, "tell me how Mr. Chastain is. Is he badly hurt? There was blood on the floor even before I hit Sloan with the statue…"

The detective to whom she had given her statement, a seasoned officer who appeared to have acquired a permanent expression of doubt, finally relented. "Wait here. I'll check with my partner."

Meg couldn't seem to stop shaking. She wrapped her arms around her body to try to quiet her twitching nerves. Around her the muted din of police business—phones ringing, computers chirping, conversations—seemed unreal.

The detective returned, his expression somewhat more sympathetic. "Mr. Chastain has been transported to a hospital."

When Meg's hand flew to her throat in alarm, he added quickly, "A bullet lodged in his thigh. The wound isn't life-threatening, but he's in surgery and they'll probably keep him in the hospital a few days."

"May I leave now? I'd like to go to the hospital."

"You won't be able to see him tonight. But he left a message for you—that you should spend the night with his mother."

"I'd rather go to my own home," Meg replied.

His expression was blank again. "That's in L.A., right? It would be better for you to stay locally. We'll probably have more questions for you tomorrow. I'll have an officer drive you to Laguna Beach."

"Could you…tell me anything about Mrs. Rhea Chastain and her brother?"

"I don't have that information, ma'am. The investigation is continuing."

When Meg reached Laguna Beach, Jessica didn't seem surprised to see her. She calmly led Meg into the house, where Huxley fussed and whined, licked her hand and sniffed worriedly at the blood on her boots.

Jessica said, "Jake called me just before he went into surgery, so I have some idea of what happened. It seems that if you hadn't had the gumption to throw the fuse switches and go to my son's aid, those two monsters might have gotten away with murder."

"Is Jake going to be all right? The police wouldn't tell me much." Meg felt as if she were speaking underwater, but Jessica evidently understood. She answered reassuringly, "Yes, he said he just took a bullet in his leg."

Remembering the sickening sound of blows, Meg knew Jake had probably played down the injuries he sustained during his fight with Sloan so as not to worry his mother. For herself, Meg wished she could be at the hospital, waiting to see him when he came out of surgery. If only she could clear the fog from her head, perhaps she could ask Jessica to loan her a car.

But to Meg's dismay, Jessica seemed to be going in and out of focus. Meg murmured something—she wasn't sure what, but hoped she hadn't expressed what she felt with every fiber of her being. *I love your son with all my heart and soul and want to be at his side. I can't bear that he's hurt. Or that it's all my fault. I would gladly have taken that bullet for him.*

Jessica said gently, "Meg, don't blame yourself. This is all Rhea's doing."

Desperately trying to hang on to some semblance of control, Meg stroked Huxley's silky head.

"Carmelita is drawing a warm bath for you, Meg," Jessica said, her voice kind, soothing. "There's a glass of warm milk laced with brandy next to the tub. I want you to drink it. Then get into bed. I'll be up in a little while."

Still dazed and shaken, Meg gratefully followed the instructions.

Her soak in a warm, scented tub revealed numerous bruises on her body, and her right ankle was badly swollen, no doubt from kicking at the back of the car trunk. At least, due to the rain, she'd had on boots, she thought, wondering what shape she'd be in if she'd been wearing tennis shoes when she kicked her way out of the car.

She sipped the brandy-laced milk and felt its fiery warmth seep through her body and calm her a little. She ached all over, but reminded herself how much better she'd fared than had Jake.

The big question in Meg's mind was, what had become of Rhea during the struggle? Everything had happened so quickly, and the house had been so dark, but why hadn't Rhea gone to Sloan's aid? Perhaps her twin, at the last minute, realized the enormity of what she was doing and had a change of heart. Meg prayed that was so.

When she emerged from the bathroom, wrapped in a fluffy terry-cloth robe, Carmelita was waiting to show her to a cozy bedroom with daffodil-yellow walls and a white four-poster bed.

For once, Carmelita didn't maintain a steady stream of conversation. She clucked sympathetically, helped Meg into bed and tucked a whisper-light eiderdown quilt over her, then withdrew.

Jessica and Huxley appeared minutes later. Jessica asked quietly, "Would you like a sedative, or maybe a pain pill? I understand you were roughed up."

"No, thank you. Just being warm and safe is all I need right now. Mrs. Chastain—"

"Jessica," the older woman corrected.

"I'm so sorry for deceiving you, Jessica."

Jake's mother stared at her for a moment, then shook her head slightly in an expression of disbelief. "I could still swear you are Rhea. You really are identical, aren't you? At least as far as looks are concerned."

"I've never seen Rhea clearly. I only met her once, on a dark beach."

Jessica's expression became grave. "I have to tell you something, Meg."

A frightening possibility occurred to Meg. "Oh, no! Sloan didn't escape, did he? Do we have to worry about him coming after Jake again?"

"No. Sloan is in police custody. It's about your sister, Rhea."

Meg waited, her heart beginning to pound again. "Yes?"

"When the police entered the house, they found her body crumpled near the top of the stairs."

"Her body…" Meg repeated, feeling dizzy again.

"She's dead, Meg. Apparently killed by a wild bullet from Sloan's gun. She had a gun, too, but it hadn't been fired. She was dressed in a nightgown, but she was also wearing gloves."

TO ESCAPE THE MEDIA frenzy over the sensational news story, two days later Jessica and Carmelita were spirited away to an unknown destination, and Meg went back to her house in Los Angeles.

She had spoken on the phone briefly with Jake while he was at the hospital. They reassured each other they were each all right, but since neither of them were alone, they didn't discuss anything else.

"We'll talk when we can meet in private," Jake had said. "Dan will take care of you in the meantime."

Meg was again interviewed by the detectives, and had to go over her story in even more detail. They listened with obvious disbelief, but did contact the Santa Ana homicide detectives investigating Mike Aragon's death, in the hope that they had turned up something to confirm what Meg had told them about her introduction to the Chastains. But the Santa Ana detectives responded that none of Mike Aragon's files had been recovered.

Dan O'Rourke whisked her away from Jessica's house, eluded the swarming paparazzi, took her to a car rental agency and rented a car for her.

The rainstorm had scoured the city of its customary umber haze of smog, and Meg drove home in bright sunshine beneath sparkling blue skies.

Arriving home, she unlocked her door and automatically stooped to pick up a couple of letters. She remembered that she hadn't opened the mail that had been delivered the previous day.

She flipped through the envelopes—bills, junk mail, as she expected. But then she came to a six-by-nine manila envelope, addressed to her in unfamiliar handwriting. There was no return address. Probably some unsolicited item she would be expected to pay for, or a CD urging her to subscribe to some Internet service. The handwritten address was a clever idea, she thought.

She almost tossed the manila envelope into the wastebasket, but curiosity won out. Ripping open the envelope, she pulled out a computer disk. Turning it over, she read the label, printed in the same script as the envelope, bearing a single word: DOMINO.

Meg no longer owned a computer. It had been sold, along with everything else of value, in order to pay off the debts from the failed restaurant.

DOMINO? What could it possibly mean? And who had sent it?

On an impulse, she reached for her dictionary and looked up the word: "Domino…a masquerade dress, consisting of a loose cloak and half mask; the half mask itself; a person wearing a masquerade costume…"

The public library had a computer she could use. She hurried out to the car for the short drive.

AT THE LIBRARY, she inserted the disk into the computer and brought up the menu. It contained only one file, titled DOMINO.

Opening the file, Mike Aragon's name, address and private investigator's license number appeared on the computer screen. This was followed by a series of dated entries, beginning with his first contact with Rhea Chastain.

"Bless you, Mike," Meg whispered. She scrolled down.

He had recorded everything—details of his first meeting with Meg, along with a sly aside about how she'd clobbered him with her groceries and how that was when he decided she could probably take care of herself among the filthy rich.

His search for Hal was covered, along with the results, although the name of the man who had supplied Hal's forged identity documents was conspicuously absent.

Mike's conversations with Rhea were meticulously reported, together with all of the data he had collected on

Rhea and Sloan. He expressed his fear that he had placed both Jake Chastain and Meg in danger, and stated for the record that he had urged Meg to end the deception when Jake unexpectedly arrived in St. Maarten.

He also reported that after the fire at the beach house he had removed gasoline cans from a car rented by Rhea in Meg's name, and stored the cans in his garage.

At the end of the file he had written the following:

Meg,
One way or another I expect our business together to be concluded today, with a visit to the police, so I'm dropping this in the mail to you now. I don't issue written reports, they tend to get lost or destroyed, or read by unauthorized people. I figure a computer disk is less accessible to snoops, especially since I always devise a name for the file that will have meaning only to my client. So I'm sending this copy of your file to your house. You might need it sometime.

MEG WATCHED as a tabloid television show regaled viewers with details of the Chastain story, amazed that their reporters had assembled so much information.

Sloan had been arraigned and was expected to be charged with conspiracy to commit murder, attempted murder, manslaughter in the case of Rhea's death, and a long list of lesser charges.

Apparently after the police received Mike's disk from Meg and confronted Sloan with it, he had given up on his initial attempt to accuse Rhea of the shooting—a futile ploy in view of the gunpowder residue all over his hands.

His lawyers had been unable to keep Sloan from talking to the media, and he was now blaming Rhea for everything.

She was the brains behind the plot, he claimed; he, the manipulated dupe.

She wanted Jake's empire, had gone to London to kill him herself, but instead had hired an assassin. When the hit man botched the job by killing the wrong man in Jake's suite, she persuaded Sloan to torch the beach house, but Jake again escaped.

Rhea had been furious when Jake and her twin took off somewhere together. She showed up at the house, told the staff to leave because fumigators were coming in. She figured Jake would return some time and she wanted him to find the house deserted. She even flipped the fuses so the house would be dark.

Late that night Rhea had learned via the staff grapevine that Jake was back, and that he had asked them to return the following day. She then ordered the exterminators to show up the following morning, and called Mason to countermand Jake's request that he bring back the staff, telling Mason he could check with the exterminators to confirm that they were going in the next day. Rhea wanted to make sure Jake would be alone in the house.

Jake and Meg Lindley had to be separated, so Rhea could take her place. Sloan's only part in the plot, he insisted, was to deliver Meg to the house so Rhea could plant the murder weapon on her twin.

The television anchorman pointed out that Sloan had unwittingly added kidnapping to the list of charges against him.

Sloan's story concluded that when he arrived at the house the power had suddenly failed, and the gun in his hand, which he was carrying only for protection, had discharged accidentally.

He couldn't explain why he had accidentally fired so

many times. One bullet had killed Rhea, another had wounded Jake.

The T.V. reporters had uncovered background material on all of the principals, including Meg and her husband. They said the murder of the private investigator who had brought the twins together was being examined for a possible connection to the plot. There was also a great deal of prurient interest in what exactly had transpired between Jake Chastain and his wife's twin during the days and nights they'd spent together.

Meg switched off the T.V. set and hastily packed her bags. It would only be a matter of time before the media showed up on her doorstep. She didn't dare risk contacting Jake now; the reporters would surely jump on any hint that there might be a relationship between them. Jake's reputation had to be protected, and the world must never learn how she loved and yearned for him.

She called Carrie Hooper, the caterer for whom she worked. "Carrie, it's Meg—I don't think I'd better work this weekend."

"Meg! I've been watching T.V....holy cow, I can't believe what you've been up to. Are you at home?"

"Yes, but I'm leaving before the reporters find me."

"You got somewhere to go?"

"No, I'll get a motel room, then hope I can find a job with somebody who won't talk to the media. I'm thinking of going back to using my maiden name."

"Well, I wasn't going to tell you this because I didn't want to lose you, but I heard from an old acquaintance of yours from your restaurant days—remember Yves? He's opened a bistro in a shopping mall. He's aiming for a really high-class clientele, you know, sophisticated French cuisine like that bistro in the South Coast Plaza mall. Anyway, he wanted to know if I could put him in touch with you. He needs an assistant chef.''

''Bless you, Carrie,'' Meg murmured, envisioning donning a chef's hat to disguise her Rhea coiffure, and losing herself in a large, impersonal mall.

She would have to inform the detectives handling the case of her new address, as soon as she found one. Her deepest regret was that she couldn't tell Jake where she was going, or explain to him that she had to disappear because she loved him too much to hurt him again.

MEG RENTED A ROOM in a private house in a modest neighborhood, a bus ride away from the upscale mall. The long hours she worked helped assuage some of the anguish she felt, but did little to ease her longing for Jake. He was in her thoughts every minute of every day. Still, she was so busy that the time passed quickly.

Then one evening when she returned to her room, her landlady said there was a telephone call for her. Expecting more questions from the detectives, she picked up the phone and heard Jake's voice. Her heart skidded joyfully.

''How did you find me?'' Meg breathed, acutely aware of her landlady hovering nearby and undoubtedly listening in.

''Mutual friends in law enforcement,'' Jake answered. ''I have to see you, but I can't move without being followed by the press. I guess you know the newshounds are still in full cry. Have they discovered you yet?''

''No.''

''Could we meet somewhere? I'll find a way to dodge the paparazzi.''

''How about outside a bistro called Yves?'' Meg was astonished that she managed to answer so calmly. ''I'll give you directions.''

MEG HAD REMOVED her white chef's smock and hat, replacing the latter with the beret she always wore to hide the fact that her bleached hair was growing out. She paced nervously in front of the bistro, her gaze searching for anyone carrying a camera.

Her heart leapt when she saw Jake coming toward her, wending his way through the crowd of shoppers. He was casually dressed in tan slacks and a leather jacket, and she noticed immediately that he was limping slightly. She wanted to race to him and fling her arms around him, but restrained herself, knowing they had to be careful not to draw attention to themselves.

His dark eyes lit up when he saw her and he quickened his pace, obviously making an effort to disguise the fact that his leg hadn't healed completely yet. When he reached her he opened his arms, and she went silently into his embrace, oblivious of the gawking passersby.

For a long heart-stopping moment they simply held each other, not speaking. There was no need for words.

Meg could have remained there forever, enclosed in the protective circle of his arms, breathing deeply the dearly recalled scent of him, feeling his warm breath against her forehead. But when he shifted his weight slightly, she remembered his injured leg, and said quickly, "Jake, let's find somewhere to sit down and talk."

"While I feast my eyes on you," Jake said, smiling. He traced the contour of her cheek, touched her lips lightly with his fingertip, as if making sure she was really there with him. "Do you have any idea how many times I've dreamed of this moment?"

They found a bench under the domed sunroof of the mall, among fully grown potted ficus trees and half barrels of flowers. Occasionally, shoppers hurrying in or out of nearby stores glanced in their direction, but failed to recognize the well-known Jake Chastain. *Nobody expects to see him in such a setting,* Meg thought.

Echoing her view, Jake said, "You covered your tracks very well. A shopping mall is a great place to lose yourself. It wasn't easy tracking you to your new address either."

"I was lucky Yves gave me this job."

"Meg, when we spoke on the phone while I was in the hospital, I'm not sure I thanked you properly for saving my life."

"From what I saw, you were handling Sloan pretty well without me."

"If you hadn't plunged the house into darkness, Sloan would have shot me. The only reason I'm alive is because he couldn't see me. Besides, I was weakening when you belted him with the statue."

"Let's not talk about that night, Jake. It's just too painful to think about. After all, if I hadn't agreed to impersonate Rhea…"

Jake reached over and picked up her hand. "All right, but keep in mind that when you save someone's life, it's yours to do with as you will."

Meg closed her eyes briefly, willing herself to have the strength to say what she knew must be said.

As if sensing her doubts, Jake said, "I love you, Meg. I have from the moment we met. I haven't been able to think about anything but you. Now that I've found you again, I'm going to make up for all you've been through. There are no more obstacles, Meg. We can be together now."

How his words made her heart sing, and how she longed to tell him how deeply she loved him in return. But she'd almost ruined his life once. She couldn't risk doing it again.

She said slowly, "You must know there's a lot of spec-ulation and nasty innuendo in the press about us. It will all flare up if we're seen together again. That's why I covered my tracks so carefully. That's why I wanted to meet you here, where the media wouldn't find us.''

Jake's expression said that he sensed what she was about to say, and he tried to assuage her fears. ''Perhaps you haven't heard yet. Sloan's lawyer is going to plea-bargain rather than risk a jury trial. That computer disk you gave to the police, along with forensic evidence they found at the scene, ties him to Aragon's murder. That should be the end of the media's interest in the case.''

''I think you're being too optimistic, Jake.''

''Another news story will break, Meg, and we'll be out of the headlines. Until then, come away with me. Anywhere in the world you want to go. I don't care where, as long as we're together.''

She turned her head so that she could look directly into his eyes. She wanted to say, *Yes, yes, I'll come with you. I love you more than life.*

Instead she forced herself to say what she'd carefully rehearsed. ''We have to face the fact that sometimes the timing just isn't right. I think that's the saddest part of life—missed connections. We didn't meet at the right time. This isn't the right time either. I'm not sure there ever will be a right time for us.''

''Meg, don't say that—''

''Please, hear me out. You are too well-known, and this case is too sensational. There will always be some reporter wanting to add more scandal—an affair between us—to the story.''

Jake said quickly, ''I understand your concern about the media ripping us to shreds, and I can't deny they might, but I can wait until they lose interest. For as long as necessary. Forever, if I have to. But that doesn't mean we can't see each other—discreetly—does it?''

"Yes, it does. We can't see each other again after today."

"Do we really give a damn what the rest of the world thinks? Let them find out I love you. I'll shout it from the rooftops."

Meg bit her lip. "Jake, apart from the trashing we'd take from the media, there're other equally compelling reasons why we can't be together."

"What do you mean?"

"There's just too much tragedy surrounding us. I need time to grieve for a sister I never knew I had. I have to deal with my guilt over Mike's death and grieve for him, too. I can't do that until I separate myself from everything that reminds me of them...especially you."

In order to avoid seeing the raw pain in his eyes, and show him her own inner turmoil, she looked down at his hands, folded around hers. Even as she spoke, she was hoping against hope that he would be able to say something, anything, to reassure her, to overcome her doubts.

At length he sighed deeply. "I understand. You need time to put everything that happened into perspective. I want to be with you so much I'm not thinking of the adjustments you have to make. How can I ask you to pretend nothing happened and come away with me now? But could we at least make a future date? Three months, six, a year?"

She was weakening, she knew, hovering on the brink of flinging doubt and caution to the wind, but that inner warning voice nagged insistently. *You can't be together now, perhaps not ever.*

What if, when he had time to really think about the upheaval she'd brought to his life, he decided they couldn't build their love on a foundation of deception and lies? What if one day he came to hate her for what she'd done? She wouldn't be able to bear it. Better to make a clean break now, while they were too much in love to worry about the tragic consequences of their coming together.

Meg disentangled her hands and stood up. Her voice sounded hollow. ''No. I don't think it would be a good idea to make any dates, no matter how far in the future.''

''Meg, don't go. Not yet.''

''Goodbye, Jake.''

He rose to his feet, tried to speak, but couldn't. He cupped her cheek, and she caught his hand and held it to her face for a moment.

Walking away from him was the hardest thing she had ever done.

Chapter Twenty-Four

Eleven months later

Yves, a swarthy, wiry, creatively brilliant French-Canadian, was bursting with excitement. He hovered over Meg's shoulder, trying to contain himself as he waited for her to pour the chocolate soufflé into ramekins and pop them into the oven.

Then he made his grand announcement.

"I've found the location for our second bistro, *chérie!* A most unique outdoor mall in San Diego, and the bank approved our loan!"

He seized her around her waist, and they danced a jig around the kitchen. When they stopped, breathless, Yves kissed her on both cheeks and gazed soulfully into her eyes.

"You know that at least half of our success is due to you, *chérie.*" Yves had originally started using the French endearment in order to avoid calling her Meg while she was still hiding from the news media, and the habit had stuck. But almost a year had passed, and the story of Rhea Chastain and her twin was old news.

The past year had been one of enormous progress, despite the heartache that Meg nurtured in private. She had moved beyond her grief and guilt. She had paid off all the debts she and Hal had incurred, she had a nice apartment and she loved her work. But secretly, she still yearned for Jake.

So many times she had wanted to pick up the phone and call Jake, but resisted the temptation. Despite the fact that she had sent *him* away, perversely, she wanted him to make the first move. Her fear was that perhaps he no longer felt the same way about her. Surely, if he did, she would have heard from him?

For the first few months she had kept track of him. It was difficult not to, since news of his various achievements reverberated throughout the business world. Sometimes she scanned the society pages and gossip columns, but Jake's name was never linked with a woman.

Then he just seemed to drop out of sight. One reporter picked up on the fact that, following his wife's death, he had merely completed the Chastain projects that had been started earlier. When they were finished, he hadn't ventured into anything new. There was brief speculation in the press that among the ruins of his personal life, he had lost interest in his global empire and gone into early retirement. Meg wondered and worried.

Now, nearly a year after she'd last seen Jake, Meg said to Yves, "I know how much you wanted a second bistro. I'm so happy for you."

"Now, to come back down to earth," Yves went on, "we have a request to cater a private party."

"You know we don't have time—" Meg began. A *Los Angeles Times* food reviewer had given them such a glowing recommendation months earlier that they now had a nightly waiting list for dinner reservations.

"Well," Yves said, "as a matter of fact, *chérie,* the party is scheduled during the period our section of the mall is going to be closed for a few days for remodeling next month.''

''Then how will the client's guests be able to get in here?''

''Ah, but the party wouldn't be held here. It's a house-warming. A new house, just finished on the Palisades. *Chérie,* we've been given *carte blanche* and offered an enormous sum of money.''

''In that case...'' Meg said, grinning.

''*Très bien!* Just *un petit problème.*'' Yves smiled wickedly. ''I shall have to go down to San Diego that day. Can you manage on your own, *chérie?* It's just a small party. Six guests only. The client's name is Mr. Ogilvie.''

THE SOLIDLY BUILT brick house was spacious, but not ostentatious, with a breathtaking view of the Pacific Ocean. The grounds had not yet been landscaped, but a swimming pool and spa had been installed.

Meg unlocked the front door with a key that had been provided. Stepping inside, she saw that like the grounds, the interior of the house was also unfinished. The hardwood floors were bare, the walls unadorned. The house smelled new, unsullied, waiting for the scents and sounds of people to bring it to life.

She smiled. The owner must be eager to show off his new home, inviting his friends to a housewarming before landscape gardeners, decorators, or the moving van arrived.

Although the house was unfurnished, a large room on the ground floor with French doors that opened to a patio had been set up as a temporary party room. There were folding tables and chairs, a buffet table, serving carts and what appeared to be a truckload of fresh flowers.

The concealed lighting was tinted a soft rose, and Meg was glad to see crisp linen tablecloths and napkins, china dishes and beautiful antique silverware and candelabra. Outside on the patio, white wicker chairs and couches were adorned with brightly striped cushions. There was also a white wrought-iron patio table with six matching chairs.

Moving into the kitchen, she noted that it was equipped with everything that a dedicated cook might need, and even many exotic appliances not usually found in the average home. She began to bring in the supplies from Yves's van.

Since Yves had taken the order to cater the party, she had not spoken directly to the new homeowner, who had expressed no preferences in regard to the menu.

Meg hummed to herself as she worked. It was fun to be the first to use this bright kitchen, with its shiny new appliances, pristine counters and sun-splashed windows. There was a greenhouse window over the sink, already filled with thriving pots of herbs. Mrs. Ogilvie, Meg decided, was a lucky woman indeed. A new bride perhaps, since her husband had ordered the catered meal? Or perhaps he was the cook in the family.

With all afternoon to prepare for the evening event, Meg baked a trio of rustic breads: rosemary, caraway, sourdough. She'd decided to begin with a roulade of phyllo and poached lobster on a bed of perfect mashed potatoes and wild mushrooms.

For any guest who didn't care for shellfish there would be an alternative appetizer of poached pears with blue cheese on wisps of *frisée* and arugula, dressed in black pepper *gastrique*.

The main course would be duck breast with fingerling potatoes, pearl onions and baby turnips.

For dessert she would offer a delicate little wrapping of *brik* dough filled with chocolate and cherries. She had also brought her own vanilla-bean ice cream.

Cooking for half a dozen people was a pleasant change

from the nightly madhouse of the bistro, and Meg enjoyed the solitude of the quiet kitchen. Yves had wanted to send a busboy to help her, but she'd declined. Nor did Mr. Ogilvie require a waiter. He would serve his guests himself, he'd said, and would also bring his own wine.

At eight o'clock she had everything ready. She slipped off her apron and was about to take her unused supplies out to the van, when she heard the front door open. A voice called, "Hello? It's me—Ogilvie."

She went out into the hall. A dignified-looking middle-aged man, who would not have been out of place presiding over a state dinner somewhere, was closing the front door. He smiled at her.

Meg said, "Hello, Mr. Ogilvie. Everything's ready. May I show you?"

"No, that won't be necessary. I know whatever you've prepared will be wonderful. I've dined at Yves, you see, although I'm sure you don't remember. You have so many faithful clients."

"Well, in that case, I'll collect my supplies and be off," Meg said.

"Please, don't leave."

He looked a little sheepish. "You see, we got you here under—well, not exactly false pretenses—but…well, perhaps the real owner of the house can explain. For myself, I can only say if his intentions had not been thoroughly honorable, his cause worthwhile and his integrity above reproach, I wouldn't have been a party to this little deception."

"Deception…" Meg repeated faintly, a faraway drumbeat beginning to sound in her ear.

Ogilvie opened the front door again and waited.

A moment later Jake appeared, carrying a magnum of

champagne. His dark gaze sought and found Meg. He smiled in a way that stopped her breath in her throat.

"Hello, Meg. Forgive the way I handled this, but I was afraid you wouldn't come if I approached you directly."

Meg's heart was singing far too joyfully to care about the white lies. How handsome he looked! He wore a cream silk shirt and dark slacks, and the sea breeze had ruffled his black hair. He looked both elegant and casual. Meg wanted to drink him in with her eyes for a long moment, then pull him into her arms and kiss him. But her feet seemed to be rooted to the spot and all she could do was murmur, "I would have come, Jake. But tell me, was Yves in on this?"

"Please don't chastise him. I presented my case in such a way that he couldn't refuse. Yves being a Frenchman and *l'amour* being of paramount importance…"

Beaming, Ogilvie said, "May I go now, sir?"

"Yes, thank you. I believe Meg and I can handle things."

After Ogilvie left, Jake explained, "He took Mason's place. Mason retired this past year."

"You still have the other house, then?"

"No. I could never live in it after…what happened there. I moved into a smaller place, but kept Mason and Cook on. I built this place and another just like it farther down the coast. I'm not sure yet which I'll keep as my main residence. I might even build another somewhere…it all depends."

They stood staring at one another in spellbound wonder.

Meg said, "You look very well, Jake. I, on the other hand, probably have flour on my nose."

He smiled. "You look like a dream come true, flour on your nose and all. I especially like your hair now that it's back to its natural color."

Meg resisted the urge to untie the shoestring that kept her honey-colored hair out of the way while she prepared food. Her hair was now almost to her shoulders.

She thought fleetingly that it was just like a man to show up unannounced when a woman was clad in a faded cotton dress and tennies, sans makeup. She said awkwardly, "I'd better get out of here before your guests arrive."

He laughed. "There are no other guests tonight, Meg. Just you, me and *m'sieur* Dom Pérignon. Although Jess would have come in a flash if I'd invited her. She's been after me to do this for a year now. I told her I had to find out how you felt about us first."

"But you had me cook for six!" Meg protested lightly. She was delighted that she evidently had the approval of Jake's mother.

"A small housewarming sounded more plausible than dinner for two. If I promise to clean my plate, will you forgive me?"

"We'll see. Speaking of your mother, how is she?"

"Her arm healed completely and she's painting again, so she's happy."

"And Huxley?"

Jake grinned. "He's a father. Four of the most handsome pups you've ever seen—five weeks old now. Say the word and I'm sure Jess will give you the pick of the litter, which she gets for providing Huxley for stud service."

"I'd love to have Huxley's firstborn son," Meg said. "It sounds almost biblical."

"Good. Jess and Huxley will be pleased to hear that. Now let's get the champagne on ice and then enjoy whatever it is that smells so good. Did you bake bread?"

It was a mild evening, so Jake took a tablecloth and the champagne bucket out to the patio table overlooking the ocean. He lit candles and carried out china and a vase of roses. Meg took the opportunity to slip into the powder room and comb her hair.

They dined under the stars, sipped the marvelous champagne and talked with the ease of two people who were completely in tune, not always agreeing but always interested in the other's opinion. The past year might never have happened. It was as if they were continuing a conversation begun only yesterday.

"Jake, there's been no word on what you've been doing for months now," Meg said finally. "Is it true to you've retired?"

"Not exactly. I've just managed to keep a low profile on my projects. Remember the abandoned campground where we hid out? It's now a camp for abused and neglected kids. There's a second one under construction in northern California and another in South America. My name is kept out of it because I set up a charitable association to handle the construction."

"But I bet you've been very much involved," Meg commented.

"Well, I had to keep busy. It's an antidote of sorts, isn't it?"

Meg didn't have to ask what it was an antidote for. She knew only too well.

Jake tried every dish and she complimented him on his hearty appetite, but even he couldn't dispose of all the food.

Meg felt pride in the meal, but being there with Jake was the fulfillment of her most heartfelt dream. The lonely months had served to define how wholly and completely she loved this man.

"You know," she remarked, "if they hadn't had to close the mall to do some remodeling, I could never have been here today."

His gaze shifted away from her and a grin plucked at the corners of his mouth.

"Wait a minute," Meg said, realization dawning. "Surely you didn't arrange that, too?"

"Well...that particular mall is one of my earlier projects. It was due for a face-lift."

She digested this information silently. Since Yves had hired her for the bistro, it wasn't as if Jake had done her any favors. Still, she couldn't resist asking, "You don't own any malls in San Diego, do you?"

He shook his head. "No, why?"

"We're opening a new bistro there. I'll be the head chef."

"Congratulations. But I hope you'll have time for other pursuits."

"What do you have in mind? I wouldn't have time to moonlight at your hotels, the way we discussed once."

Jake stood up. "That isn't what I had in mind. But we'll talk about it later. Now will you excuse me for a minute?"

He disappeared. Minutes later the haunting beat of a tango drifted through the open patio doors.

Meg stood up and walked into the house, drawn by the lure of the sensuous music.

Jake waited for her in the empty living room. He had dimmed the lights, and rows of flickering candles now adorned the mantelpiece and hearth. He extended his hand to her. "May I?"

Meg looked down at her tennis shoes.

"Take them off," Jake said.

Slipping off her shoes, Meg melted into his arms, feeling a fire ignite in her veins. They moved slowly to the music, her socks sliding easily on the highly polished wood floor.

Her heart pounding, Meg whispered, "I dreamed of dancing with you again."

Jake murmured, ''You're light as a feather in my arms, and so beautiful you take my breath away.''

One of the dramatic pauses in the music gave him time to kiss her forehead, then her eyelids, and press his lips lightly to the hollow of her throat. Every sensory nerve in her body responded.

He held her close, guiding her around the uncluttered floor of the softly lit room, gliding, hesitating, dipping.

Then all at once, although the music continued, they were standing still, wrapped in a close embrace. They began to kiss, and the kiss went on for a very long time.

At length, breathless, they broke apart.

Meg said, ''Could this be the beginning for us, Jake? Are you all over...''

Jake halted the question with another quick kiss. ''Yes. I am. Are you?''

She nodded. ''I realize now that we couldn't have avoided the outcome, sad though it was. And wishing it could all have worked out differently doesn't help. At least we found each other.''

He placed his hands on her cheeks, holding her face tenderly. ''I memorized your face, thought of you every single day, longed for you. I want to spend the rest of my life with you. I love you, Meg, more than I can ever express.''

He kissed her again, a passionate meeting of lips that expressed more desire than any words.

''Marry me, Meg, please,'' Jake breathed. ''Right away. Let's not waste another minute apart.''

''Oh, Jake, there's nothing in the world I want more...I love you so much, but I have an obligation to Yves. The new bistro—I can't let him down.''

''I wouldn't want you to. Your loyalty and integrity are part of what I love about you. Meg, my darling, I can run my business from anywhere I choose. We'll find a house in San Diego near your new bistro.''

Grinning, he added, ''Of course, I'll probably show up at your new place for every meal so I can enjoy my wife's cooking.''

''I'd like that. We'll need a house with a big fenced yard for Huxley II.''

''And maybe a firstborn of our own to play with him?''

Meg said softly, ''I hope so, and by the time it takes us to make one, the bistro will be established.''

''So the answer is yes? Say it, Meg. Say you'll marry me.''

''Yes, oh yes, *yes!* I will marry you, Jake.''

They rocked back and forth with the music, bodies close, hearts beating in unison, moving to ancient erotic rhythms that no longer belonged to the tango, but to one man and one woman, pledging with bodies and minds their endless love.

After a moment, as if with a will of their own, Meg's fingers reached for the buttons on his shirt. She slipped her hands inside the soft silk and felt the hard planes of his chest, felt his heartbeat beneath her fingertips.

Jake's hands found the zipper on the back of her dress and she shrugged it from her shoulders, so that it slid to the floor. She gasped with pleasure as their bare flesh finally fused, then he bent to kiss the hollow at the base of her throat again, and slowly traced a delicious path with his lips to her breasts.

They were both breathing rapidly as his tender touch explored her body, caressing each soft contour, awakening nerve endings, bringing her to such an exquisite peak of desire that when he swept her up into his arms and carried her out into the scented night she could only whisper his name, over and over again.

Then he was setting her down on the cool cushions of a patio couch, swiftly discarding the rest of their clothes, and bending to whisper against her lips, ''I'll love you forever, Meg. This is our true beginning.''

As they made love under the stars, Meg knew that the past was behind them now, and the future was theirs alone.

BROTHERS OF ROCK RIDGE

by award-winning author Aimée Thurlo

The dark, sexy and mysterious Redhawk brothers
become a family once again to track down their foster
parents' killer and their missing foster sister. But Ashe and
Travis have no idea what dark danger—and steamy
passion—awaits in their hometown of Rock Ridge....

REDHAWK'S HEART
#506, March '99

REDHAWK'S RETURN
#510, April '99

THE BROTHERS OF ROCK RIDGE—
As different as night from day...
but bound by a vow to protect
those they love.

*Available at your favorite
retail outlet.*

Look for a new and exciting series from Harlequin!

HARLEQUIN

Duets™

Two __new__ full-length novels in one book, from some of your favorite authors!

Starting in May, each month we'll be bringing you two new books, each book containing two brand-new stories about the lighter side of love! Double the pleasure, double the romance, for less than the cost of two regular romance titles!

Look for these two new Harlequin Duets™ titles in May 1999:

Book 1:
WITH A STETSON AND A SMILE
by Vicki Lewis Thompson
THE BRIDESMAID'S BET
by Christie Ridgway

Book 2:
KIDNAPPED? by Jacqueline Diamond
I GOT YOU, BABE by Bonnie Tucker

**2 GREAT
STORIES BY
2 GREAT
AUTHORS
FOR 1 LOW
PRICE!**

Don't miss it! Available May 1999 at your favorite retail outlet.

HARLEQUIN®
Makes any time special.™

Look us up on-line at: http://www.romance.net

HDGENR

HARLEQUIN®

I N T R I G U E ®

COMING NEXT MONTH

Look us up on-line at: http://www.romance.net